BALTIMORE

ALSO BY MIKE MIGNOLA

Hellboy: Seed of Destruction (with John Byrne)
Hellboy: Wake the Devil
Hellboy: The Chained Coffin and Others
Hellboy: The Right Hand of Doom
Hellboy: The Conqueror Worm
Hellboy: Strange Places
The Art of Hellboy

ALSO BY CHRISTOPHER GOLDEN

The Myth Hunters
The Borderkind
Wildwood Road
The Boys Are Back in Town
The Ferryman
Straight on 'Til Morning
Strangewood
Of Saints and Shadows
Angel Souls and Devil Hearts
Of Masques and Martyrs
The Gathering Dark

BALTIMORE,

or,

THE STEADFAST TIN SOLDIER AND THE VAMPIRE

by Mike Mignola & Christopher Golden

BANTAM BOOKS

BALTIMORE
A Bantam Spectra Book / September 2007

Published by
Bantam Dell
A Division of Random House, Inc.
New York, New York

Book design by Glen Edelstein

Library of Congress Cataloging-in-Publication Data

Mignola, Michael.
Baltimore, or, The steadfast tin soldier and the vampire / Mike Mignola & Christopher Golden.
p.   cm.
ISBN 978-0-553-80471-3
1. Vampires—Fiction.   2. World War, 1914–1918—Fiction.   I. Golden, Christopher.   II. Title.   III. Title: Baltimore.   IV. Title: Steadfast tin soldier and the vampire.
PS3613.I38B35 2007
813'.54—dc22   2007000193

Printed in the United States of America
Published simultaneously in Canada

www.bantamdell.com
RRH   10 9 8 7 6 5 4 3 2 1

For Bram Stoker, Mary Shelley, Herman Melville, Hans Christian
Andersen, and my wife, Christine.
—M.M.

For Maurene Golden, Denis Golden, Brian & Mary Golden, Gerry Golden,
Terry & Diane Golden, and George & Elaine Sacco, and in memory of
Richard Golden and of my father, James Laurence Golden, Jr. Your
unwavering support and enthusiasm have always meant the world to me.
This dedication is long overdue.
—C.G.

ACKNOWLEDGMENTS

The authors would like to express their profound gratitude to Anne Groell, editor extraordinaire, for her tireless energy and enthusiasm, and for insights that truly gave *Baltimore* a little something extra. Our thanks also to Josh Pasternak and to Glen Edelstein and the entire Bantam team. Special thanks, of course, to our spouses and children, for putting up with us. And a special thanks to Guillermo del Toro. He knows why.

BALTIMORE

PRELUDE:

REQUIEM

"There were once five and twenty tin soldiers,
all brothers, for they were the offspring
of the same old tin spoon."
—The Steadfast Tin Soldier
by Hans Christian Andersen

ON A COLD AUTUMN NIGHT, under a black sky leached of starlight and absent the moon, Captain Henry Baltimore clutches his rifle and stares across the dark abyss of the battle-field, and knows in his heart that these are the torture fields of Hell, and damnation awaits mere steps ahead.

On one knee he pauses, listening, but the only sound comes from the chill autumn wind that carries with it the stink of death and decay. Baltimore gestures to the men picking their way through the darkness behind him, then moves in a crouch toward a small rise that could be a mound of war-torn earth . . . or a hill of corpses.

He falls to one knee behind the mound, which is indeed an innocent pile of dirt, excavated in the process of digging a trench. But Baltimore feels no relief at the discovery, save that the small mound provides better cover than corpses would have. Bullets pass through putrefying flesh far easier than through hard earth.

In the thick of the night, only a madman would attempt to cross the ravaged No Man's Land that separates his battalion from the Hessians. The blasted tundra is furrowed with dank, muddy trenches and strewn with the bodies of the dead. Bales of barbed wire are stretched in winding serpents across the field.

Yet madmen they are. The battalion commander has determined that someone must traverse that damned earth in the dark and bring the fight to the enemy. Desperation demands it. Without some twist of fate—brought by gods or men—the dawn will find them in circumstances most dire.

The mission has gone to Captain Baltimore.

He has led his platoon away from the safety of the battalion camp, out of the forest that now seems so far behind them, and fifty yards into No Man's

Land. Ahead lies at least four times that distance before they will reach any decent cover. The Hessians are camped in thick woods on the other side of the battlefield.

Baltimore knows that he stands at the very edge of the world. How else to explain the dread that slithers in the hollow of his chest and wraps itself around his soul? He must be on the threshold of Hell, for he can conceive of no patch of ground that could be farther from home and family and comfort. Yet this is the nature of war. To become a soldier, to spill blood and evict human souls in the name of faith or country, means traveling so far from home that home becomes as distant and cherished a memory as innocence.

He yearns for them both, even as he realizes at last—only now, only here—that they are lost to him forever.

As a boy he had kept to his room on rainy days and played with his tin soldiers, had cast them as enemies and caused them to kill one another on the battlefield of his blanket. But tin soldiers do not bleed. They go back in the box and live to fight another day.

Soldiers of flesh and blood also end up in a box, but theirs is of heavy pine. Baltimore has seen far too many soldiers bleed, and go into that wooden box in pieces. Dread flows in his veins now, making it difficult for him to move. Death waits for him on that ravaged ground and he has no wish to meet it. His bones ache with a chill that is more from terror and sadness than the November air, and he can scarcely breathe.

He raises a hand and signals his men, first to the left and then to the right. In two lines they hurry forward, flanking his position on both sides. Their motion is barely a whisper to disturb the darkness, yet to him they seem far too loud. As they come nearer he can hear the soft tread of boots upon hard earth and the chest-deep grunts of grim men tired of killing.

They take shape in the darkness, figures topped with the flat plate helmets of the allied forces, carrying rifles at the ready. Nearest him is Sergeant Tomlin, whose rifle lies cradled in his arms like a newborn.

The night sky is hung low with billowing clouds. Only the barest hint of light filters through from the heavens. Tomlin's eyes glint in the dark, and now that he is close, Baltimore sees the urgency in the man's features. His skin prickles with fear, and his chest aches with the pounding of his heart. Baltimore has never been a coward. Yet now he hesitates, in the worst place imaginable for such a pause.

With no other choice, he nods, raises his hand, and signals again.

Ebon shapes move out across the field. Baltimore and Sergeant Tomlin split up, go around the earthen mound, and even at that distance the sergeant exists as little more than a dark patch of moving shadow. Baltimore clutches his rifle so tightly that the grip pains him. His legs move seemingly of their own accord, carrying him across the torn-up earth. He nearly stumbles over a dead soldier, his body burnt so badly that it is impossible to tell whether he had been friend or foe. The dead man's face has run like melted wax.

"My God," he whispers to the night.

Tomlin scurries left to meet up with his detachment and Baltimore tears himself away from the gaze of the dead man to join up with the detachment on the right. Soft grunts and the shush of canvas and cotton uniforms can be heard up the line where Tomlin's group convenes, but the night has swallowed them.

In a crouch, Baltimore steals along the ruined ground, his men falling in around him. He lifts a hand, glances around for Norwich, the corporal with the wire-cutters, and finds the man right beside him, the twin handles of the tool jutting from his pack.

One by one they reach the barbed wire—a tangled, coiled mess as tall as a man. Baltimore drops to one knee. With a gesture, he signals to Corporal

Norwich. The man hands his rifle to the private beside him and slides the wire-cutters from his pack. Swiftly, and as silently as possible, Norwich sets to work on the barbed wire. Farther up the line, Tomlin's detachment will be doing the same.

Baltimore stands and peers at the wall of darkness on the far side of the battlefield. The trees nearest the open ground are stripes of shadow against the deeper black of the forest.

Norwich has progressed halfway through the six-foot mesh of barbed wire. Where he's already cut, the wire has pulled back like the flesh around a wound.

The corporal snips a wire that whips back and lashes his cheek, tearing flesh. Norwich groans loudly, drops the wire-cutters, and claps a hand to his cheek, but he does not shout or curse. Baltimore races toward the break in the barbed wire. He signals to the private holding Norwich's rifle and together the two men drag Norwich out of the breach by his legs.

The corporal's eyes are wide with pain and a seething, oddly directionless anger. Blood paints black streaks on his cheek and jaw, seeping out from the hand he presses to his wound.

Baltimore gives Norwich a nod of approval for the effort he's made to keep quiet. Then he gestures to the private who helped him pull Norwich out of the wire, a silent command for him to pick up the cutters and continue the job. The private hesitates a moment, as though hoping the order had been directed at some other soldier. Then, reluctantly, he crawls into the barbed wire and picks up the cutters.

A shadowy figure of grays and blacks moves nearer, emerging from the clutch of waiting soldiers. He doffs his flat plate helmet and Baltimore sees it is the medic, Stockton. The man reaches into a pouch strapped over his shoulder and pulls out a small kit. Quickly, as the skinny private snips wire after wire, opening a path through the barbed coils, Stockton cleans Norwich's wound and smears a coagulant paste over it. There is nothing more to be done. The placement of the gash makes a bandage troublesome in the field.

Stockton takes one last look at the wound but in the dark it is impossible to discern any real detail. The medic gives Captain Baltimore a thumbs-up and moves in a crouch to join the other soldiers awaiting the order to move out. A black silhouette in Mercury's helmet hands him his rifle.

The skinny private emerges from the wire, moving low. He's finished the job Norwich had begun. They have a path now.

Grimacing, Norwich stands and takes the cutters back, slipping them into his pack. He and the private turn an expectant look upon their captain. Baltimore nods, and signals them forward. Private Macintosh takes point. Baltimore could not have mistaken the silhouette of that giant brute for any other. The captain falls in with his men, fifth in line as they step quickly through the gap in the tangle of barbed wire.

Once they are through, they spread out, making a line along the inside

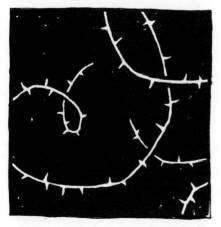

of the wire. Baltimore surveys the pitted and scarred field of battle ahead. The wind kicks up. He shivers as the chill cuts through his uniform, slicing to the bone.

Less than ten feet ahead lies a trench that gapes like a wound slashed in the world. The blackness in that pit makes the night seem bright in comparison. To his left, Tomlin's detachment will have

made it through by now and spread out so that the platoon is all together. They will be awaiting his order, as if there is any other possible choice but forward—down into the trench and up the other side.

Baltimore raises his hand to signal the advance.

In quick succession, three soft pops puncture the night, followed by a strange whistling that ends when a trio of flares explode into brightness above the battlefield, casting the entirety of the scene in a garish white light, such that every corpse and trench and divot in the earth stands out in perfect detail.

The platoon is strung along the line of earth between barbed wire and trench, completely exposed.

Dread and fear turn to rigid ice in his veins and Baltimore freezes, legs locked in place like one of his cherished tin soldiers, feet welded to its base. He has failed his country, and the men who follow him. His gaze follows the flares as they rise to the peak of their arcs and seem to hang for a moment like angels on high.

Ten or twenty feet to the right, one of his men curses. The voice sounds as though it comes from a thousand miles away. They might as well have been separated by such distances—all of them—for in the moment when death comes, each man is alone.

Awash in white light, Baltimore looks down even as the trench comes alive with movement. The Hessians who have lain in wait rise, rifle and machine gun barrels swinging up to take aim.

A tin soldier cannot move.

He stands at the ready, rifle in hand, but it will take the hand of the child to move him into action against his enemy. The  *battlefield is a heavy blanket striped two shades of blue, wrinkled and ridged with hills up which the platoon of tin soldiers must be made to charge.*

The war hesitates. It breathes with a light spring breeze flitting through the room.

The boy has gone for now. Allies and enemies are frozen on the brink. The great force that moves them all has abandoned them in the midst of this scene and terror grips the tin soldier. Paralyzed, he can only wait for the battle to start again. Once the boy returns, his fate will be decided. Perhaps he will survive, perhaps not, but it is the unknown that gnaws at him.

The bedroom window is open a crack, letting that spring air swirl and eddy into the room. Sunlight marks out an elongated rectangle upon the floor, cut through with a quartet of windowpane crosses. The laughter of children carries in on the breeze. The boy is outside, playing with others, when on that blue-striped blanket, the fate of two tin armies hangs frozen in the balance.

If the boy would only come in, if Henry would play with them and bring his laughter into the room, the tin soldier knows that all would be well. With the boy in the room there is warmth and happiness. There is safety. But in this petrified moment, anything can happen.

Anything at all.

The tin soldier cannot move.

A new sound enters the room. Harsh, chuffing laughter. This is no childhood merriment. It comes not from the green spring day outside the window, but from a shelf high on the wall. From within a wooden box, whose sides are painted and etched with grinning jester faces. A crank handle juts from one side of the box, unmoving.

But inside the box, something stirs.

The goblin Jack shifts inside his wooden box and there comes a thump thump thump of its wooden head striking the walls. A tinkle of jangling, happy music blats three notes, but the crank does not move. The laughter comes again—a harsh, barking staccato, and the soldier knows there is something to fear more than losing his life, more than losing the war...

The gunfire punctures the air—a harsh, barking staccato. The platoon are black silhouettes cut out of a brilliant white background. The angel-flares float languidly downward, drifting on the autumn breeze. They begin to flicker almost in rhythm with the machine gun fire, turning the slaughter of Baltimore's men into a gruesome zoetrope—a Grand Guignol of shadows and light.

Cries of pain and death rise all around him. Baltimore turns to the left and sees Sergeant Tomlin and another man stagger backward in a marionette dance of bullets and flesh. They are driven into the barbed wire and thrash there, tearing their flesh with each new motion. Bleeding. Dying.

To the right, the skinny private stands straight as though at attention, the top of his skull missing and a hole where his nose should be. An entry wound. Already dead, he still clutches his rifle and marches three steps forward before tumbling down into the trench with the Hessians who have murdered him.

The tin soldier cannot move.

Baltimore does not realize he has been shot until he feels hot blood sliding down his thigh and his left leg gives out. He does not even raise his rifle as he stumbles, attempting to hold himself up. The gun remains clutched in his hands, a useless bit of metal.

A fresh barrage of gunfire comes from the trench. And as he spins, falling, he sees the faces of the Hessian soldiers, dark with dirt for camouflage, loading their rifles and feeding ammunition into their heavy machine

guns. As the flares begin to die, he sees the men of his platoon moving toward him, Stockton and the giant Macintosh forming around their captain. They return fire, but the ten rounds in the magazines of their rifles will not be enough.

Baltimore falls.

The tin soldier cannot see, but he can still hear the rasping, insinuating laughter of the thing in the carved box, the hideous Jack. The sound is like some terrible machine, a devil's factory. He knows that up on its shelf, in the box, the Jack stirs still, amused and waiting for its chance to emerge.

What it will do then, the tin soldier does not know. But he dreads the moment he will hear the bright, jarring calliope of its handle being cranked, for then he will know the Jack is about to be freed.

For now, the laughter is horrid enough.

And then it ceases.

Time passes, though the soldier knows not how long. He feels the cold, unyielding press of his comrades all around him, tin arms and legs beneath him and pressing down from above.

They are back in their box, of course. The boy has gathered them up and packed them away until the mood strikes him for another war. To the boy, it is so simple, so innocent.

It is a comfort, being back in the box. Stifling, yes, for he is contorted in there, on his back with his legs jutting upward and all of those other tin men on top of him, rifles jabbed against him. But it is safe in the box. There are no enemies here. The two armies are one. Brothers of tin.

It is safe. Even pleasant.

Or it would be, were it not for the cold night and the pain radiating out from his lower thigh where the bullet has pierced him, and the stink of blood and rot.

It begins to rain.

In the box . . . to rain . . .

The cold rain rouses him. Frigid tears trickle across his face and Baltimore becomes aware of the rise and fall of his chest. He can breathe, which means he is not yet dead. The metallic stink of blood lingers in the air; the rain is unable to wash it away.

His eyelids flutter open and he shifts his gaze, trying to work out where he is and how he has gotten there. Other scents fill his nostrils now—the rich smell of damp earth, the thick odor of unwashed bodies. Pain throbs in his left leg, as though someone were jabbing a bayonet deep into his flesh.

Perhaps it is this, even more than the chill rain, that has woken him.

Baltimore finds it difficult to breathe. He lies at an angle such that his legs are elevated and his head hangs backward. His thoughts come slowly, as though he has drunk too much whiskey and woken up in the middle of the night, not quite sobered. His mind feels numb and muddled.

Why is it so difficult to breathe?

The darkness remains, so he has not been unconscious long enough for morning to arrive. Yet as he fights the disorientation that threatens to drag him down into oblivion again, Baltimore realizes that the darkness is not quite so complete as it had been. Dark shapes lie heavily upon him. Cold, damp, rough material touches his face. He lies on a series of small bumps

and ridges that feel like a pile of stones.

Muddled as his brain is, the truth swims up in his thoughts and a breath of despair escapes his lips.

He is in a trench with the dead, clothing sodden with blood and icy rain. The stones beneath him are the jutting elbows and knees of the soldiers who followed him to their deaths. He shifts a bit, forcing his head up, and is rewarded with an explosion of pain in his injured leg. Now, though, he can see that the weight on his chest that has made it so hard to breathe has a face. In the gloom of the stormy night, he can see the gash on Corporal Norwich's cheek. The dead man stares at him with still, tarnished eyes.

Pain stabs his leg again and he wonders at the extent of his injuries. Baltimore blinks and shifts himself, finding a grip on the dead around him. The effort makes his head spin and he pauses to let the feeling pass. He has lost a great deal of blood.

He fights the urge to call for help. There is no way to know if anyone still lives on the battlefield, but if so, it seems far more likely that they will be Hessians than allied soldiers. And what if some of his own battalion do hear him? If they send someone out to attempt to retrieve him, the Hessians will cut them down as well.

Images of his men being slaughtered flicker through his mind, and the guilt weighs so much that it threatens to push him deeper into that hole. He had been frozen, unable to help.

Not that it would have mattered. One more gun would not have saved them, these men whose blood soaks the ground. Now he wishes he could have remained frozen, to avoid the pain and the cutting truth of his failure.

Cold. Baltimore is so very cold. A sleepy numbness comes over him. Silence is better. Safer. He has lost too much blood already, he is sure. Death will not be far off.

Yet he does not want to die in the trench.

Steadying his breathing, trying to clear his mind, Baltimore pushes upward, braced against the dead on either side. His uniform crackles with dried blood. Pain shoots through his leg and he lists to one side. His head rests against the back of a dead soldier.

Again he catches his breath. He has to force his eyes to stay open. His mouth feels dry and he can feel the pull of unconsciousness, but he slides his left arm up between two corpses, one of them the scarred Norwich, and shoves the dead corporal aside.

He can see the sky.

Freezing rain spatters his face and helps to keep him conscious. Fresh air fills his lungs, cold and bracing. Clouds still lie heavily across the night sky but there are breaks through which he can see dim stars, and to the east the horizon has begun to lighten.

If only he can free himself of this tangle of dead men, he will lie peacefully upon the ruined earth. If he remains still, perhaps the pain will not be so bad, and he can let his eyes close, let himself go into that eternal sleep.

He wonders if he will live long enough to see the sunrise, and hopes that he will.

The dead seem to close around him, as though they do not want to release him. A frantic pulse races through him and Baltimore moves. He draws his good leg under him, braces himself again on the dead, and drives upward. Pain drags a scream up his throat but he keeps his teeth clamped tightly and it emerges as a groan. He cannot feel his left leg below the knee, but at the back of his thigh he feels a trickle of warm, fresh blood, and it troubles him.

His hands scramble for purchase. He pushes himself up through legs and arms, body shaking with the effort. His thoughts blur again but Baltimore remains conscious enough to avoid looking at the faces of the dead. The more he touches them, the more he feels their ghosts around him. Accusing specters seem to float just at the edges of his vision.

"I'm sorry," he whispers.

The pain in his leg is like a hammer to the bone, crushing him as he grips the walls of the trench and, with his good leg, uses the mountain of corpses to climb out. He emerges from the trench on a ladder of his own dead soldiers.

He tries to blink away the pain that blinds him, thinking at first it is the rain that blurs his vision. Then black oblivion sweeps him down into its embrace . . .

. . . and again the cold rain awakens him.

For a moment he lies there, incapable of moving, and wonders if the Hessians have seen him emerge. He has heard neither shout nor whisper nor footfall, and so he gathers he has not been noticed . . . or he truly is alone.

The wall of barbed wire looms to his left. Men of his platoon are tangled in the barbs, crucified there, splayed wide and punched through with bullet wounds. One of the men has had his throat cut, perhaps to end his misery, or simply to silence his dying cries.

With a deep breath Baltimore tries to turn over. Blackness swims around the corners of his eyes and when he opens them again the horizon has brightened slightly. Dawn grows nearer every time he drifts.

He lies back to watch the eastern horizon, waiting for the sun. Waiting to die.

Only . . . there are things in the sky.

He blinks again. His thoughts feel soft, swathed in cotton. The haze grows worse. His eyelids flutter but he tries to

keep them open, watching the sky, wondering if the shapes there are mere hallucination or spots on his vision, but they remain. And they move. They fly.

Kites. They are kites, like the one he'd had as a boy, but with shorter tails.

The kites circle and drift and glide and soon they come lower, fluttering down over the battlefield... over the dead. The icy rain runs down his face and neck and fills the orbits of his eyes and he has to blink it away again. He feels oddly peaceful.

When he grows aware once more, Baltimore stares up at the sky. The storm clouds are still dark, but in the breaks between them the stars have faded almost entirely. The horizon has turned a rich, dark blue—the indigo that promises morning.

But not yet.

A flapping noise comes to him across the tormented field and abruptly he remembers the kites.

He lets his head loll to the right. Something moves and shifts in the trench. More than one thing. Black wings arch up, spattered by rain. There is the sound of slapping leather. Not birds, then.

Something other.

The pain seems mostly gone from his leg, along with all other feeling. The numbness there seems as though it is spreading. He doesn't even feel cold anymore.

The noise again... he rolls his head to the left. One of the creatures perches on the coils of wire between two of the dead soldiers. Its tented wings seem too large for its body. It ducks its head toward one of the soldiers, its weight making it bob on the wire as its head darts toward the corpse, studying it more closely.

It seems like the strangest dream.

Baltimore sighs softly.

The creature flinches and turns to look directly at him. Its eyes gleam a hideous, luminescent crimson in the predawn gloom. The ears and snout remind him of a bat, but the creature is huge and terrible. Its slippery, red mouth is lined with long, silvery needles for teeth—all wet with blood.

They are eating the dead.

As Baltimore blinks again, forcing himself to remain conscious, he sees the creature dart its snout forward and tear a chunk of flesh from the throat of a private that all the men had called Topper. Baltimore has never known his real name. The creature yanks back and a strip of skin comes away with the gobbet of bloody meat. It cocks its head and chokes down its prize.

"My God," he whispers.

The creature flinches again and turns, the barbed wire swaying under its weight. It tilts its head and stares at him with a dreadful curiosity in its crimson eyes. The things in the trenches and elsewhere on the battlefield pay him no mind, enraptured by their feeding upon the carrion that had once been his platoon. But this is the nearest, and it has more than noticed him.

It hops down from the wire.

All the muddiness is swept away from his mind now. Baltimore trembles, his breath coming in hitching gasps. He manages to draw up his right leg but has not the strength to propel himself away. His face flushes with the heat of his terror and he stares down across his body and watches the thing crawling across the sodden, churned-up earth in a jerky, scrabbling walk, pulling itself toward him on folded wings.

If he screams, he will draw the attention of the others.

If this creature tears his throat out, it will not matter.

But if he can kill it . . .

His fingers flex as if with a mind of their own, wishing for a rifle. He could lay it across his chest to sight it, can practically feel himself pulling the trigger, the kick of the weapon as he fires. But he has no rifle.

The creature drags itself across the ground in that grotesque hobble, wings spreading. The rain strikes them, obscenely loud. Baltimore locks eyes with it, his breath coming shorter and faster. His right hand shakes so hard his fingertips drum the ground.

It creeps toward him, inches away from his left side, from his hip, and he feels suddenly sure that it moves so slowly to relish his fear. The creature lifts a clawed talon and reaches out.

It *touches* him.

Baltimore can hear the sounds of flesh being torn from the corpses in the trench and on the ground around him, can hear the rain hitting the ground, spattering their wings, but he can only stare into those poison eyes, lit by some unholy light.

It begins to crawl onto him, its wings almost caressing. Its claws are on him, its cold body draped across him, as intimate as a lover's touch. Then it bares its picket-row of teeth and he sees the blood that stains its mouth, the bits of flesh caught on those needles. It inches upward, body pressing against his groin.

He meets its gaze and at last understands, staring into its eyes, that this is no animal, but a creature of malice, with a dreadful awareness.

Baltimore screams.

Wild, mad-eyed, he whips his head around in search of some weapon. At the edge of the trench, tumbled from the outstretched hand of a dead soldier, is a rifle, its bayonet gleaming with cold droplets of rain.

With the last reserve of his strength—perhaps the last bit of life remaining to him—he forces himself to lunge for the blade. The creature's claws dig into his flesh, cut through his uniform, and it clings to him even as he

snatches the bayonet from the end of that rifle. His wounded leg shifts, spilling fresh blood, but he has moved beyond pain now.

The creature hisses.

He thrusts out his left hand and grips its throat, would have plunged the bayonet into its chest had it not lunged at that very moment. Its jaws come at him, eyes on his throat, and he slashes the blade upward, slicing it from horrid mouth to snout to brow.

The creature falls away from him, flapping and writhing on the ground. Screaming, as no animal could scream.

Then it rises, shaking in fury, blood streaming from the cut in its face. Its eyes no longer glow crimson. They are dull, soulless things—gray and flat as stones. Yet he can feel the hatred in the thing, and it sears him.

The hunger has gone from the devil. Only the fury remains, and the glitter of its sleeping intelligence, now awakened.

The creature wipes its talons across its wounded face and flicks droplets of its own blood out across the battlefield. A rictus grin pulls its slashed lips away from a row of narrow, sharp teeth and it comes at him then. It bends and clutches his wounded leg, lifts it, and Baltimore gasps, certain its jaws are about to tear into his flesh.

Instead, with a soft grunt, it *breathes* into the open wound above his knee. Its breath comes out in a mist, the same crimson that its eyes had been, with a stink worse than the dead and a moist, putrid heat.

Baltimore clutches the bayonet tightly, but feels the last of his strength leaving him. Blackness swims at the edges of his vision. But if he loses consciousness now, surely he is dead.

The creature throws back its wings and howls at the storm clouds as though appealing to some ancient, primal god.

The ground shifts beneath Baltimore. He feels it tremble as he stares at the carrion-eater. The creature turns to hiss at him, blood spilling from the gash in its face, soaking into the thirsty earth along with the rain.

The other creatures crawl across the ruin of the battlefield, converging upon Baltimore. One takes flight, circling above the rest.

He cannot scream. Fear shakes him, but he cannot muster the strength even to quake with it. His eyelids are heavy, his head lolling as he tries to fight the black oblivion that smothers his thoughts.

Too much pain. Too much blood lost. Death has come for him, and he will welcome its release.

The creature grins as it bends over him, droplets of its blood spattering his chest and face. Then it spreads its wings like a shroud and springs into the sky, flowing into the night, as black as shadow. Its wings flap with a languid elegance as it rises higher and higher.

In silence, the rest of its kind take flight as well, pursuing the first— their broad leather wings beating and thin tendril tails dragging behind. They wheel westward, disappearing into the gray-black clouds.

Moments later, the sun appears on the eastern horizon, casting a bright golden light upon the hellish landscape of war. It silhouettes the clouds with morning haloes, and limns the corpses, tangled in barbed wire and strewn along the ground.

Blackness fills his vision, blotting out the morning, and at last he succumbs to its embrace. Slipping into unconsciousness, Captain Baltimore feels like he is flying.

Numb, unmoving, once again the tin soldier, he lies upon the heap of his brothers and feels the welcome darkness swallow him at last.

ARRIVAL:

KYRIE

"The first thing they heard in their new world, when the lid was taken off the box, was a little boy clapping his hands and crying, 'Soldiers, soldiers!'"
—The Steadfast Tin Soldier
by Hans Christian Andersen

EMETRIUS AISCHROS HAD FOLLOWED the canal nearly forty miles, all the way from the ocean, and he cursed every step. At the port where he had left his ship behind—for such a large merchant vessel had far too steep a draft to travel the canal—the air tasted sweet. And even in the town the flowers grew wild and colorful. On the farms just a short way inland, crops grew tall and healthy and the breeze whispered across the fields with the blessings of the harvest spirits.

Now, as he followed the wide path alongside the canal, his boots trod upon scrub brush and weeds and broken glass. A mile ago he had stepped over the first dead bird, and they became more common with every yard. On the opposite bank of the canal loomed a strange encampment of mad-eyed, dirty-faced men dressed in tatters. Their shelter had been constructed of detritus thrown off by passing boats. Indeed, the main body of their hut was the rotted hull of a fishing trawler.

They stared hungrily at him as he passed. Aischros stared back, letting them see the hard glint in his eyes, so there would be no mistaking who was predator and who was prey. He did not bother to push aside his heavy wool coat to share a glimpse of his dagger. The merchant sea captain carried his bag over one shoulder, dark cap set low over his eyes to shield him from the sun. One look at him ought to tell them he would be armed, and capable in a fight. The breadth of his shoulders and the scars on his face were clue enough.

Besides, he thought, no one would be fool enough to enter the City unarmed.

Aischros returned his gaze to the brown waters of the canal. A stink rose from it far worse than simple sewage. Death and rot, shit and rust, the stench carried them all, and yet something else lingered under that smell— a natural, noxious odor like the gas from the boggy marsh in Crossley, a place he hoped never to visit again.

Though the sky above was crystal blue and the spring breeze was cool and fresh, the sun shone down fiercely, cooking the seaman and the slow-churning water, so that the wind was not sufficient to carry away the stink.

When he reached the City, it would only get worse.

It loomed ahead like a monolith, blocks of gray and black stone with only the smallest windows visible, high up on the walls. The buildings huddled together with their backs turned, as though engaged in some conspiracy against him. The effect unsettled Aischros. Even from a distance the City seemed a massive fortress, the shadows between buildings so narrow that a spider of claustrophobia skittered along his spine just from looking at them.

Ahead, the canal curved slightly leftward and disappeared beneath an archway that comprised the substructure of the building above. Once upon a time it had been a bridge, but now the entirety of it had been closed in, as though the City had consumed it. As he approached, Aischros saw a small window open above the archway and small hands thrust a bucket out and upend it, spilling its contents into the water. From a distance he could not see if it had been food scraps or excrement, and he preferred his ignorance.

Trickles of sweat ran down the back of his neck. He ought to have removed his jacket now that the sun had grown so brutal, but he kept it on. The cold, dank darkness of the arched tunnel ahead did not look especially warm.

As he trod the worn path alongside the canal, two fat rats ambled out of the darkness. Aischros frowned and stared at them, wondering why the vermin would emerge from the bowels of the City. They darted to the right into a tangle of scrub grass, and as he watched them go he noticed for the first time the strangely shaped things that jutted out from that poor shelter.

As he drew nearer, the details became clearer, though he wished they hadn't. What thrust from the brush were human legs—one foot covered in a dark shoe and the other bare and pale as chalk. Stiff. Dead.

The corpse twitched as the rats gnawed upon it, trembling with their ministrations.

A shout came from within the tunnel. "Damn, Nick, not so fast! Give me a chance."

A boy emerged from the shadows beneath the arch. He wore threadbare clothes, torn and stained, and his hair was a shock of wild black. The path beside the canal became a stone ledge when it entered that dark tunnel, and the boy paused on the rough, hardscrabble ground outside the City, looking around.

"Pick up yer feet, ye lazy sod," he called back into the tunnel. "The rats'll get all the good bits if ye don't hurry it up."

A second boy came out from the tunnel, twice as dirty and half the size. He couldn't have been more than seven or eight and his thick blond hair was matted with dirt. Though the larger now followed after the rats, striding toward the corpse without hesitation, the little blond boy glanced around with wary menace. He saw Aischros immediately, but the mariner did not slow.

"Nick," the other boy muttered, his voice carrying along the embankments of the canal.

But the elder scavenger did not respond. He used his feet to shoo the rats away from the dead man, giving one of them a hard kick, then crouched by the corpse. He glanced once at the City wall looming high above, and Aischros understood for the first time that the dead man had been dumped out a narrow window. Whether he had died before or been killed on impact did not seem to matter much—not when these young vultures had arrived to strip him of anything they might find valuable.

"Nick!" the younger boy snapped.

This time the older one looked up sharply. The moment he spotted Aischros, he grinned and stepped away from the corpse, a tobacco tin clutched in one hand.

He made a small sound—maybe a word, but mostly a snarl, and clearly a warning. He slid the tin into one pocket, and when his hand emerged, a knife glinted in his grasp. The other began to hiss, but neither of the scavengers moved. For his part, the captain continued without hesitation, expressionless as he studied the dark beads of their eyes. Other than the filth that streaked their faces, their pallor was sickly white, reminding him of several strange fish his nets had once dragged up in the Adriatic—things that had let curiosity lead them up from the sunless depths.

As he drew nearer he saw the boys' eyes were a lifeless, lightless black, their features thin and stretched into a natural sneer. In appearance, they were uncannily like the rats they had pursued from the shadows.

Beneath the brim of his dark hat, Aischros narrowed his gaze and glared at them, unblinking. His life had been one of violence and scars, some of which they would have seen had they glanced at his hands, and he had no fear of vermin—whether they walked on four legs or two.

As he approached, unwavering, the boy with the knife lost his churlish grin and backed away into the shade of the embankment beneath the bridge, the corpse he'd been robbing all but forgotten. His eyes were wide and skittish and he held the knife out in front of him, as much talisman as defense.

The younger boy hissed, glaring at him from the edge of the tunnel. He twitched with each step as Aischros grew nearer and then, at last, when the seaman had come within twenty feet, darted up the embankment beside the canal and joined the other. Aischros paid them no further heed, but he remained aware of their position, in case they should suddenly grow brave.

He shifted the weight of his rucksack and tilted his head back to gaze up at the massive bulk of the City looming ahead. From this perspective it almost appeared to be one single structure of shadows and stone and narrow-eyed windows. The bright sunshine and the blue sky added no color to the walls. Even the decorative stonework, faded and eroded and chipped away by time and mischief, seemed only to create the impression of a gigantic tomb.

The tunnel yawned ahead. At home as he was upon the sea, Aischros disliked the idea of being enclosed within that arched passage with the thick, grimy water. Whenever possible, he was careful to avoid rivers and lakes, and the canal was no different. Being so close to it, in the dark . . .

He glanced once more at the sun, marked its place in the sky, and knew he had no choice. Already he had missed the appointed time, as set down in the letter he had received nineteen days past. Noon, the letter had instructed, but the sun had already reached the midpoint of the sky and he had not even entered the City yet. There was no time to find another way in.

A shiver raced through him, in spite of the sun.

From the corner of his eye he noticed a shadow upon the canal and a moment later it fell across him as well. Aischros turned to find a barge passing him by on the canal. Heaped upon it were wooden crates, but its center consisted of a pile of something—perhaps fresh soil or manure—beneath a thick tarp. The bargeman stood atop the heap, propelling his vessel along with a pole. As Aischros watched, he slid it from the water and thrust it down again, then moved to the left, brought the pole up, and thrust it down on the other side of the barge, navigating the foul water.

For the first time, Aischros paused. He stared at the barge as it passed. The bargeman did not look up at him...did not look up at all. His long gray beard and hair were greasy and tangled. Cloaked in a colorless tunic that hung on his thin frame, he hardly looked strong enough for the work, but the pole rose and thrust once more, proving the matter.

The barge passed into the shadows beneath the bridge, and Aischros held his breath. Out of the sunlight, in the gray half-darkness just inside the tunnel, the heap at the center of the barge altered in aspect. It now appeared to be a mound of gray corpses.

The figure on top of the pile of dead men turned to glance back at him. In the shadows the bargeman seemed hooded, dark and silent as the ferryman on the Styx. His eyes gleamed, even as the barge slid into deeper shadows and then into darkness.

For long seconds, Aischros stood at the place where the path beside the canal turned from dirt to stone. He stared into the shadows, awaiting what,

he knew not. When the rat-boys began to stir, as though they might have mustered some courage, he set forth again.

He stepped from the sunlight and into the darkness of the tunnel, into the bowels of the City.

Once upon a time, the place had been a riot of vivid color and conversation. Bright banners had flown and well-dressed ladies and gentlemen had strolled the cobblestones as though on a promenade. Every morning, Market Square had been full of vendors hawking their wares. The aromas of exotic spices and flowers filled the air. Carts laden with fruits and vegetables lined the square. Aischros recalled the scent of winter oranges and the taste of ripe mangoes. There had been nectarines that dripped with the mead of gods, or so it had seemed to him then. He had tasted

pineapple for the first time in Market Square, and had found the largest, most delicious tomatoes and onions he had ever seen before, or since.

Butchers and fishmongers had an entire corner of the square devoted to their fresh offerings. Little girls wandered amongst the stalls, selling flowers from baskets they'd woven with their own hands. Musicians had played all through the marketplace. Aischros recalled a man with a horn and a lovely woman in a lemon-yellow dress who had played violin.

The whole City had been alive then. Men had gathered in parks and pubs and argued about politics with a sense of hope for the future. Newsboys had shouted the headlines from street corners, waving newspapers with the gravity of miniature prime ministers and presidents. Laughing mothers and daughters had exited shops, arms laden with packages containing the latest fashions from Paris and Milan. It had been on these streets that Aischros had seen his first automobile, trundling its way amongst the carriages and horses.

Hope. Life. Color.

All gone now. Eradicated.

The City was quiet and heavy with despair. The banners were mourning black. Aischros wound his way along filthy cobblestones, past broken windows and the faded signs of unattended shops. The buildings leaned inward,

blotting out the sun. From outside the City, there had seemed a protective quality to the way the stone and wood structures huddled together over the streets, but beneath those looming façades, he felt only menace.

He heard no laughter, no debate. A dog barked, somewhere nearby, and while passing a pub he heard an anguished cry and the sound of glass shattering. Aischros paused, staring at the darkened door of the tavern, and considered going to see what had caused that shriek. But he knew his intrusion would not be welcome. Strangers were met with suspicion or open hostility in these dark times.

He hurried on, trying his best to ignore the way the City had fallen into corruption and ruin since he had last passed through. When he came to the sunlit Market Square, he could almost hear the echo of its past joy, could almost smell the ghost of the wonderful scents that had drifted on the air.

But now it smelled of piss and sewage. In the shadows of an alley beside what had once been a butcher shop, he saw gray figures huddled beneath blankets, watching him with dead eyes.

By the time he had turned onto Powderhouse Street, Aischros no longer allowed himself to lift his eyes except to check his location. The few people he passed on the street gave him a wide berth. It occurred to him that the best thing to be done now would be for someone to put the City to the torch—burn her to the ground and sow the earth with salt.

When he came to the inn, its beckoning doorway seemed a mercy. Anything would be better, he thought, than having to spend another moment on the streets of this dead City. The place had become its own tomb, every building a grave marker with dirty windows.

Aischros stepped through the door of the inn, only to find it no improve-

ment at all. He had been to the inn once, long ago, before the war. Like the City, it had been alive then, bright with discourse and ideals, trembling with the creativity that had thrived within. Now only the ghost of imagination remained.

Poets and actors, writers and artists, had gathered here to argue and laugh and dance, to taste absinthe and ale and blur the edges of reality. To imagine worlds and possibilities.

Now it was all dust and grime and

filth, and the place stank of faded glory. Portraits on the wall were cracked and hung at angles apropos for images of opium addicts and suicides. Ideals and imagination had failed, as had their creators. Once the place had been vivid with life. Now it existed as a suckhole, a drain of failed humanity.

He did not have to wonder what had happened here. This was the world now that the plague had come. The war continued, but the plague had made it a specter of itself, attended to only by those who couldn't bear to admit

that it no longer mattered. Aischros stood just inside the door of the inn and understood immediately that the pallid men and women who gathered there lacked even the courage to take their own lives.

They only lingered, haunting the place.

As he entered he heard the words in the air, saw them stealing surreptitious glances at him even as they pointed to a certain chair where a great poet had drunk himself to death, a certain fireplace where a novelist had set his manuscript ablaze and wept over the ashes. Nothing remained but half-formed ideas.

Aischros passed the huge fireplace on the left, masonry so rough that it seemed to have thrust itself out of the earth. He wondered how many manuscripts had been burned in frus-

34   *Mike Mignola & Christopher Golden*

tration there. Now, though, no fire had been laid. The fireplace was dark and cold, as was the air of this place.

He had relished the vibrant life at the inn when last he had visited the City, just a handful of years ago. But the whole world had been different then—before the war, before the plague.

Gray, pantomime people stood lined up at the long mahogany bar at the rear of the place. Beyond them, the bartender frowned, as though Aischros represented some unwelcome species. And perhaps he did: the living. These were not plague victims like the pale, feverish, dull-eyed creatures huddled in shadowed doorways throughout the City, but they were no more alive. He wondered how many afternoons and evenings he would have to spend in this place before all the spirit and spark were drained from him and he became as gray as the rest.

This being early afternoon, some of the tables between the door and the bar were empty. Others were occupied. He had never seen either of the two men he had come to meet before, but he knew them the moment he laid eyes upon them, for they had color in their cheeks. The rest of the patrons were like the inn itself, dusty . . . *dim.*

Aischros stroked his thick mustache and the stubble upon his chin, far too many days from seeing a razor, and paused to study the two men for a moment. One was quite handsome, dressed in a gentleman's suit. A golden chain disappeared into a small pocket in his vest—his watch, no doubt— but its conspicuousness made him either bold or stupid. His sophistication and noble bearing were marred by a wide swath of scar tissue visible upon the right side of his neck and jaw and the diminished right ear, whose lobe must have been seared away by the same fire.

His companion cut a very different figure, small and slender, with hair as red as a fox pelt. The red-haired man had grim features, ordinary save for their harshness, but he was far from ugly. Aischros had not looked at himself in a mirror in some years, but knew well the scarred terrain of his own homely face.

The red-haired man raised his right hand in a small salute of welcome. The ring and fourth fingers were missing.

Rucksack still slung over one shoulder, Aischros strode to the table. The eyes of the other patrons were upon them, but they had not even the spirit to maintain interest in newcomers and already many of them had gone back to the drone of their conversation and the dull taste of weak whiskey.

"You are the two men to whom Lord Baltimore referred in his letter?" Aischros said, voice low and thick with the accent of his Hellenic origin.

The nobleman stood, the picture of courtesy, and extended his hand to be shaken. "Thomas Childress, Junior, sir. And this gentleman is Doctor Lemuel Rose, among the finest surgeons on the continent."

Doctor Rose raised an eyebrow and gave a dismissive shake of his head, as though finding this assessment of his reputation somehow amusing. Instead of holding out his truncated hand to be shaken, he produced a cigarette with his left and struck a match to light it.

"Demetrius Aischros," said the seaman, taking Childress's hand. He had a firm grip, and Aischros liked him immediately, in spite of his obvious wealth and charm.

Doctor Rose drew in a lungful of smoke from his cigarette and then gestured toward a chair.

"Join us," he said, the words expelled along with the smoke.

"I'll fetch you a pint, shall I?" Childress asked. "Or will it be whiskey?"

Aischros knew the ale here would be as flat and flavorless as the inn itself. Perhaps the liquor would be no better, yet he felt certain it would at least be wet, and his throat was dry from his travels.

"Whiskey, I think. I would be grateful."

"Excellent. I won't be a moment." Childress gave them a small salute and made his way to the bar.

In his absence, Aischros and Doctor Rose shifted awkwardly and glanced at each other. Childress had an easy way about him, amiable but intelligent as well. A man used to discourse. In Doctor Rose, Aischros saw a man unaccustomed to such niceties. They had that in common, at least, for the seaman had little use for courtesy on shipboard.

The small man held his cigarette between slender fingers, studying Aischros now over the embers that burned on its tip.

"How do you know Captain Baltimore?" Doctor Rose asked in another expulsion of smoke. "You're not a soldier."

"I'm a sailor. At the height of the war, I offered my ship and my services to the allies. I ran the Channel with her, taking the boys to the meat grinder and bringing home what was left. I carried many a wounded man home from battle. Lord Baltimore was among them. We found we were men of similar disposition. I'd had my fill of the war then, and wanted a respite from the sea. We had become friends, and so for a time after that journey, we were traveling companions."

The doctor nodded. "You knew him shortly after he'd left my company, then. After I'd finished with him."

"You knew him during the war?"

Doctor Rose smiled. "Oh, yes. In the Ardennes Forest. I'm the one who took off his leg."

Aischros blinked at the surgeon, not knowing how to reply. A moment later Childress returned with a pint of warm ale for himself and whiskey for the captain. The three men toasted one another and the absent Baltimore.

"I presume we're waiting for him to arrive," Doctor Rose said.

They looked at one another and, one by one, glanced at the door, as though the words were some theatrical cue. When Baltimore did not appear, Aischros took a drink of whiskey. It was as tasteless as he had imagined, but was indeed wet. His parched throat was grateful.

"And you, Mister Childress? We have just been discussing how we came to know Lord Baltimore. What is your relationship to the man?"

Childress narrowed his gaze. He took another sip from his own ale and glanced once more at the door. "I've known Henry most of my life. Our families were quite close when we were children. A life of privilege, it was. But I can't say I know him better than any other man, despite the duration of our acquaintance. And I confess I have not seen him in many years. I was quite surprised to receive the letter that summoned me here."

Tendrils of smoke curled up toward the rafters from Doctor Rose's cigarette. Aischros studied him, then glanced at Childress.

"Do either of you know why we have been . . . ?"

He wanted to say *invited,* but truly, the tone of the letter had been more of a summoning.

Childress shrugged, some of his earlier bonhomie evaporating. "Henry's note asked only that I appear here at the appointed date and time. He said I would meet two other men of his previous acquaintance and that if fate willed it, he would join us here."

All three glanced toward the door again. Seconds passed in companionable if curious silence. At last, Childress sat up a bit straighter and raised his glass for a taste of ale. When he set it down, the amiable gent had returned, and Aischros realized that this was at least partially a façade. A hollow sadness lurked at the back of the man's eyes.

"All right, then," Childress went on. "Until we ask him, we can't know why he contacted the three of us, but there's another question that's got me curious. Henry Baltimore sends off his mysterious missives and we all come at a run. I know why I'm here, to honor old friendship. But what of the two of you? Why are you here?"

Doctor Rose smiled thinly and glanced at Aischros. The seaman stroked his mustache and considered the question.

"Curiosity," he said. "Loyalty, perhaps, to a man I once called friend. But truly it is the mystery. When I knew him, Lord Baltimore shared with me a terrible story about the war...a tale of evil. I might never have believed him, except that I have seen terrible things in my life, both in my travels with him, and on my journeys across the sea to Mogador and Gaaldine and Socotra, from the Ivory Coast to the Strait of Malacca. A sailor sees many oddities traveling the world. Wonders and horrors alike."

Childress nodded knowingly.

Doctor Rose studied Aischros almost as though he were afraid of the man. "He told you how he acquired the wound that cost him his leg."

"Yes. At first I believed he had hallucinated much of it from—"

"Loss of blood, and fever," the doctor said, and when he laughed there was a dry rasp in his chest. He drew a puff from his cigarette and let the smoke furl out from his nostrils. "Precisely what I thought. At first."

Childress leaned both elbows on the table and looked first at one man and then the other. "Tell the tale, then, gentlemen. For I've heard only whispers, but they make my soul uneasy, like many things I know of Henry Baltimore."

The doctor and the sailor looked at each other. Aischros gestured to the slender man.

"You were with him then. In the heart of the war."

With this invitation, Doctor Rose nodded.

"I was. And I shall never forget it."

THE SURGEON'S TALE:
OFFERTORIO

———

*"All the soldiers were exactly alike with one exception,
and he differed from the rest in having only one leg."*
—The Steadfast Tin Soldier
by Hans Christian Andersen

1

Doctor Rose took one last long draw from his cigarette and then stubbed it out on the table. His pint of ale he ignored entirely. He felt the eyes of his companions on him, but it felt to him as though they were far away now. His thoughts tumbled down into the dark well of memory, where he could still feel the chill and smell the stench of fire and death that he'd encountered in that hellish landscape of the war.

"This was in the days before the plague, when we still thought the Great War was the worst thing that could happen. A wide field, a clearing in the Ardennes, had been turned into a slaughtering ground as our boys fought the Hessians. Nothing but mud and blood out there with the barbed wire, smoke from the rifles, and the screams of the wounded from the trenches. For weeks that battle went on, and we all knew attrition would decide the victor. Both armies would simply keep killing, right until the last man. Unless measures were taken.

"One night, with barely a sliver of moon and cloud cover making the battlefield darker than anything I've ever seen, Captain Baltimore was ordered to take his platoon and cross No Man's Land. As I understand it, the Hessians were waiting for just such a gambit, hidden in trenches with machine guns at the ready.

"Baltimore was the only survivor of that mission. And even that, gentlemen, was a very near thing.

"It was early morning when they put him on my table. When I was through with him, I doubted he would survive another hour. But he proved me wrong. He was unconscious much of that first day and night, and delusional during the brief moments he was awake. His leg was not so badly damaged, but he had lost a great deal of blood. Far worse was that gangrene had set in—"

"So quickly?" Aischros asked.

Doctor Rose narrowed his eyes. The captain's rough, homely features and the scars upon his face made it easy to think of him as a simple brute, but he was no fool.

"Yes. Even at the time, I thought it odd.

"It was two days before he was fully conscious. I went to examine him that morning and found him awake, and he told me his awful tale. Evil had touched him, he said, on the field of battle, but it had not ended there. It had visited him again in his fever dream the night before. His fear, he told me, was that what had been begun might never end . . ."

Adrift between dreaming and waking, Baltimore heard dim voices around him and shivered with a chill draft that came and went as though with the opening and closing of doors. In that limbo between sleep and consciousness he shifted weakly, instinctively trying to escape the terrible ache in his bones.

His eyelids fluttered open from time to time in an ebb and flow of meager awareness, but even those moments were blurred with disorientation. The stink of blood and antiseptic made his nostrils flare. He lay beneath white starched sheets, the feel of them so familiar that in his fugue state he thought himself a boy again; young Henry, the sickly child so often forced to take to his bed, embarrassing his father with his delicate constitution. Thin and wracked with fever, too weak even to lift a spoonful of soup to his lips, he lay in his bed and waited for his mother to come, to put a cool, soothing hand on his brow and kiss his nose, and promise him that one day he would be strong. One day her little Henry would have his father's lands and title, and become Lord Baltimore.

Yet in some primal part of his brain he knew that this was illusion. In addition to the voices that drifted to him in the fog of his fever, there were screams. There had been no screams in his home as a child. His father would not have countenanced screaming. And these were not the cries of children or the fury of an angry wife. They were shrieks of agony and panic.

Subconsciously, Baltimore tried to cling to the illusion. Better to be that sickly child than . . . what? When he shifted, trying to find comfort on his starched bed of nails, his left leg sang with pain, as though it were filled with broken glass. His breath came in hitching gasps and his brow furrowed. The only vaguely conscious thought in his mind was the knowledge that he was not *aware*. His mind swirled in a sea of disorientation and he struggled in those near-wakeful moments to reach the surface.

When awareness came, it arrived in a whirl of confusion. He took a long, shuddering breath and his eyes opened halfway, a film blurring his vision. Several times he blinked but could only partially focus, even then. His hearing seemed muffled, the only sound audible to him the damp, ragged rhythm of his own breathing.

Vision wavering, he fought to remain conscious as the fever attempted to drag him down once more. His nostrils flared and he shivered with disgust at the stink of death and decay that surrounded him—a miasma of putrid odors that eradicated all other scents.

For a moment, the darkness claimed him, and he lost himself within its embrace.

Minutes or hours later his eyes blearily opened.

Around the flat, hard bed upon which he lay there were curtains, some of them hanging open, others closed. The curtains were shades of white and gray, yet streaked with dark stains that he felt sure must be blood. A crimson handprint marred one. They were drawn haphazardly and Baltimore let his head loll to the right. Afternoon sunlight streamed through a stained-glass window whose colors depicted an angel with a flaming sword driving Adam and Eve from the Garden of Eden.

He gazed upward then, and through the haze of his dimmed vision saw the rafters high above; he knew the place. His battalion had taken a church to use as a makeshift hospital. He had hoped never to see it from within, not even for prayer.

The pain in his leg seared flesh and bone and sent jolts of agony up through his entire body.

His head lolled to the left. The stench became immediately worse and his stomach roiled with nausea. Between two curtains he had a view into the battlefield hospital. Pews had been arranged so that patients not as badly wounded could be stretched out upon them. Others, bandaged and bloody, lay upon beds and tables, some half shielded by curtains.

The church echoed with screams of pain, of sorrow, and of madness.

A soldier and a nurse passed, carrying between them a corpse wrapped in a blanket. The soldier stumbled and nearly fell, and though the fog was once more closing in around him, fever about to claim him, Baltimore craned his neck to see what had gotten in his way.

A human forearm lay on the stone floor, burnt and broken, the flesh ravaged. But the stump showed an even cut.

Baltimore could not breathe.

The floor was spattered with bloodstains, some still gleaming wet. Deeper into the church he could see an area surrounded by screen curtains that hung ten or twelve inches short of the floor, and visible beneath them were other severed limbs with sheer, gore-encrusted ends. A hand. At least two arms. The wreckage of a leg, still wrapped in a shred of uniform.

People moved behind those curtains, shouting to one another. More screams erupted in the church and he knew they came from that hidden place, where the surgeons were at work at the often futile task of trying to save lives. From beneath those curtains, blood ran along the cracks between the stones in the floor.

He scowled in revulsion and turned away. As he shifted, fresh spikes of pain shot upward from his left leg.

Baltimore froze. His eyelids fluttered, vision blurring badly, but in that moment he recalled with utter clarity a terrible scream that he had heard while deep in his fugue state.

His own.

He had opened his eyes and seen a nurse and a medic above him, and only when he saw that the medic was bent over him did he feel the man's powerful grip on his arms. Holding him to the table. He had glanced downward and another man had been there, a thin doctor with fiery red hair whose hands were coated with fresh, bright blood.

"No," Baltimore grunted now. And, weak as he was, he forced himself up on his elbows and stared down at his lower half, covered in a blanket striped in two shades of blue.

The shape of his body under the blanket was wrong. He tried to move his left leg, and it shifted. Just the stump. The rest of the leg, from a point just above the knee, was gone.

Impossible. He felt it. The pain in the lower leg, that shattered glass, cutting, searing agony . . . he had felt it. As he tried to move it now, he could *still* feel it.

A small rose of blood seeped into the blanket where it touched the stump of his leg. Fresh bleeding. A memory slithered into his mind; the kites feasting upon the dead of No Man's Land, the remnants of his platoon, the thing that had crawled on top of him. He trembled as images came to him. His knife had flashed out, slashing the demon's face. It had roared pain and fury to the storm-laden night sky, and then turned on him with those eyes like polished stones.

He could still see its open mouth, rows of long needle teeth bared, as it lifted his leg and *breathed* into his wound. It had felt like maggots wriggling inside the flesh of his thigh and in that moment he knew it had poisoned him.

Slowly he sank back. His eyes closed, the church hospital disappeared from around him, and for a time he drifted in nothingness, not even the screams of the ravaged and dying able to reach down into the fog of his fever.

He slept fitfully, consciousness touching him only in brief and erratic instants. The pain in his leg was a ghost, haunting his dreams. And ugly dreams they were—nightmares of dead Hessian soldiers staring up at him from trenches half-filled with blood, rifles aimed at his face. Dreams of unnatural black things flying across the predawn sky, circling above his ancestral home, perched outside his bedroom window, and him that boy again . . . in that bed, in that room. Out the window the ancient oak—whose arms were wide enough to lift the entire manse—was filled with black creatures, its branches bent under the weight of that devil's flock.

When consciousness returned to Baltimore, night had fallen. He knew not how many days and nights had passed since he'd been brought there. The screams of the day had become moans in the dark, and though an icy chill gusted through the church as if the doors had been thrown open to winter, the stink of death had retreated.

Yet Baltimore was not soothed.

He felt the maggots again, not merely on the stump of his leg, but all over his body, something crawling on him. Whether it was the breath of the devil or merely the evil taint of its regard, he felt it there, close with him. Though his eyes were heavily lidded with sleep and the dying embers of his fever, he knew this was no nightmare.

So drained he could barely feel his body, could not lift a finger in his own defense, he rolled his gaze to the left.

A man stood by him, though he knew it was no man. The devil was gaunt and gray, colorless save for the red slash of a knife wound that slit its face from brow to chin. Its right eye was a dark hollow, an empty socket. Somehow this was the creature that had plagued him on the battlefield, the thing whose breath had infected him. Now it stood on legs and was shaped like a man— wore a man's clothing and a man's face—but that eye was the same terrible, vacant black as the creature's.

When it grinned, the cuts he had sliced in its lips peeled open, glistening crimson.

Baltimore sighed—a long exhalation that he knew would be his last. The gray devil bent over him and he smelled the rotten-meat stink of its breath and the charnel smell of the battlefield on its clothes. Even the sickly child he had once been had never been so helpless.

The creature bared its teeth, but came no closer. It reached up and traced a finger along the crimson stripe that gashed its face.

Yet somehow he had no fear. This monster had come to finish the job it had begun on the ruined, blood-soaked earth of the Ardennes. Baltimore lay there, a man with one leg and no strength to fight. *So be it,* he thought.

"When you go from here," it whispered to him, "you must remember this. We were content to prey upon the dead and dying, but you...you have made it a war between us.

"Remember."

He felt himself sinking into the cra-
dle of unconsciousness once more and
twisted on the stiff cot beneath him. The
effort only weakened him further and he
could not keep his eyes from closing.

When they flickered open again, he
was alone in the cold and the dark.
Barely able even to move his head, he
shifted his gaze from side to side, searching for that gaunt, gray figure in the
shadows of the church. But he could see only curtains and the still forms of
patients lying on pews and cots and tables, asleep. Or dead.

Someone wept in the dark.

On a pew partially obscured by a filthy curtain, a wounded soldier lay
with his eyes open, staring at Baltimore. His head was wrapped in blood-
soaked bandages. A sheen of sweat covered his face, beads sliding down pale
cheeks like tiny tears. His flesh was gray, his eyes dull as stones. The soldier
was not dead, but that gaze was lifeless and soulless as a shark's.

Whatever had happened to the soldier, it was more than just a wound,
more than just a fever.

In that gray flesh and those lost, flat eyes, Baltimore saw the touch of the
devil.

2

Doctor Rose fell silent. His throat was parched from having related to his companions the tale Captain Baltimore had told him years before. He often dreamed of his time in that battlefield hospital, and remembered it well. The stones had absorbed the screams of the dying without ever echoing back a reply from the god in whose name the church had been erected.

He took a deep draught of ale, then slid the glass onto the scarred table. Childress and Aischros scrutinized him, both men wearing darkly curious expressions. Doctor Rose withdrew a cigarette case from the inside pocket of his jacket and carefully removed one with the remaining fingers of his right hand. He returned the case to its concealment and then produced a small box of matches.

Childress sat up a bit straighter in his chair, this handsome man the most robust creature in the room. Any other place, he would have drawn the attention of the women in the bar, for both his looks and his obvious affluence. Here, the women noticed only the bottom of their empty cups, and only then so that they could be filled again.

A barmaid entered from a narrow passageway at the back of the room and carried plates of food to a pair of thin, older gentlemen in threadbare suits. They had about them the look of disgraced scholars. No steam arose from the plates, but that came as no surprise. In a place as leeched of life as this, the food would never arrive hot.

Even so, his stomach growled.

"In all the time I traveled with Lord Baltimore, he never told me that story," Aischros said. "Only bits of it; fragments, like a nightmare he'd had."

"It sounds quite like a nightmare, in fact," Childress said, eyes narrowing. "There is no more to the tale?"

Doctor Rose cocked his head. "I feel quite certain there is. However, Captain Baltimore left my care the day after he related these events to me."

The ugly sailor took a sip of his whiskey and wiped at his lips. "Why tell you? Of all those he might have spoken to, why did he choose to tell the man who had sawed off his leg?"

A frown creased Doctor Rose's forehead as his stomach rumbled again. "Are either of you hungry?"

He caught the cigarette between his teeth, slid out a wooden match, and struck it on the table. It flared to life and he glanced at his companions as he drew the first inhalation of smoke. The tobacco was a powerful Turkish blend that he rolled himself, and the flavor filled his lungs as he exhaled.

"After that tale?" Childress replied. "I think not."

Aischros, the sea captain, was not so discerning. "I've eaten little today. I'd welcome a meal."

"Anything they serve here would be tough as shoe leather, and just as flavorful," Childress said.

Aischros smiled, which pulled at the many small scars on his face and only served to make him all the uglier. The sea had hardened and weathered him, but it had given him an air of unmistakable nobility as well.

"I've eaten worse," the captain said. "Sometimes, no flavor is best."

Doctor Rose pushed his chair backward, the legs scraping the wooden floor with a small shriek. He took another long pull at his cigarette, and as he exhaled, he began to stand.

Childress held up a hand. "Hold on a moment."

The doctor raised an eyebrow, halfway up from his seat. The cigarette dangled between his fingers.

"You didn't answer Demetrius's question."

Doctor Rose slid back into his seat. He held the cigarette up and stared at the glowing cinders on its tip. "I could not say with any certainty what prompted the young captain to share his story with me. Perhaps he felt a—"

He paused, and his two companions leaned in.

"Go on," Childress prodded.

"It is an incredible tale. Most would not believe it," Aischros said, his accent blunting every word. "Why did you?"

The doctor sat back, his truncated hand falling to the table, his cigarette almost forgotten. He looked at the two men again, and understanding seeped into him. They were brothers, of a sort. He had been about to suggest that Baltimore had told him the hideous tale of the demon on the battlefield because the captain had sensed a kind of kinship with him. But he did not have to explain that to these men. The expectant look in their eyes made that clear.

"Wouldn't *you* have believed him?" he asked.

Aischros lifted one corner of his mouth in a warped smile, and then glanced at Childress.

"The illness Henry told you he'd seen in that patient," the blond man said. "What was it?"

The doctor splayed the fingers of his left hand on the table, feeling the rough-hewn wood. Unbidden, they slid over to grasp the matchbox that still lay there. He picked it up, tapping it on the table.

A sickly tremor went through him.

Aischros uttered a low, dismayed grunt. "Is that not obvious?"

"I can only tell you what I believe," Doctor Rose replied, a weak, false smile touching the corners of his mouth. "Captain Baltimore told me that he had seen that same look on other faces there in the church in the Ardennes, in the hospital— several patients and at least one nurse. The dull eyes, the gray flesh.

"I did not believe him then, but in the years that have passed since, I have come to realize the signs were there; that the early days of the plague had been upon us, and Baltimore had recognized them. Though, of course, he could not have known what was to come."

Silence ensued once more. It was a dark thing to contemplate, the beginning of the plague. The spread of that illness that had so many, even in this City, sleeping in alleyways to escape the touch of the sun on their gray, mottled skin.

Childress glanced at Aischros, then back at Doctor Rose.

"What did you see?"

The doctor narrowed his gaze. "See?"

"Henry told you that story for a reason. It wasn't that you were the only one around. Something about you made him feel like you would believe him. There's a cynical aura about you, Doctor, and a discomfort as well. It sets you apart from others. I confess it feels familiar to me. So, I ask you again, what did you see?"

Doctor Rose ran his tongue over the dry skin of his lips. "A story, then."

"Before you begin, Doctor," Aischros said, "and I hope you'll forgive me for asking, but was it losing your fingers that stopped you being a surgeon?"

Lemuel Rose's eyes went wide and he became positively jovial as he stubbed out his latest cigarette.

"No, good Demetrius. Opium ruined me as a surgeon. A wonderful retreat, opium. But costly. My decline was swift, from the heights of medical society to the drudgery of addiction. When I could no longer pay my debts, that was when they took my fingers."

He slipped a wooden match out of the box and struck it against the rough wood of the table. It flared to life and he held it in front of him, as though he could see all of his past in the flicker of that small flame.

"A story, gentlemen. One I rarely tell without the persuasion of the poppy. But I shall tell you, and perhaps you will believe it."

Scant months into the war, I was stationed in northern Gaul, doing my best to patch up the grim, determined men who had sworn an oath to shatter the

Hessians' dreams of conquest. Already, many lives had been spent in the effort, but hopes were high. The men who had come to war considered it a noble calling. This was before the allies had begun to feed their boys into the jaws of the hungry lion of war. They were soldiers, in those early days, not children.

I sewed them up when I could, cut off their limbs to save them if I had no other choice, and closed their eyes for them when their ghosts had slipped away. It was bloody, desperate, hideous work, and yet their courage was contagious. I felt young and strong and full of hope; certain, as they all were, that we would crush the Hessians before winter arrived.

How foolish we all were. A generation of naïve boys.

We were camped in a small river village near Escaudain, where we had taken over a schoolhouse to use as our hospital. Though the people of the village were still there, they seemed only to haunt the place, ghosts in their own homes. Even now, I feel certain that they were grateful for our efforts. We were fighting a war for their freedom, after all. But they resented our presence as well. As if we had brought the war to their doorstep instead of the Hessians.

The most bitter of all was a young woman named Marie Alena, who had been the teacher in the school before the windows were covered to keep the enemy from seeing light within; before the screams of the wounded and dying echoed from its walls; before their blood stained the floor. I have never returned to that place, and never shall. But it would not surprise me to learn that after our departure, they had razed the schoolhouse to the ground.

I had become a surgeon to save lives. A hospital ought to be a place of healing and wonder. War obliterated all such illusions. Those who emerge from hospital more or less as they entered are fortunate, for they have been to the necropolis and survived. The soldiers I healed were sent back onto the battlefields because the war had not finished with them yet. The hospital and the war were conspirators, you see. The one feeding the other, and being fed in return.

The dead were shipped home alongside those who could no longer fight, who had lost an arm or a leg, and whose hearts or souls had been killed, even

if what remained of their bodies still lived. War and the hospital sent home corpses and hollow men.

But madmen were kept on. Some commanders treasured them. Lose a limb, you could no longer fight; lose your mind, and they'd put you on the front lines. The men whose minds were shattered either made the best killers or the best shields. They were superlative at the two things soldiers were built for—killing and dying.

None of this comes as any surprise to the two of you, I know. Mister Childress was a soldier, and you, Captain Aischros, carried home the ravaged boys the Great War had ruined. I merely remind you of these things so that you will understand how taken aback I was to be approached, one cold, misty morning in the early fall of that damnable year, by a Lieutenant Agnar, of the Nordic forces.

Rumors had flown for weeks that the Norsemen were making their way south, and that they'd had great luck dispensing with any resistance the Hessians had placed in their path. The enemy had not concentrated any great mass of troops that far to the north, and the Nordic warriors overran them easily. They arrived in northern Gaul and joined their forces with the rest of the allies. One such detachment had been assigned to our battalion, but I only learned of this when—while washing the blood of a dead sergeant from my hands—I turned to find Lieutenant Agnar watching me.

It was a strange morning. The village was quiet. The sergeant had died of complications during surgery to remove shrapnel from his lungs, but he'd been wounded in the previous day's fighting. Two days earlier we had shipped home several men who could not return to battle, and so that morning the hospital's only patients were those recovering from minor wounds.

Soon, the medics would arrive with the freshly wounded, but in those few morning hours it felt as though the entire encampment and the village itself were holding their breath.

Lieutenant Agnar wore the thick, layered uniform of the Norsemen and had the build, coloring, and bearing of his Viking ancestors. He identified himself and inquired as to whether I was the Doctor Rose he had been told to seek. When I confirmed that, indeed, I was, he gestured behind him and

brought forth into the hospital another Nordic soldier—a gaunt young man with troubled eyes.

When the young soldier, apparently of his command, came up beside him, the lieutenant wrinkled his nose as if he had only at that moment noticed the stench of blood and death and putrefying meat that had saturated the walls of the schoolhouse.

"Fix this one," Agnar said, "or I will cut his throat myself."

He cast a baleful look at the soldier, took two steps backward—as though he had no wish to turn his back on us—and departed.

I gazed at my new patient, and he at me. His eyes were wide and I saw in them some frenzied quality, but not madness. Or so I thought.

"You don't look injured, Private," I told him.

He replied with a mordant laugh and shook his head. "No. I have perfect health."

His accent was thicker than his lieutenant's, but he spoke English well enough. When I prodded him, he gave his name as Harbard, but it was clear he was reluctant to speak to me. Several times he inquired as to the time, but seemed dissatisfied with my assurance that it was early morning. He went to the window to seek the position of the sun, but the gray mist that hung over the village and the river made it difficult to judge the time of day in that fashion.

"What is it you fear, Private?" I asked.

"The coming of night," he said without hesitation, glancing away from me, unwilling to meet my eyes.

"There is something that appears after dark that frightens you?"

"Yes," he said softly. "Oh, yes."

In the gloom, I had failed to notice how dark the hollows were beneath his eyes. Now I moved nearer to him and they seemed almost painted there. I wondered how many nights he had gone without sleep.

"Am I to understand that your lieutenant brought you to me because he believes you insane?"

Though I had offered counsel to wounded soldiers before, I had never been asked to treat a man with a mental condition. They were kept on the battlefield. There was no asylum in war for the mentally ill.

Private Harbard shook his head, glancing again out the window, searching for the reassurance of the sun. "No. He wants you to believe that. But he is also afraid of the night; afraid that when tomorrow comes, I will be the only man alive—again."

Though his words chilled me, I endeavored to conceal my reaction.

"Given Lieutenant Agnar's instructions," I said, "perhaps you ought to dispense with the portentous allusions and tell me precisely what it is that caused him to bring you here."

The private insisted that I would never believe his tale, and I—naïve as I was then—assured him that many true stories begin with those words, and that I would keep an open mind.

He perched on a chair, somehow managing to look even more tired and gaunt than ever, and took a deep breath before he began, as though merely by telling the story he had somehow surrendered to whatever tormented him so dreadfully.

"Fifteen days ago, my company entered a village in the northlands. We were journeying south to kill Hessians—to stand with you against the Hun. It was a quiet, pretty village in the hills, a place where the old gods are still worshipped and no one ever thinks to go anywhere else. A light snow fell, early even for my homeland, but amounted to nothing.

"The people did not want us in their village, but they let us sleep in their barns and replenish our water from their wells. One of the elders of the village lived in a large stone house with a stable full of horses, and he invited Sergeant Egill, the commander of our company, to sleep beneath his roof. But when we wanted food, they resisted. The whole company became angry and threatened them. The villagers were not troubled by our anger. They seemed entirely without fear of us, and this only made us more furious.

"The sergeant met with the elders. These were our people, and we did not want to fight with them. We were on our way to war to protect them from the Hessian wolves who were marching northward and would, in time, take their daughters and burn their homes. The whole world has heard what cruel masters the Hessians have been to those they have conquered. Sergeant Egill tried to reason with the villagers, to tell them that we all must stand together. If we were to fight for them, food for our journey was the least they could offer.

"Still they refused. A dry place to sleep and fresh water were enough, they said. Winter was coming and they needed all that they had. And, they claimed, they did not need our protection from the Hessians, for the village was defended by Bjame, a terrible demon-bear. They appeased the bear with sacrifices and in return, they said, Bjame would allow no harm to come to them.

"We laughed, the other men and I—mocked the villagers for their old beliefs and old ways. The elders ignored the sergeant's demands. He gave them a single night to change their minds, and warned them that the consequences of refusal would be ugly.

"Later, the sergeant had Hafporr and Skagi pass word that we should meet in the village square. Most of the soldiers in the company were large men, and I looked on them as I would the heroes of Valhalla. Yet they prized me above all, for I was the best tracker, the best hunter. When we needed meat, they trusted that I would kill it for them.

"Sergeant Egill gave Skagi six men and told him to keep watch in the village. The rest of us he led into the forest, determined to find any bear that might have its den nearby and drag its  carcass back into the village to show them what sort of protection all of their sacrifices had bought them. The sergeant kept me with him and I searched for signs of bear. The others spread out through the woods.

"It was not long before I found the trail. The sergeant and I followed it, the autumn moon bright. I smelled the blood even before we discovered its source. A shape lay across the path before us. It might have been just a raised tree root, if not for the stink of death that lingered in the trees all around us. As we neared, we saw that it was a human arm, and scattered about the forest floor ahead were other parts. The sergeant stepped in a pool of blood and slid in it, almost falling.

"We did not find the dead man's head. The torso had been cracked open, the innards strung from the branches of the trees. In the quiet of the forest, we could hear blood dripping. Though tattered and stained, the uniform bore the insignia of our company.

"The sergeant's voice was grim and low. 'Find it,' he said.

"'No need,' I told him. For now that I'd grown used to the stink of blood, the other powerful scent around us had made me realize the truth. The corpse was bait.

"Before I could tell the sergeant that the beast had never left the spot, it rose up from behind a felled tree to our left—an enormous, ancient bear, its hide crossed with scars that gleamed in the moonlight. Sergeant Egill whispered something I could not hear, entranced in some way I still do not understand. The barrel of his rifle drooped instead of rising. Bjame thundered toward us.

"I pulled the trigger and the machine gun jumped in my hands. I realized I was holding my breath but could not force myself to gasp for air. I shot the beast six, perhaps seven times. One bullet went through its left eye and burst out the back of its skull. It lumbered on, roaring, and then it fell dead, collapsing on top of the sergeant, breaking his left arm and two fingers on his right hand where he clutched his rifle.

"Though it did not move, its huge chest heaved like a bellows. Its one milky eye stared at me. It started to shift, to drag itself off the sergeant, who cried out as his broken bones ground together.

"I drew my knife and circled behind the bear. Grunting, it tried to follow me with its one eye. I stabbed it in the back, twisted the jagged blade in the bone and gristle of its spine. It shuddered and I climbed onto its back. Carefully I reached down and slit its throat; hot black blood spilled out onto the ground.

"Dying, it found some well of strength. With a hiss of air bubbling from the wound in its throat, it threw me from its back. I rose up quickly, but the monster was too close. It fell upon me as I brought my blade up. The knife pierced its belly and I ripped upward.

"I blacked out, smothered beneath the beast, but soon I came awake to the sound of gunfire and found Sergeant Egill and some of the other men from

the company standing nearby, shooting into the dead creature. The ancient bear twitched with each bullet, but it had been dead for long minutes by then.

"I had killed it.

"The men cheered me and painted my face with its blood. They dressed my wounds. The bear had died even as it fell upon me. I'd been fortunate. Or so I thought.

"The sergeant had the men tie ropes to the bear and drag it into the village. Men and women fled at the sight of us, some of them weeping. Screams of horror rose as the bear was dragged up to the front of the stone house of the village elder who had given the sergeant a bed, where we set fire to its great, stinking corpse.

"In the morning, we took what food we wanted and no one in the village attempted to stop us. The black, charred remains of the bear were still smoking in the street. We had stripped away their primitive beliefs and mocked them, but still we were furious at the way we had been treated, so we stole the horses from the elder's stables. The old man attempted to bar the way, and Skagi shot him. Sergeant Egill would have done it if he'd still been able to hold a gun.

"We left the village then, still damning the souls of its people, though we had murdered their god.

"The afternoon of the second day out from the village, I became feverish. I remember little, save the hands that put me on the back of a horse, and the steady ambling gait of the beast beneath me as the company continued southwest to join the war against the Hessians. Word came by messenger of the movement of other Nordic units, and in my fever

dreams I heard a few words here and there, enough to know that ten thousand men had been sent to battle. Our company, fewer than thirty, was small in comparison. A family.

"Three days ago, the morning sun woke me. My fever had broken. I felt strong and full of life. Ready for war.

"Even as I opened my eyes, the stench overwhelmed me. The scent was familiar. Blood, and death, and the animal stink of the demon-bear. I stood and turned in a circle, gazing at the carnage that surrounded me. Sergeant Egill lay nearby, head torn from his body, a few inches of spine jutting from the stump. The clearing where we had been camped was strewn with ruined corpses and parts of men and horses alike. Most had been torn open, organs dragged out of them, and—

"Enough. You understand.

"Now, understand this.

"I wandered a day and a night until I joined another company making its way here. This very morning, the nightmare became true again. I woke, as before, covered in blood, the only survivor in my camp.

"Lieutenant Agnar had gathered all of the units under his command into a battalion of brave Norsemen, and they discovered me on their way here this morning. I washed in the river, clothed myself in the uniform of a dead man, and now I am here. I told Lieutenant Agnar my tale. I thought he would execute me. I hoped he would.

"But he does not truly believe me, Doctor Rose," the young private said, staring with his haunted eyes. "And I fear that, tonight, it will happen again, and instead of a single company—a few dozen men—I will wake in the morning and find my hands painted with the blood of hundreds."

A glass shattered near the bar. The innkeeper cursed someone as the son of a whore and a ripple of weary laughter went through the place.

Doctor Rose blinked, becoming aware of the rest of the inn for the first time in long, long minutes. His throat felt dry and he lifted his cup and took a long swallow, only to curl his upper lip in disgust. The ale had been flat and warm before; now it tasted even worse.

"You didn't think he was a lunatic?" Aischros asked, raking the back of his hand across his stubbled chin.

"I confess I thought him disturbed," Doctor Rose replied. "But not a lunatic. If these men had been murdered, surely some evidence would have surfaced. The facts would be known, if not the explanation for them."

"And what was the explanation, Doctor?" Childress asked. "Surely you pursued the issue."

Aischros held on to the arms of his chair and settled into it with a creak of wood, as though preparing for rough seas.

"The superstitious might think the demon-bear pursued the soldier and tormented him," Aischros said, in his growl of a voice.

Doctor Rose lit another cigarette and inhaled, tapping the matchbox on the table.

"Yes," he agreed. "But Private Harbard had other ideas..."

3

You must understand that, until the war intruded, I had lived what could only be called an ordinary life. Privileged, yes, but ordinary. As a surgeon I had seen dreadful things, borne witness to the depravities and cruelties of humanity, and the vagaries of fate in the form of disease and happenstance. Terrible as it was, the war represented only an amplification of that ugliness. My experience had always been one of the real and the tangible. Consequently, I approached the young private's claims with a rational mind, and considered only two possible hypotheses. Either he was, indeed, delusional, or the northern village whose god Harbard had slain had been exacting a terrible vengeance upon him.

Since the latter seemed highly unlikely, I could only presume the former. I confess that Private Harbard's tale had chilled me, and his gaunt frame and vacant stare lent the story a certain veracity. Of course, I told myself that I was a man of medicine, of science, not a superstitious fool.

Through the open windows of the schoolhouse where we had set up our hospital, I heard men shouting and the rumble of truck engines, and I knew that they carried the wounded from the morning's bloodshed. The troubled young man must have seen in my manner that I was about to dismiss him, and a kind of wild panic lit his face. He became quite animated, and reminded me of the warning from Lieutenant Agnar.

My mind had already sped forward to the surgery I would doubtless be performing in moments. Several nurses bustled into the schoolhouse, going about their preparatory work as though we weren't there.

"Doctor, you must believe me," Private Harbard said. "The lieutenant will tell you that these massacres were quite real. Either the demon-bear punishes me, or it has passed its curse to me and I have wrought these horrors with my own hands. I cannot sleep in this camp tonight; the risk is too great. If you had seen the slaughter—"

I held up a hand to forestall any further conversation. "I must see to the injured, Private. But I agree that something must be done to solve the mystery you have presented. With apologies, I believe there must be some other explanation for all of this, some unknown perpetrator. But the truth should not be difficult to determine. Doctors Hendron and Kenney will attend to the hospital late this afternoon, and you and I shall venture northwest into the forest, far away from the camp, from the village, and from the field of battle."

The private shook his head worriedly. "I'll tear you to pieces," he said.

His tone unsettled me, but I did not let him see how much.

"I will find myself a perch high in a tree and watch over you through the night. If anything at all odd should happen, I will be there to witness it."

Then the medics rushed in, carrying the first of the day's wounded on a stretcher. The man had both hands clamped over a gaping wound in his abdomen and prayed swiftly and softly, as though the words were a mantra.

"Return an hour before nightfall," I instructed Private Harbard. "I shall be prepared."

The words echo in my mind to this day.

My work that morning and into the afternoon is a blur to me now, just as it was then. I recall one hulking soldier who had a bullet lodged in the jowls of flesh beneath his chin. He seemed not to have felt the wound at all, but when I removed the bullet, he bled so fiercely that I could not close the many layers of fat and flesh quick enough to save him. I am certain there were amputations and sutures and burns, but I remember nothing further.

By the time Private Harbard returned, I was exhausted. Yet I readied myself for the venture, as promised, and we set off immediately, striking out to the northwest—first along a hunting trail, and then into the deeper

woods. Strange as the circumstances might have been, I exulted in this opportunity to escape from the stench and the screams of the hospital.

Shortly before nightfall, we came to a clearing that suited our purposes. At my companion's insistence, and feeling faintly ridiculous, I tied his wrists and ankles with thick rope, and then bound his arms to his sides. With some difficulty, I managed to climb a tall oak at the southern edge of the clearing. Its trunk was split, and I situated myself in the crux, perhaps eighteen feet above the clearing.

Harbard lay on his bedroll, tightly bound, and I kept watch from my perch. Exhausted as he was, it did not take him very long to get to sleep despite the discomfort of his bonds, and envy set in rather quickly. The young private was taller than I, and his hair blond, but otherwise I suspect we were mirrors of each other. I have always been thin—some would say gaunt—and as tired as I was, I imagine there were dark crescents beneath my eyes to match his own.

Hours passed. I drew a thick blanket like a shawl around me, but the cold wind and the songs of the night birds lulled me. Had I not prepared, I would certainly have fallen asleep there in the embrace of the tree. But I had brought smelling salts with me, the very sort I had often used on patients, and when I felt myself succumbing to weariness I administered the scent.

I had long since lost track of the time, but it must have been after midnight when I heard a low, rhythmic growl, as if from some lumbering beast.

I took a sharp breath, and regretted even that small sound. If I gave away my presence, it would be to my peril. Whatever else I might have believed, I felt sure of that.

Holding my breath, afraid to make any movement at all, I peered down into the clearing below. My heart thumped so loudly in my ears that it took a moment before I was able to locate the source of that steady huffing noise.

It came from Private Harbard.

A shudder of relief went through me and I cursed myself as a fool. The rhythmic growl was nothing more than the sleeping soldier, snoring. His breathing had changed as he slept, and the ragged noise had sounded bestial.

His story had made me even more uneasy than I had realized, and I began to regret going out into the forest with him. I ought to have just told the lieutenant that he was delusional and let Harbard's own commanding officers deal with him. Instead, I was stuck in a tree, muscles and bones aching, cold and frustrated.

I muttered a curse under my breath and shifted my position, preparing to climb down and wake the young Norseman, to demand that we return to camp immediately.

The snoring grew louder, and even more bestial: a steady growl.

The soldier's bound, sleeping form twitched once, twice, a third time. He lay on his side, and in the moonlight, his profile was quite clear. He looked peaceful, and very young.

He twitched again, and his mouth opened. It stretched impossibly wide, though his lips did not tear. Dark forms jutted from his throat, pressing those jaws open, forcing them farther apart.

I cannot say that what I felt was terror, precisely. It was as though I had been transported out of the world that I had always known. Frozen with astonishment, barely aware now of the danger to myself, I watched as the soldier's mouth was stretched wider still by huge paws, with claws like knives.

In moments, the bear began to emerge. It crawled out of the soldier's mouth and then stood, sliding his skin off as though it were a suit of

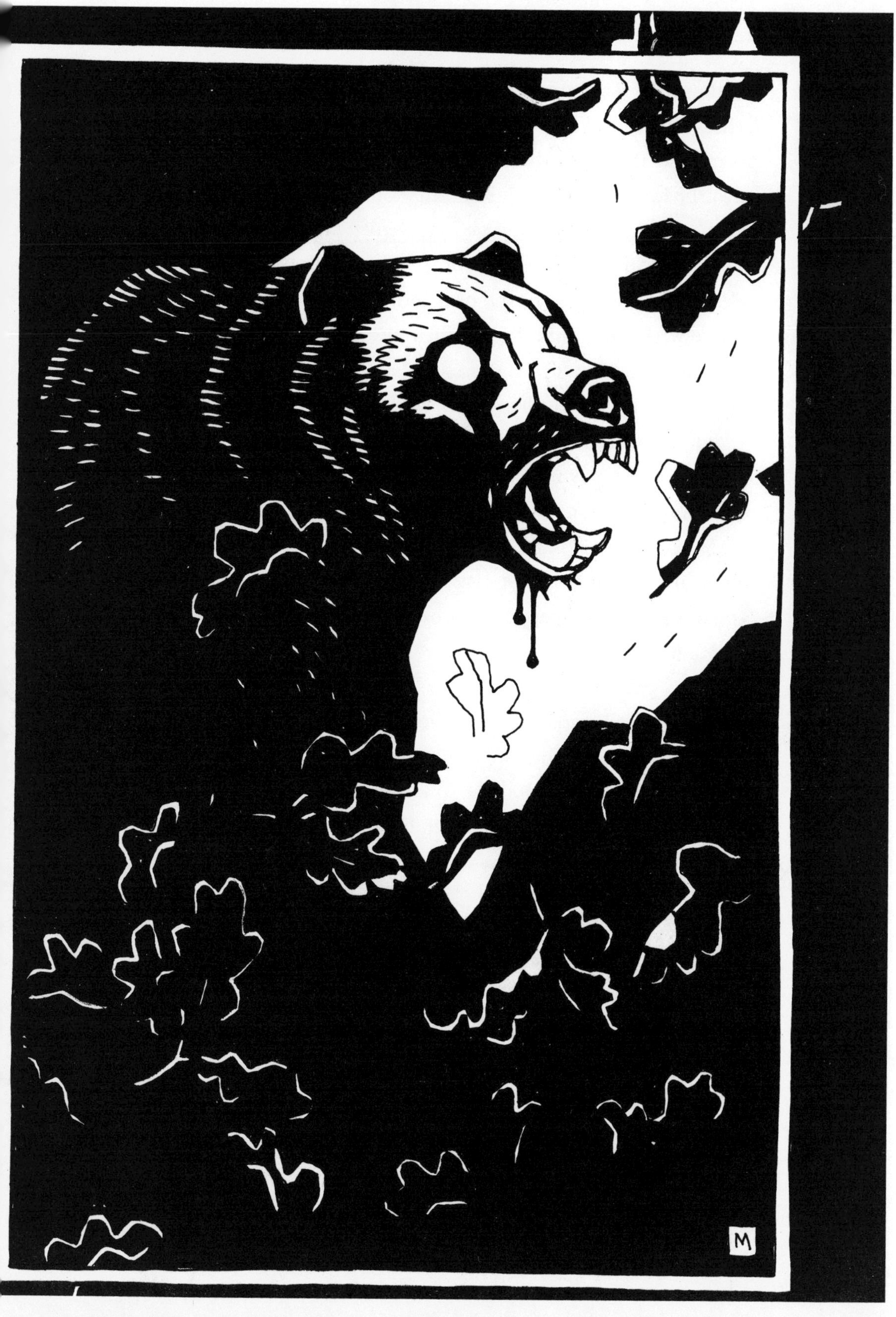

clothes. It stood ten feet high and its eyes glowed in the moonlight. Monstrous and unnatural, it stepped away from Private Harbard's skin, his uniform, and the ropes that had bound him, sniffed the air, then started off into the forest.

The wind had been my savior, I believed, carrying my scent away from the beast. All through the night, I waited, paralyzed with fear and wonder. Then, just before dawn, the bear returned with its knife-claws and muzzle coated with blood, and slipped back into the skin and uniform of the soldier. The ropes that bound his wrists and ankles were still in place. Those I had used to tie his arms to his sides had slid down around his waist.

Somehow, Harbard was still sleeping.

Doubt me if you will, gentlemen, but this is no tale passed down through generations. I witnessed it all with my own eyes.

Morning coaxed me down from the tree, and I sat and watched the Norseman sleep. When at last the private woke, and I had untied him, he asked me what had happened. I had no choice but to be truthful.

Rather than surprise, he greeted the news with resignation and determination.

"It is what I feared, Doctor," he said. "And so, I must ask you to indulge me one last time. When we return to camp, please tell the lieutenant that I am to be returned to combat."

Stunned, I asked what he intended to do. I could not keep his secret and

be a party to further slaughter. Private Harbard vowed that no more of his countrymen would die because of him. He had a plan.

I did as he asked.

On the battlefield, that very afternoon, he surrendered to the enemy and was taken prisoner.

The following morning, there was no gunfire from the enemy line. Cautious, thinking that the Hessians had withdrawn from the battle, allied troops made their way across the battlefield to investigate.

In the enemy encampment, they found a massacre. Not a soul had been left alive. Despite the carnage—as if wrought by some animal—they found no sign of a bear or any other beast. But they brought back the strangest thing—took it to us at the hospital to confirm that it was, indeed, what it appeared to be.

The skin of Private Harbard, still in his uniform.

The smoke from Doctor Rose's cigarette curled lazily in the gray afternoon light. A muddle of low, dreary voices surrounded them.

Doctor Rose smiled at his companions.

"The world was no longer ordinary to my eyes. That, my friends, is why I believed the tale told to me by Captain Baltimore."

THE SAILOR'S TALE:
SANCTUS

———

"On the table where they were being set up were other toys, but the chief thing which caught the eye was a delightful paper castle. It was altogether charming, but the prettiest thing of all was a little maiden standing at the open door..."
—The Steadfast Tin Soldier
by Hans Christian Andersen

1

Aischros sat forward in his chair and studied Doctor Rose, transfixed by his tale. The wood creaked beneath him. Decades at sea had made him lean but thickly muscled, and he had been tall and broad to begin with. The chair seemed barely up to the task of holding him.

Childress had his elbows on the table, chin resting atop steepled fingers, and he regarded Doctor Rose with grim interest. For his part, the doctor seemed unburdened now, having told his tale, and he set down the wooden matchbox he had been tapping through the telling.

When neither Aischros nor Childress questioned him further, Doctor Rose stubbed out his cigarette.

"Now then, Demetrius, shall we have the serving girl fetch us something to fill our bellies?" the doctor asked.

The mariner arched an eyebrow. After the story the man had just told, it seemed quite surreal that none of them remarked upon the strangeness of it. Had three other men been gathered there, surely such a conversation would have taken place. But Aischros knew that Lord Baltimore had called him and the others together for a reason.

Aischros nodded. "Poultry, Doctor. Whatever they have. I find savory pies suspect, because cooks can hide anything in them. And I don't imagine the steak here is anything less than burnt black. However dry a piece of chicken might be, though, salt can cure it."

"Very good," Doctor Rose replied, standing, clutching the matchbox in his left hand. "And you, Mister Childress? Have you changed your mind?"

Childress seemed to come awake. He sat up and smoothed the front of his coat, and straightened his tie. Aischros thought that the color in his tie seemed somehow less vivid than when he had first joined the men at the table. Perhaps it was the lengthening shadows of afternoon, or perhaps simply the effect of lingering too long in such a dreadful place.

"You know," Childress said, "I think I will have a bite, after all. I gather all three of us are patient enough to wait until Henry arrives or the innkeeper ejects us. If you gentlemen are going to dine now, I might as well join you. Some sort of stew, for me, I think. There's little chance of it being hot, but it will, at least, not be burnt."

Doctor Rose smiled, inclined his head, then turned to seek out the serving girl.

"Do you believe him?" Childress asked, when Doctor Rose was out of earshot.

Aischros narrowed his eyes. "Don't you?"

He rose, needing to stretch. Bones popped in his back and shoulders and he let his head roll, loosening the muscles in his neck.

"Another ale?" Aischros asked.

Childress gazed balefully at his glass a moment, then looked up. "By all means. It's awful, but perhaps if I drink enough, this place will not seem so sepulchral."

Aischros laughed. "Maybe. And maybe it will only grow more so."

"Pleasant bloody thought," Childress muttered.

The mariner shook his head in amusement, and went to pick up another round of drinks from the bar. This time, there would be no whiskey for him. As he sipped, it began to taste more like mule piss, instead of less. Ale all around, then, and flavor be damned.

When he returned, Doctor Rose and Childress were in the midst of conversation. Aischros slid the glasses of ale onto the rough tabletop and took his seat, the wood creaking another warning. His companions had interrupted their conversation upon his approach and now they turned to regard him in silence. Cigarette clutched in his ruined hand, the scar tissue over the stumps of Doctor Rose's missing fingers shone a ghostly white.

"What is it?" the mariner asked, troubled by their scrutiny.

Doctor Rose leaned back, as comfortable now in the rigid wooden chair as a sheik upon a bed of velvet pillows. "You've already said that Baltimore entered your company after departing mine. Mister Childress and I were hoping you would share the story of your travels together."

Aischros drained a third of his ale, then set the glass down. He was pleased to see that it was cold enough to begin a ring of condensation on the wood. Even so, it had no flavor. He dragged the back of his right hand over his stubbled chin and his mouth, wiping away a thin film of ale. It had no froth, for it was flat.

He ran his hands over the pitted, scarred table, then settled more deeply into his chair.

"By the time I carried Lord Baltimore back from the war aboard my ship, I'd had my fill of those ruined men and their dead eyes. He was one of them, yes, but there was something different about him. He seemed somehow apart from the other wounded men on that journey. They kept away from him as much as the cramped confines of my ship would allow, but they didn't appear to be aware of this. The man had a strange light in his eyes, my friends, and at night he insisted he be kept on deck so that he could watch the sky, as if afraid some attack would come from above.

"I asked him, that first night, what he was looking for. 'Kites,' he said. Only later did I understand what had him so frightened. All those years ago, I thought it was just shattered nerves. Despite his injuries and his missing leg, the morning seemed to rejuvenate him. As his fellow soldiers still gave him a wide berth, I struck up a conversation with him.

"With the sun high and warm and the sea shining blue, Lord Baltimore behaved differently. He seemed of good cheer, hopeful, and eager to return to England and his home. He knew a hospital in London where he believed he would be able to acquire a wooden leg, and he thought to travel there and rest a while before returning to the island on the Cornish coast that was his ancestral home.

"It had been a very long time since I had visited London, and I had never explored farther north by land. Most of England was unknown to me. The sea had been my life, and I knew I would never leave it for very long, but the idea of leaving my mission behind for a time and visiting a place where there were people who were not killing and dying every day was a powerful temptation.

"I shared these thoughts with Lord Baltimore on the third day at sea. Though the sun shone brightly and the sky was clear, he cast an anxious glance skyward.

"'Demetrius,' he said, 'it will be no easy task for a one-legged man to travel to London. If you'll give over command of your boat to your mate for a while, I'd be grateful for your company on my travels.'"

Captain Aischros shifted in his creaking chair. Doctor Rose and Mister Childress had listened to this part of his tale without taking so much as a sip of their ale.

"He was afraid," Childress said quietly.

Doctor Rose slowly nodded his assent. "When the curtain of the world is pulled back and we realize how much of what lies behind it is unknown to us, fear is the only rational response."

The doctor puffed on his cigarette and glanced impatiently toward the small door that led to the kitchen; a display of nonchalance that Aischros believed to be an act. A mask.

The words could have applied to Baltimore or to Doctor Rose himself.

Aischros stared at his ale but did not attempt to reach for the glass. He felt comfortable in that wooden chair. Though he knew it must be illusion, it seemed to him that the whole inn—perhaps the entire City—rolled beneath him like the unfathomable sea.

"You traveled home with him, then?" Childress asked.

"In time," Aischros replied. "We journeyed first to London, and spent several weeks there, while Lord Baltimore had a wooden leg made. It was a curious appendage, different from any other that I had seen before or have since. He could afford the finest work, and certainly it must have been. The hospital supplied him with a temporary leg, a stump of a thing, and with it and crutches he was able to move around fairly well. I saw much of London in that time and, though he often attempted to remain behind, I usually managed to convince him that I needed him as a guide.

"It did him good, I thought, to be out amongst people. The man rarely discussed his experiences in the war, but more and more I came to realize just how heavily it weighed upon him. No ghosts tormented him, but the horrors that had befallen him in the Ardennes Forest haunted him far more than any ordinary specter.

"Still, he seemed to be improving. He did not look at the sky so often, or stare at shadows as though he expected them to move. I had great hope that the traces of the man I saw beneath that grim exterior would emerge completely.

"Then, one afternoon, several days after he had been given the unique leg that had been made for him—not some sea dog's peg, but a hinged, jointed limb carved from the finest wood—we saw a coachman sitting up on his seat at the front of a carriage. He seemed nearly dead, slumped there with the reins in his hands. He was not, of course. His eyes were open and he was breathing, but his flesh had a gray hue to it and a sheen of sweat covered him. His eyes were wide and dull and black—"

Doctor Rose coughed and reached for his ale.

Childress stared at Aischros. "Early signs of the plague."

"As you say," Aischros agreed. "From that point on, we noticed it everywhere. And word was spreading quickly. The whispers said that the plague was devastating, moving throughout the continent. It was worst on the battlefields, but the cities were troubled with it as well. Promises were made. In London, the authorities claimed that the English Channel would keep them safe, that the plague had not reached their shores yet. But Lord Baltimore and I had already seen proof that this was untrue.

"We left London and struck out to the northwest. At last, Lord Baltimore was headed home."

* * *

On a perfect day, five weeks after Captain Aischros had delivered Lord Baltimore once more to English soil, the two men arrived at Boscastle Harbor. It was a picturesque township—the only natural harbor along twenty miles of rocky Cornish coast—and beneath the blue sky and the golden sun of that day, to Aischros it seemed a storybook place.

Baltimore quickly arranged for a local fisherman to ferry them out to Trevelyan Island, where the family's ancestral home had stood for over three hundred years. Throughout their travels he had expressed many times the desire to send a letter ahead of his arrival, but had always decided against it. His family, he told Aischros, would worry too much; better to surprise them with his early return from war than have them fret about his condition for weeks in anticipation. If he could adjust to life with only one usable leg, his family would follow suit.

"I can only imagine what horrors my mother, my sister Helen, and my dear wife would conceive if I informed them of the loss in a letter," he had told Aischros as they departed London by coach a week before. "Better they see that I return to them, if not whole, at least healthy."

Now, as the fishing boat made its way through the harbor and along the inlet toward open water, Aischros looked at Baltimore and those words returned to him. The ocean breeze whipped at Baltimore's hair and the color had risen in his cheeks. The sight of the little village with its pretty houses, chimneys rising high on both sides of the valley around the harbor, had raised Baltimore's spirits significantly. As the fishing boat carried them out from the protection of the rocky mouth of the harbor and into the rough seas off the Cornish coast, a smile blossomed on the younger man's face that Aischros thought must be the only true, untainted happiness he had ever seen in his companion.

In that moment, he did look healthy. But it was the first time Aischros would have made such an assessment. Baltimore did not have the gray, sickly pallor of the plague victims they had seen in their travels, but he certainly did not seem well. Whatever invisible specter haunted Lord Baltimore, it had not departed as Aischros had hoped. Instead, it lingered in the man, tainting his every word and gesture.

Or it had, until now.

Aischros could not help smiling in return.

"Home at last, eh?"

Baltimore glanced at him. They stood at the aft of the boat, out of the way of the crew.

"I married less than a year before departing for the continent—for the war," Baltimore replied. He held on to a thick railing, managing his balance admirably. "I do not think I shall ever leave again. My parents wish for a grandchild, and my wife longs to hold a babe in her arms. For the first time, I understand the desire. Once, I wanted to journey around the globe—see the whole world—but I believe I'll be content now to have Trevelyan Island and Boscastle Harbor be my world, and count myself a lucky man."

Aischros looked past him and saw the rocky coast of the island rising up from the water to the northwest. Beyond the craggy face, Trevelyan Island was thickly forested, an oasis of green in the vast sea. The roofs of several elegant homes were visible here and there, but the greatest of these was an entire ridge of stone and wood that could only have been the estate of Lord Richard, the twelfth Baron Baltimore, which one day his son, Henry, would inherit.

"It seems a lonely place," Aischros said.

Baltimore seemed unable to tear his gaze from the sight of home, but he shook his head. "No. A quiet place, yes. But there are other families on the island, those who settled there under the protection of the first Lord Baltimore, and servants, of course. There were not many children, but I had friends, growing up.

"Most of them are gone now, of course. Off to war, or simply to find a larger life. Some of their parents have remained, but several of the houses are empty now. For me, this was never a lonely place. It was simply home. I enjoyed the quiet. Some of the fondest memories I have are of times spent alone, playing with toys that my father had . . . had given me."

His voice had faltered, and Aischros watched as Baltimore raised a hand to touch his forehead as though a sharp pain had come upon him.

"Are you all right?" the mariner asked.

Lord Baltimore glanced at him, and all the ruddiness the wind and his homecoming had brought to his pallor had faded. "Yes. Sorry. Just felt a bit disoriented suddenly."

"Perhaps we ought to sit. The sea's a bit rough."

Baltimore smiled thinly. "Says the man who's been aboard ship his entire life. Don't you ever get homesick, Demetrius?"

Aischros shrugged. "I don't have another home."

"You don't talk about your childhood."

"Never really had one. Not the way you mean. Hard parents, hard luck, and hard work. I went to sea the first time at ten years old, and I've drifted with the tide ever since. Traveling with you has been the longest I've spent on dry land in one go in all those years."

Baltimore seemed touched by this. He reached out and gripped Aischros's shoulder firmly. "And I've been grateful for the company. It's all hard times now, isn't it, with the war and the plague? We've just got to take care of our own now."

The fishing boat rocked on the surf as her captain steered her toward a stony beach on the low side of the island, where a formidable-looking dock thrust out into the water. At the aft railing, the two companions kept their footing with ease, in spite of the rough sea.

"Yes, sir. It's all we can do, in such times," Aischros agreed. He nodded toward the island. Close as they were now, it was easy to make out most of the upper floor of the Baltimore estate, its ancient stone façade making him think of an abbey or monastery. The windows glinted in the sun, brilliant and inviting.

"And now you're home," the mariner said.

A troubled expression eclipsed the sunlight on Lord Baltimore's face a moment. "You're going to stay with us a while? You'd said that you would. Let Trevelyan Island show you a bit of hospitality. Hot meals and a comfortable bed. It's the least I can do."

"I'll stay for a few days. But this little taste of the sea's got me yearning for *my* home, and my ship."

As the crew brought the fishing boat into the dock, the two men lapsed into companionable silence. Lord Baltimore seemed overcome with relief at their arrival and Aischros did not want to disturb him.

The mate put a plank down so that they could descend to the dock. Aischros followed Baltimore down, concerned that his friend might not be able to manage with his wooden leg, but he had become quite acclimated to the false limb and made it to the dock without incident.

As Aischros went down the plank he glanced to the north and for the first time noticed a blackened, burnt area of the woods. The ruined shell of a home stood in its midst, gutted by fire. He wondered how the blaze had started.

Baltimore spent a moment speaking with the captain of the fishing vessel, then turned and beckoned to him.

"Demetrius, come. These gents are going to bring our things up to the house. Now that we've arrived, I can't be patient another moment."

Aischros smiled. Whatever cloud had passed over Baltimore's heart had dispersed. The fishermen would carry their bags and the various gifts that Lord Baltimore had purchased in London for his family to the Baron's estate.

The blunt stump of his wooden leg pounded the boards of the dock as he hurried toward the pleasant, narrow, winding lane that led up into the woods toward the sprawling manse.

There were no gates at the entrance to the grounds and gardens of the Baltimore estate, but a pair of granite posts had been erected on either side of the lane, spanned by an iron arch, from which hung a wooden sign bearing the family coat of arms. When Aischros and Baltimore passed beneath the arch, they saw a woman coming down from the house in a black dress. With the blue sky above and surrounded by the vivid green of the lawn and the trees at the edges of the property, she seemed almost wraithlike—a sliver of the night; darkness gliding into day.

"Elowen?" Lord Baltimore said, his voice a harsh rasp.

Aischros glanced at him, saw the concern etched in his companion's features, and then looked toward the woman again. She was young and fair, though she wore her hair pulled back severely, and she wore a look of great anguish.

Could this creature truly be the vibrant, laughing girl Baltimore had spoken so often about, his beautiful Elowen?

"Lord, please, no," Baltimore whispered, hurrying as best he could, limping now on his wooden leg.

Aischros kept pace with him, but said nothing. He was not a fool. He knew the black dress was a symbol of mourning.

"Ellie?" Baltimore called, and Aischros saw him shift his gaze, just for a moment, from his wife up to the front of the house. It was dark and quiet, as though it stood empty now, though surely there must have been servants within.

Elowen Baltimore shook her head in sadness and raised a hand to her mouth as she froze, there in the lane, staring at her husband's wooden leg.

"Henry," she said. "Oh, my darling Henry."

They went into each other's arms and Aischros could only stand back and lower his gaze to the ground, offering them that courtesy.

"I saw the boat coming in and I told myself it couldn't be you. But I've placed my hope upon every vessel that's come to the island since the day you

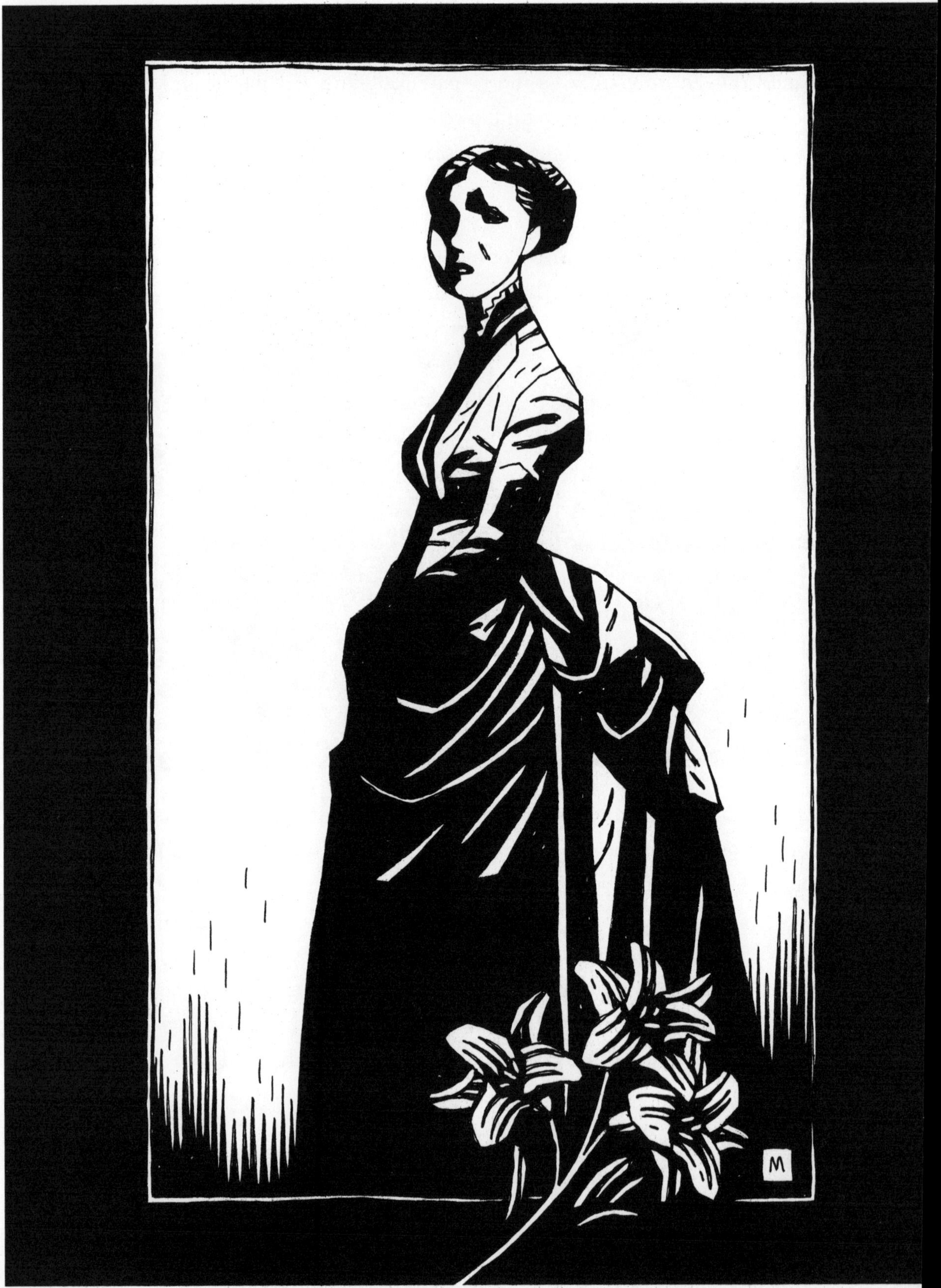

left. At first, I thought I imagined you, that my wish had given me an illusion ... but it is you, Henry. It really is."

As she spoke, Aischros could hear the hitching in her voice, so that when he glanced up, the tears that streaked her face surprised him not at all.

Baltimore pressed his forehead to Elowen's. "What's happened, Ellie?" he rasped, and there was a dreadful certainty in his voice. The specter that had so long troubled him had descended fully upon him now.

"Where is everyone?" Lord Baltimore asked.

Elowen raised a shaking hand and covered her mouth, tears running freely. She twisted the hand into a fist as though that was the only way she could force herself to uncover her mouth, to speak.

"The plague, Henry. It's claimed them all. Your parents, and Helen, too. They're all gone now."

Baltimore stepped back from her as though struck. Aischros wanted to reach out to him, but it was not his place. A shroud of grief for his friend closed around him.

"No," Baltimore said. He cocked his head and searched his bride's face, eyes pleading for her to tell him that this was some mistake, or some terrible prank.

"I'm sorry, my love," Elowen replied, her hand upon her heart. "We'd had word that it had begun to reach England, but never imagined it could strike as mercilessly as it did here. Others on the island were taken by the sickness as well. Kenan Howel was the only survivor of his household. He left them all in the house and set it ablaze; burned it to the ground, thinking he could keep the plague from spreading. Half of our servants died, and several fled for the mainland. It's passed now. No one else has become ill in nearly a month."

Baltimore flinched. He had begun to shake as well, but not a tear fell. He grew paler still and stared at his wife.

"When did this happen?"

"It's been almost six weeks now. I prayed every day for your safe return, Henry. I've been so alone."

Courtesy and propriety warred within Aischros. He knew he ought to offer his condolences and introduce himself, and took a step toward Lady Baltimore to do precisely that.

"Henry?" Elowen said, taking her husband's hand. The worry in her eyes was alarming.

"No," Baltimore said, once more shaking his head. His entire body began to tremble. "No."

He collapsed there, in the lane in front of his childhood home. Lady Baltimore tried to hold him up, but his fingers slipped from hers and he slumped to the ground.

She followed him to the ground, black dress pooling around her as she knelt by him.

"Henry!" Aischros shouted, the first time he had ever called Lord Baltimore by his Christian name.

Elowen held her husband's face in her hands, speaking to him in low tones, telling him he could not leave her alone again. Aischros fell to his knees beside his friend and felt his throat for a pulse. The man's chest rose and fell steadily.

Surely, Lady Baltimore had noticed him previously, but now for the first time she gave him more than a glance. Her gaze upon him was desperate.

"What's wrong with him?"

"His heart still beats. He is breathing," Aischros replied. Then he frowned, studying Baltimore's face. "His eyes are open. He may still be conscious. I've seen such things before, with soldiers coming home from war. I'd thought he would be all right, but this news . . . it was too much for him."

Elowen glanced up toward the house and Aischros understood at once. He slid his arms beneath Baltimore and lifted the man off the ground.

"Come. We'll bring him inside."

And though she was now the Baroness Baltimore and he only an ugly, dirty, lowborn foreign sailor, she did not hesitate at all. He had arrived with her husband, and she would not question their acquaintance. Aischros had met other highborn women who would not have been so accepting, even under the worst of circumstances.

"Thank you," Elowen said as they hurried toward the stone manse. "I couldn't have carried him myself, particularly with that—"

She gestured toward her husband's wooden leg, and Aischros saw the pain in her eyes. That the woman had not also collapsed after what she had endured—and now, seeing her husband missing a limb, and succumbing to his own grief—it spoke volumes of her fortitude.

"It's nothing," he said, only because it would have been rude not to speak.

"What is your name?" she asked.

"Demetrius."

Baltimore had begun to mutter feverishly to himself, but the words were impossible to decipher. As they arrived at the door, Elowen touched his forehead with the back of her hand.

"He's so warm," she said.

Better than cold, Aischros thought, but did not say.

Then, just as she opened the door and he carried Lord Baltimore across the threshold, the disoriented man spoke more loudly.

"The Jack-in-the-Box is laughing again," he said, eyes staring at nothing, lost somewhere in his mind. "I think he may get out."

2

As he told his story, Aischros felt as though he could see the past unfolding before him. He gazed into a gray corner of the inn and the spiritless men throwing darts seemed to drift like smoke, the wall disappearing so that he could bear witness to that terrible day for a second time.

"What did you do?" Childress asked.

Aischros blinked, and the dart-players and the wall resolved themselves to solidity again. There was no window to the past in that corner, only the deepening shadows as the late-afternoon light dimmed further. It was nearly twilight, and the faded spirit of the place ebbed into a deeper gloom. He and his companions might be ruddier of complexion than the gray souls that occupied this place, but in that strange hour before dark, he felt like just another haunt.

"Demetrius?" Doctor Rose said.

"Hmm?" Aischros said, turning to them.

The scrutiny of his companions brought him fully into the moment, though the disquieting feeling of the memory lingered.

"What did I do?" he echoed. "What could I have done? Lord Baltimore had become sickly and feverish. At first, his missus thought he only needed to rest and to confront his grief over the loss of his sister and their parents. But when three days had passed with no change, and a parade of doctors from the mainland could give her no cure and no comfort, Lady Baltimore determined only to wait until the fever passed.

"I remained under that roof for nearly a week, no more use to her than the doctors. By then I had been a month and a half away from my ship, and now longed to return to the sea, to have a purpose. I felt lost there, on Trevelyan Island.

"I feared for my friend, and worried for his wife, who would be alone now in that great house, with only her servants for company. But I felt I could not stay another moment. I promised to return with my ship before the year was out.

"Lady Baltimore said that she was grateful for my help, and my loyalty to her husband, but I could see in her eyes that she thought my departure some betrayal. It made me hesitate, but guilt was not enough to make me stay.

"It was nearly four months before I returned. By then, the evil that had only begun to taint Trevelyan Island upon my first visit had consumed it entirely, and Lady Elowen Baltimore was dead."

The cemetery stood on a bare hill at the northwest point of Trevelyan Island, surrounded by trees on three sides, with the fourth overlooking the cold, gray Atlantic. Demetrius Aischros walked the winding path amongst the graves of the island families, his gaze drawn again and again by the view of the sea. There was nothing but churning ocean as far as the eye could see, as though one might follow it until the end of the world. But to him, the endless sea was a siren call. Even now, it tugged at him, and he knew he would follow it until his final days.

Exposed to the elements, the cemetery was buffeted by brutally cold winds that swept across marble and granite gravestones and rough earth without mercy. Aischros turned up the collar of his peacoat and thrust his hands into his pockets. His cheeks stung, but where his flesh was striped with scars, he felt numb.

No rain fell, but the gray sky hung low and threatening, and though it was early afternoon, the gloom was thick as dusk. The sooner he could leave this godforsaken place, the better. But first, he had to pay his respects.

He had returned to his mission, working for the allies, ferrying fresh soldiers to the front lines and bringing the mangled veterans back from battle, only half alive. With each voyage, he had been haunted by the feverish mutterings of Lord Henry Baltimore.

And every time he had to look at another young man who'd been mutilated on the field of battle, or seen a woman or child with those black eyes and the gray, sweat-sheened face of the plague, he'd felt the weight of his failure to return. He had wondered what had become of Lord and Lady Baltimore, but had devoted himself to the war, telling himself it was out of duty, that he had abandoned his mission too long already.

In his heart, he had known the truth.

He did not want to return because he feared what he might find.

By then the plague had spread so far, claimed so many, that soldiers had thrown down their weapons and slogged home through mud and forest and over mountains to rejoin their loved ones, to hold their sons and daughters and wives while so many died. The Hessians and the allies were still at war, but the fighting was, for all intents and purposes, over.

Without the military to pay him to ferry men back and forth, Aischros had no choice but to return to merchant shipping and fishing to survive. But he had known he could no longer put off fulfilling his promise to return here and look in on Baltimore.

He had found the sprawling manse empty, hollowed of all but a terrible dread that seemed to loom in every stone and beam. The island had been all but abandoned. Only two homes still seemed occupied. One was a small cottage with smoke rising from the chimney; but when he knocked and called, no one came to the door, as though they were hiding from him—from anyone. He found the second house after trying nearly every dwelling on the island, knowing he ought to flee, but determined to fulfill his promise now that he was here. The place was inhabited by an obese old woman, her two fisherman sons, and a menagerie of snarling, hissing cats.

After securing a promise from Aischros that he would leave before nightfall and would never fish the waters around their island, the old woman told him that Lord Baltimore had departed Trevelyan after the death of his wife, and not been heard from since.

The news had struck Aischros hard. Lady Baltimore had seemed so alive, alight with intellect and hope and love for her husband, that he could not imagine her dead. The world seemed comprised mostly of dull, lifeless people now; even those not touched by the plague seemed diminished by it. Those who still lived vividly were rare and precious.

He had no way of knowing where Baltimore had gone, but knew he could not leave the island without visiting the family tomb where Elowen Baltimore had been laid to rest with her husband's parents and sister and ancestors.

Aischros cast a final glance at the rough northern seas and then continued along the path through the cemetery. It ended ahead, at the highest point on the windblown hill, where the massive Baltimore family crypt was set against the trees that bordered the cemetery. The tomb was half lost in shadows and the rest seemed to blend in with the gray gloom of the day and the promised storm. The black iron door seemed cut out of the fabric of the world, as if by stepping through it he might enter the realm of death itself.

"Superstitious fool," Aischros muttered to himself, teeth chattering as the wind whipped him. He laughed softly and shook his head, but it was forced. He would not be able to shake the dread that enfolded him until he set sail again and was far from Trevelyan Island.

At the front of the tomb he stopped and stared up at the letters carved from stone. BALTIMORE. Aischros crossed himself and folded his hands in front of him, regret and fear and guilt uneasy within him.

"Save your prayers," a voice said.

Aischros flinched, startled, and took two steps back. He narrowed his

gaze and tried to see into the shadows to the right of the crypt. A figure seemed to resolve there and Aischros shivered. Had the man been there all along? He told himself it had to be, for it was impossible that he had simply coalesced from the shadows, no matter how it had appeared. He must have been in the trees behind the crypt, watching as Aischros moved through the cemetery, waiting for him to approach.

He must have been.

"Who are you?" the mariner demanded.

The figure came toward him, a monk in a hooded brown robe, tied at the waist with black rope. Light glittered in his eyes like candle flames and his cheeks were flushed. His age was impossible to determine, save that he was old, his skin like papyrus. He had a long hooked nose that seemed suited to his thin, nearly skeletal build.

He wore a dour expression, stern as a schoolmaster.

"The time for prayer has passed."

Aischros nodded. "So you've said. What do you know of it?"

"A great deal."

Hope and curiosity arose together. "You know where Lord Baltimore's gone?"

"Only where I hope he has gone. Only the purpose I hope he has undertaken."

"Riddles," Aischros snarled. Anger made his chest rise and his hands curl into fists. "I've beaten men for clever answers."

The monk spread his hands and bowed his head. "I give you the only answers I have."

Aischros frowned, wondering if the man was as much a lunatic as he seemed.

"All I want to know is what happened here. How did Lady Baltimore die?"

Again the monk bowed his head. When he looked up, the glittering light in his eyes had died and they were lost in the deepening gloom. A gust of wind whipped up off the ocean and Aischros shivered, pulling his collar up higher. Even as he did so, he felt a thick, icy drop of rain on the back of his right hand, and thunder stampeded across the sky.

Cold rain began to fall, pelting the cemetery all around them.

"Tell me," Aischros said, staring at the man.

Protecting himself from the cold and the rain no longer seemed important. A block of ice had begun to form in the middle of his chest, and he was far colder within than without.

Rain dampened his hair. A frigid line ran down the back of his neck like a frozen tear.

And the monk began to speak.

"Lord Baltimore lay abed for weeks, lost in fever and hallucination. His lady wife could make no sense at all of his ramblings, save that he thought himself a child again, sick in his bed and cared for by his mother. He asked for the toys of his childhood, those things that had given him comfort, and it pained Lady Baltimore's heart to know that she could not provide them.

"Doctors came from as far as London and Edinburgh, but no help could be found. Time, they all said. Time would heal him, or nothing could.

"Though lost in a fog of dementia, grief for his plague-lost family driving him into a world within—where he could hold on to them forever—Lord Baltimore remained dimly aware of the true world around him, of his wife's tears and prayers and anguish. There were moments of lucidity, in which he knew he must find the strength to rise from his fever, in which he damned himself as a self-indulgent fool. His heart was crushed, crippled by all he had lost, but in the  moments where he felt Lady Elowen's presence, it began to come alive again.

"His mother and father were forever lost to him, but his wife still held him close. His sister, Helen, was dead, but Elowen needed him to live.

"His moments of lucidity came with greater frequency, though his fever lingered. He lay in bed, seeking within himself the strength to rise. The horrors of the previous months were chains that held him there. Slowly, he freed himself from their weight.

"One morning, he managed to smile at Elowen, and she wept and held him, and for hours she did not leave his side, even as he slipped back into the numb, barely conscious state in which he had lingered for days upon days upon days.

"That very evening, not long after dark, Lord Baltimore surfaced from his fever to find a maid knocking at the door to his room. The maids often appeared in his room and he had seen them, like phantoms, drifting in and out, dusting and changing linens and opening the window to give him fresh air. They never spoke to him, even in his more lucid moments. They seemed skittish in his presence.

"That night, a maid called Hedra—a young girl whose family had served the Lords Baltimore for generations—rapped upon his open door several times. When he turned his head to look at her, awake and aware, she jumped and laid a hand upon her heart, so startled was she to have his eyes upon her.

"'What is it, girl?' Lord Baltimore asked.

"'A doctor to see you, sir,' Hedra replied. 'Lady Elowen asked me to see if you were able to receive him.'

"Lord Baltimore declined. He told the pretty young maid that he had no desire to see another doctor for as long as he should live. Hedra paused, hesitant to speak her mind, but then forged on, telling him that this particular doctor seemed different from the others. She had overheard him, you see, telling Lady Baltimore that he was a specialist in cases such as Baltimore's, that while they might mystify other physicians, he knew precisely how to deal with such an affliction.

"Still weak, but for the moment alert, Baltimore surrendered. If his wife wished him to see this newcomer, he would do so, for her sake if not his own. He was about to say just that when Hedra provided one final observation.

"'He must have been in the war, too, my Lord. He's got a terrible scar all down the right side of his face. Bright pink, it is,' Hedra said, and she shuddered.

"It was her shudder, he told me later, that filled him with a dreadful certainty. He knew, in that moment, that it was no doctor that awaited him downstairs; knew, in truth, that it was nothing human.

"Terror gripped him, unlike anything he had felt before. He threw aside his grief just as he did his bedclothes. Hedra squeaked in alarm at the sight of her one-legged master in his dressing gown, but Baltimore turned upon her a furious glance and raised a finger to his lips to hush her. His weakness lingered, but the panic that raced through him flushed from his body any vestige of the disorientation that had troubled him for so long.

"Baltimore snatched up his wooden leg—where it stood leaning against the wall by his bed—and strapped it on. Hedra looked away with a whimper, and kept her face turned from him as he hurried from the room, stumbling twice—nearly falling. He steadied himself on the wall and then hurled himself to the stairs, clutching the balustrade and then the banister, descending swiftly, wooden leg pounding every other step.

"He stumbled the last few steps, barely catching himself at the bottom, in the grand foyer. The front door hung open, swaying in the wind as a storm began to howl out in the darkness of the night. Wild and disheveled, unwashed and still feverish, Baltimore turned to see a hideous tableau on display in the parlor.

"On the floor, Lady Elowen lay dead, her throat torn open and her blood quickly pooling around her head. Her limbs, he told me later, had been twisted at wrong angles, so that she looked like some discarded wooden puppet.

"The sight stopped his heart, turned it to cold iron. At the top of the stairs, Hedra called down to him in her quiet voice, asking if everything was all right.

Baltimore staggered toward the door, gripping its frame, and he stared out at the night, then up into the evening sky.

"He caught a glimpse of the thing, my friend. A horrid, winged thing, blacker than the night itself. It was familiar to him. He knew it, as surely as he knew the scars on the stump of his missing leg.

"And then it was gone."

The monk stood in front of the Baltimore family crypt, hands hidden in the sleeves of his robe. The frozen rain pelted his hood loudly. Other than the rustle of the wind in the trees and the incessant shushing of the ocean, it was the only sound.

Aischros could feel the dampness of the rain beginning to soak through his peacoat. His hair was plastered to his skull, and rain ran down the inside of his collar. The cemetery had grown darker, not only with the storm, but with the onrush of night.

For long moments, he could only stare at the monk, grieving for Lord Baltimore and for the death of his beloved Elowen, yet also filled with a different sort of dread—and an unease that sprang from a mystery of his own past. The monk's eyes gleamed blackly beneath his hood, and the way he studied Aischros, the mariner felt sure the man knew exactly what the tale had reminded him of.

"So that's where he's gone? In pursuit of this creature?"

The monk glanced behind him, pausing a moment to study the face of the crypt. He lowered his head briefly, as if making a silent prayer, then turned to look at Aischros again.

"Not at first. After Elowen's funeral, what was left of Henry Baltimore roamed this cemetery like a hollow-eyed ghoul. He stared out over the ocean for three long days, and spent each of those nights seated on the step in front of the crypt. Just there." The monk pointed, his bony finger indicating the marble step in front of the heavy iron door of the tomb.

"He had surrendered, I believe. He sat and waited each night for death to return and claim him at last.

"On the third night, he heard the shriek of metal upon stone, and turned to see her gray, bloodless face looming out of the darkness of the crypt behind him."

Aischros stiffened, eyes wide, staring at the monk. "You're mad."

The monk shook his head, the patter of rain upon the fabric of his head dulled now, the wool sodden.

"No. I am many things, but I am not mad.

"Baltimore had endured too much. He had lost all of the love he had ever known. His soul had been ripped from him, and his whole self hollowed out, leaving only a void within.

"Elowen dragged herself from the crypt, eyes wide and black. Her limbs were still twisted at impossible angles but—once more like a marionette—she lurched and swayed forward. She grinned at her husband. In the moonlight, the jagged rows of her little needle teeth gleamed as though made of silver.

"So empty was he, that Baltimore would have gone to her, happy to surrender his life as long as he would die in her embrace.

"But that is where I entered the tale.

"I had watched the scene unfold from the shadow of a nearby grave marker. In that moment, I knew that Baltimore was lost. I rushed to come between them, shouting his name. Startled, he tried to push me away but I shoved him backward and turned upon the horrid, flopping creature, lifting the iron cross that I wore around my neck.

"The creature that had once been Elowen hissed and tried to lift her broken arms to shield her face. She lurched away, dragging herself on the rough earth toward the ocean. Even as she moved, her body changed. Her bones

popped like gunfire and her flesh shifted with noise like a flag unfurling in the wind. Her skin was black as oiled leather. Her arms were wings now, and whole. She propped herself up and turned to hiss at Lord Baltimore and me.

"Nothing human remained in her. Elowen had been transformed into a thing—a carrion bird fit for feasting only upon the wretched refuse of Hell itself. I glanced at Baltimore and saw the recognition in his eyes. He knew this thing, or one like it.

"'Vampire,' he said, and I agreed.

"I slipped the iron cross from around my neck. I had filed its long bar to a dagger point and I held it out to him. I did not have to explain to him what he must do. The knowledge passed between us without a word. He took the cross from me and fell upon the creature, stabbing it over and over before at last piercing her heart.

"The thing fell still then, and with a whisper of moving flesh it became the corpse of his wife again, now strangely whole. I could not see his face, or hers, for he cradled her so close to him, rocking her and singing quietly to her some melody that must have been special for the both of them in happier times, but now sounded like a dirge.

"His voice broke and he threw back his head, raging at the sky. In that one long cry of anguish and fury, I could hear the twisting of his heart and the withering of his soul. Then he quieted, and lifted her from the ground. Limping on his wooden leg, he carried her back into the crypt. When he emerged, he slammed the iron door behind him

and went to search the ground where she had lain in the moonlight.

"I said nothing, but I could hear him muttering to himself. Somehow, her wedding ring had been lost. It would not lie with her remains; nor would he ever discover it.

"He might have left her there out of ignorance, but I had seen such horrors before. Far too many of them. I helped him to carry her from the crypt once more. We brought her to the bluff overlooking the ocean, and there we set her afire. The flames consumed her greedily, and as her bones blackened and her flesh crumbled to ashes that the wind carried out over the water, an ebon shadow in the shape of a bird rose from her corpse. It would have flown from her, but I had reclaimed my iron cross from Baltimore and drove it back into the flames.

"Moments later, a gray bloated thing slipped from within her charred ribs, fat and grotesque as a toad. It attempted to crawl away, but once more the power of the cross forced it back to the fire.

"As the last of Baltimore's love was burned away, I told him of vampires, and the path I had taken that had led me to him. I had recognized from the first, you see, the true nature of the plague."

The rain had begun to slow, but Aischros felt sheathed in ice now, the water streaming down his skin, inside his clothes. The wind battered him and night had fallen in earnest. He had glanced at the crypt and then at the place on the bluff by the ocean where he imagined the fire had blazed. Now, though, he could only stare at the monk. Frozen as he felt, still his blood ran colder still.

"You're saying the plague is . . ."

The monk narrowed his eyes, almost scoffing. "Of course it is. This is no natural disease, but the predations of leeches!"

The snarl in the man's voice made Aischros flinch, and now that strange illumination returned to his eyes, the tiny pinprick flickering of candle flames.

The madness of prophets, he thought.

"It is my purpose to bring the truth, to carry a warning from town to town. But I am a man of God, not a man of war. I may spread the word, but the Lord needed a soldier to stop the rise of evil."

Aischros regarded him warily. "And God has chosen Lord Baltimore for this task?"

"You doubt the truth," the monk said, his robe so completely soaked now that it clung to his frame, making him appear more skeletal than ever. "Baltimore doubted me at first. He did not want to hear the words, though he recognized them. He had already borne witness, had known the nature of the plague even as I did. He told me his tale, just as I have related it to you, and then he hung his head back and stared at the sky.

"'If God has brought all this upon me, has made me suffer as no man should ever have to suffer, then He is no less devil than the Devil himself. God can go to Hell!' he cried.

"I held up the iron cross with which he had ended his wife's unholy resurrection and with which I had driven the taint from her at last. 'You are no

less a weapon than this, my friend,' I told him. 'God has honed you with hammer and anvil, a blacksmith at the forge. He has made you suffer as He did Job, so that the world might be spared far worse.'

"Then I shared with him the vision that had revealed the truth to me and, in time, led me to him. It was sunset on a warm Sunday evening and I was tending to my garden. A chill passed through me and I felt faint. The plants I had been cultivating withered and blackened. When I looked up, I saw a figure striding toward me out of the sunset, wearing a red crown, clutching a gold scepter in its right hand, and carrying a coffin under its left arm. The light of that sunset washed crimson over the land, flowing across the hills and fields in the color of blood.

"Its scarlet cloak unfurled behind it like wings, and where the shadow fell the land was nothing but graveyards and battlefields. Wherever the darkness touched, the soldiers began to rise from muddy trenches where they had been left to rot. Graves split open and cadavers crawled free. They followed in the wake of the Red Death.

"Many could not walk. Too long in the ground, they crumbled to dust and loose bone and scraps of burial cloth. From these, winged shadows

emerged and took to the air to follow the creature, black shapes against the red sunset. And through it all I could hear, across the land, a rapid, mocking laughter that sounded like gunfire.

"I fainted then, and when I came to my senses, I lay upon crushed flowers and stared up at the night sky. The dead had not risen. The world had not yet been infected with the touch of the Red Death. But I knew that the time was coming."

The rain had ceased. In the night sky, patches of starlit dark could be seen through the clouds. The wind died. And yet Aischros felt colder than ever. He felt as though he were rooted to the spot; as though he would never be able to move again.

"What did Baltimore say when you shared this . . . vision?"

"He knelt by the pile of ash and bone that was all that remained of his wife, and he promised her that he would never rest, not even in death, until he had scoured the taint of that evil from the world."

Aischros stared at the monk, the mad light in the man's eyes nearly extinguished.

"And if I believe all of this . . . you were chosen to receive this vision, yet you passed this mission to Baltimore . . ."

"Not I," the monk replied, and there was a terrible weariness in his voice. "I have told you already. God required a soldier. I am only a messenger. Even if I wished to take up the soldier's mission, I could not. My fate is elsewhere. I have foreseen it. I will go on warning all who will listen, but I cannot save them. In a town not far from here, my message will turn them against me. My death will be hideous. They will stone me and hang me from a tree."

Aischros shook his head. "Then why go at all?"

Beneath his hood, the monk seemed to smile. "It is the role He has chosen for me. I fulfill it. We all have a role to play. Yours will come in time."

"What are you talking about?" the mariner demanded, the ice in him melting suddenly, as a heat rose unbidden from his belly. "What do you mean by that?"

"In time," the monk replied. "For now, go. The sea awaits."

With that, the hooded man turned and slipped into the shadows beside the crypt. Aischros saw the thin figure move into the trees, but then he was gone. He took two steps after him, thinking he would pursue the monk into the trees, but the wind rose again and the trees whispered, and he found himself unsettled by the darkness.

He made his way down from the cemetery along the winding path.

He sailed that night by the light of the moon, and never set foot upon Trevelyan Island again.

3

"Good Lord," said Doctor Rose, the sardonic mask slipping a moment. "I'd no idea his family had met such an awful end. But what of the monk? Did you ever discover what became of him?"

Aischros nodded, not looking at them. "He died just as he had foreseen."

The mariner's eyes were unfocused. He felt as if he were looking through them, beyond the walls of the inn. The recollection of his time on Trevelyan Island lingered with him, and he knew that, having told the tale, it would be some time before he could distance himself from it again.

"I never knew how it all happened," Childress said. "Only that Henry's family had died, and Elowen had been murdered."

At his speaking of Lady Baltimore's name, Aischros flinched and looked up. A soft smile of remembrance touched his lips. Elowen had been a kind of epiphany to any who met her.

Doctor Rose opened his cigarette case and offered him one. Aischros shook his head and the doctor held out the case to Childress. The man hesitated before accepting. But when the doctor struck a match and went to light the cigarette, Childress flinched away from the flame. He frowned deeply, then reached out to take the match.

Mister Childress had no love of fire; that much was clear. He rubbed his palm across the burn scar on his neck and frowned.

"How well did you know them?" Aischros asked him.

Childress let his smile bloom. "All my life. Trevelyan was my home. My heart is filled with memories of a time when it was like paradise. But I was gone a very long time, and the last time I returned there, I saw what it had become. I try not to think about that. I want to remember it as it was in my youth...and Henry and Elowen that way as well."

"It seems you also have something to share with us," Doctor Rose said.

Childress nodded, his humor fading, the way Aischros supposed it must in this gray, dull place.

"I wonder," the man said. "Was this what Henry had in mind, having us all meet like this—that we, who each know only a part of him, would share these tales?"

Doctor Rose frowned and looked toward the door of the inn. Aischros and Childress did the same. It did not open. Of Baltimore, there was no sign.

The gloom had deepened. Evening would arrive soon. The serving girl had begun to light oil lamps and the innkeeper was trying to light a fire in the hearth. A heavy iron chandelier hung from the ceiling, boasting dozens of small lightbulbs, but no one even attempted to turn it on. Somehow Aischros felt sure that the electricity did not work at the inn. If he had to wager, he'd bet that it had simply ceased functioning at some point, and no one had bothered to have it fixed.  Or perhaps it had never worked at all. Such a modern thing as electricity would have seemed out of place in this decrepit purgatory. The ghosts would not have allowed it.

"Is he dead, do you think?" Doctor Rose asked. "Did he send us those notes to gather us here so that we would eulogize him?"

Aischros grunted softly and shook his head. "He's been dead for years. Since that night. But he can't rest. Don't you see? He promised."

"You speak in metaphor, though," Doctor Rose replied, almost worriedly. "You don't mean he's truly dead?"

"What is that? Truly dead? His blood pumps, he breathes and walks and eats. Does that make a man alive?"

Neither Childress nor the doctor had an answer to that.

"Your story, Mister Childress?" Doctor Rose asked.

"In time," he replied, turning to focus on the mariner. "First, however, I feel certain there's another story that Demetrius must tell."

Aischros grimaced, the weight of dread still upon him. "What do you mean?"

"Come now, my friend," Childress said, lifting his glass of ale in a kind of toast. "You believed that monk's every word. It was plain in your face and your choice of words. You shared a bond with Henry that he obviously felt quite strongly. And you believed Doctor Rose's incredible account. He's told us of the experience that allowed him to accept Henry's story. What gave *you* such faith in impossible things?"

Aischros lowered his gaze a moment, then looked up. "I have tried to forget."

Childress took a sip of ale and grimaced. He set down the glass. "It's a day for remembering things best forgotten."

The mariner ran a hand over the stubble on his chin, his fingers tracing several of the myriad thin scars on his face.

"All right," he said, looking at Doctor Rose and then back at Childress. "Once. And then never again."

The mariner let go of the arms of his chair and sat forward, staring at them. "It could not have happened, but it did. I know that it did.

"I was a young man—only nineteen—but already I had been at sea for years. It would be some time still before I had a ship of my own. I worked on a merchant ship that sailed out of Greece, but the captain was a drunk. He'd shallowed her on the rocks off Capri, on the Italian coast. It would take months to repair, and no one knew if the owner would decide to scuttle her instead. I couldn't wait. I had to eat, and I had to have something to send home to my mother.

"The mate gave me the name of a friend who captained a boat that sailed out of the port of Genoa, and a letter to introduce me to the man. The mate had decided to stay with the captain until a decision was made regarding the damaged ship. I'll never forget his kindness to me, or what it led me to."

I traveled north with only my pack and bedroll. It was early summer and the weather was perfect. I kept the ocean in sight for nearly the entire journey, staying wherever they'd have me along the way. I had been paid what was owed me for my work on the merchant ship, but I wanted to hold on to as much as I could, for my mother's sake.

Those were the last peaceful days I ever spent on dry land.

Perhaps a week and a half after I left Capri, I came upon a funeral procession moving along the road from a small fishing village toward a cemetery on the hill above the town. The church bell rang in the village. Dust rose on the road from the scrape of the mourners' feet. They were like a sea of black cloth. The women wept and cried out to God, their grieving sobs clutching at my heart. I saw several who could barely stand and had to be helped along by others.

It seemed to me as though the entire village had emptied for this funeral procession. The priest at the front sang a Latin dirge. Most of the women had covered their heads with black veils. Somehow, the faces of the old men were the worst, carved with silent pain. Though I was young, I had seen men die. Yet never had I seen such grief. Sorrow seemed to rise with the heat off the road and waver in the air.

I stood aside to let the procession pass by. The funeral was a public thing, but the pain of all of those people seemed so private that I dropped my gaze, staring at the ground. It seemed wrong for me to witness their mourning.

Yet my curiosity gnawed at me. Who was this dead man to cause such sadness? The dust from the road stung my eyes and as I wiped the grit away, they began to water. Blinking, I was compelled to lift my gaze. I could not help studying the last of the mourners as they walked by, and as I did, I noticed something.

These stragglers did not howl with grief and they did not weep. They walked slowly, carrying some invisible burden, and as I studied their eyes I understood that it was not sorrow that weighed upon them, but fear.

I might never have spoken, but one of the men in the rear of the procession cast a puzzled glance at me. Whether or not it was intended as an invitation to speak, I took it as such. Shouldering my pack and bedroll, I stepped into the road. The wailing of the grief-stricken carried back to us from farther along the road, but only those stragglers saw me.

"Excuse me," I said to the man, whose face was so weathered by life on the sea that it was impossible to judge his age. "What dreadful thing has happened here? Who has died?"

My Italian was fairly pitiful. I had been at sea for several years and learned enough of the language—as well as Spanish, French, and English—to communicate while in port. But there were too many Italian dialects for me to learn the language well. Still, I knew enough to make myself understood, and to decipher what was said in reply.

"Cicagne took him."

I blinked, eyes still watering. Perhaps the man thought me touched by what I had seen, for he paused to speak with me. An ugly woman I took to be his wife lingered a few feet away, and several others stopped as well. I did not like the attention I had drawn, but the man's words confused me, and curiosity has gotten me into trouble all my life.

"Who is this Cicagne?" I asked.

A dark look crossed his face. He glanced toward the village as though afraid that something might be coming up the road after him. "Cicagne is not a man; it is a town, up the coast. The people cry today more for themselves than for Alberto Gnecco. He was a coward and a liar, a filthy man—"

The man's wife hissed at him, and there was such venom in her eyes that I prayed I would never marry such a woman.

"He was a father and a husband!" she shouted.

"A poor father. A poor husband," the man replied, shaking his head. "Cicagne called to him. The town calls sinners, and they must answer. It lures them to their deaths. Most of the villages nearby, the people know better than to let themselves be drawn there. But the more sin there is in a man's heart, the harder it is for him to resist."

"You're an old fool!" his wife cried, the wind off the ocean whipping at her black mourning dress. "My cousin was no worse than any other man. There is sin in all of us, and Cicagne will draw in anyone that passes by. No heart is without stain."

I held out my hands, hoping to calm the couple. "I still don't understand. How did he die?"

The early-summer sun baked the road, but I saw the woman shudder as if in winter. She crossed herself.

The man had gone pale. "No one knows. He was found on the road to Cicagne, broken and bloody."

I thought this a poor reason to suspect some diabolical power had killed the man. More likely his injuries had been inflicted by bandits, or someone he had wronged. If he'd gone off to Cicagne and been killed there, it made little sense that he would be found brutalized on the road between the village and town. Of course, I did not voice these doubts. It would have been an insult.

"I'm traveling north," I said. "Cicagne lies in my path."

The man stepped back from me as though I had spit on him. He seemed about to speak, then waved a hand at me and scowled, starting up the road in swift pursuit of the funeral procession. The others who had paused and witnessed this exchange fell in behind him.

Only his wife hesitated. She stared at me with such pity as I had never seen, this ignorant village woman who had likely never been farther from her doorstep than the cemetery, and never would. Yet she looked at me as though I were some slow-witted fool.

"Stay by the sea," she said. "I beg you. Do not follow the hill road. Cicagne has taken too much. Sin soaks the very earth there. It's all that remains of the place."

With that, she turned to hurry after her husband, a black shape in the dust of the road and the shimmering heat of the sun. I watched her go, struck by the conviction of her words. Like the grief of the mourners, her fear came from deep within her, and it chilled me. I shivered, just as she had, then cursed myself for a fool.

Superstitious nonsense, I told myself. The man had been murdered on the roadside, not in that cursed town. As I passed through the village, nearly empty while the people attended the burial of Alberto Gnecco, I thought of dozens of other such dire legends I'd heard, both as a child in Greece and in the time I'd spent as a sailor. Some illness had struck this Cicagne, I felt sure, generations past. A poisoned well, something that would have driven the people out.

For nearly two hours I continued north. The sorrow I had witnessed on the road clung to me. But as I walked, I felt the sun on my arms and the back of my neck, and it seemed to burn away that strange disquiet. Several times I passed narrow roads that branched away from the shore, disappearing into the inland hills. I passed fields and farmhouses, and in the distance I saw what must have been a vineyard once, though it seemed a wretched, withered place now. Abandoned.

I kept to the coast. The breeze off the water was pleasant, but it was the sight of the blue-green sea that I cherished. It comforted me, so that I did not mind walking. A cart passed me, a tinker going north, and he offered me a ride. Tempted as I was, I chose to walk. At that pace I would reach Genoa by nightfall, or not long after.

I thanked the tinker, then followed his cart as it grew smaller and smaller on the road ahead. The rocky coast was jagged and steep. The cart vanished over a rise far ahead, and by the time I reached the spot, the tinker and his horse and cart were long gone, as though they had never been there at all.

I stood on the rise, the sea crashing on the rocks off to my left, and stared at the road ahead. A narrow road cut away from the sea, leading up into the hills. The fields were wild and overgrown and the hills were thick with trees. But amongst the trees I could see the peaks of several roofs and two small towers that could only have been churches. From the road, it seemed a peaceful place. The church towers had been built with stones of different shades, and had a beautiful pattern of white and pink marble.

I could only think that this was Cicagne, but how this pretty town could cause such dread was a puzzle to me. I continued along the cliff road, but paused at the fork where the road to Cicagne began. A broken post jutted from the ground at the split in the road. In the high yellow grass, I saw what must have once been the sign, pointing toward Cicagne. It was faded and tangled in grass, as though the earth were slowly claiming it. I wondered how many years it had lain there, untouched.

An odd feeling came over me, and I became aware of a low sound that I realized I had been hearing for several minutes without being conscious of it. Only as I stopped and truly listened, forcing myself not to hear the crashing waves and the wind and the seabirds, did I realize it was music—a tinny, distant melody, nearly stolen away by the wind. It was a jaunty tune—a flute, I thought.

I gauged the position of the sun in the sky and the distance to Cicagne and I felt sure there was time for me to visit this odd town and be back on the road to Genoa by nightfall. Once again, curiosity had gotten the better of me.

Convinced as I was of the foolishness of the local superstitions, still there seemed no doubt that the town was abandoned, and I wanted to know why.

With the sea at my back, I struck out along the narrow, rutted road—little more than a cow path, really—that curved up into the hills. Perhaps half an hour later, I entered the woods and could no longer see the town, except for a glimpse or two of the beautiful marble church towers.

After a day in the sun, the woods felt cold. The shaded path through the trees had retained much of the coolness of the night before. At first it felt pleasant, but there was a stillness in the woods that I found unsettling. I heard no birdsong, and nothing moving through the underbrush, as I would have expected. I was a sailor and no expert on forests, but I had traveled through woods before, and the oddness of the quiet there was inescapable.

That was my one moment of hesitation. If there were no animals in the woods around the town, perhaps whatever illness had forced the people to abandon the place still remained. Would I get sick just from visiting? The idea seemed ridiculous. How could any disease have lingered so long? I determined to be careful what I touched while in Cicagne, and that I would not refill my canteen there, even if I found a spring or pump.

Another minute of walking and I emerged from the woods, where the impression I had gotten of Cicagne from the coastal road was borne out. Several small houses had been built near the woods. Beyond them was the town proper. Two- and three-story structures stood in staggered rows on either side of the road, which was laid with stone. Many of the buildings had shops on the first floor, wooden signs hanging from iron arms above their doors, with apartments above. Some were whitewashed, others of stone, and all had roofs of terra-cotta tile. Their shutters were all painted in bright greens, reds, oranges, blues, and yellows. Balconies protruded from the second and third stories, some enclosed in a fashion I'd only previously seen in Spanish towns.

Between those houses near the woods and the main part of the town, a cemetery stood just off the road to the east. A stone wall ran all around it, and at the front was an iron gate, which hung open. Over the top of the wall I could see dozens of smooth stone markers. The graveyard seemed an ugly contrast to the beauty of the town. There were no ornate tombs or statues, no marble gravestones, only those plain markers of slate or granite, entirely bare of any name or other symbol to indicate the identity of the dead.

In the center of the cemetery was a dark, weathered tree stump so broad it could have served as a king's dinner table. It had been cut long, long ago, and there was not another tree or stump on the grounds.

Curious, but aware I'd find no answers there, I continued on. Cicagne was odd in so many ways, but the overall effect was truly beautiful. It was like no other town I had ever seen. Several of the buildings were painted in such fanciful, ornate fashion that they reminded me of miniature storybook castles.

The two towers I could see ahead, at the center of the town and the peak of the hill, only added to the effect with the pink and white marble designs built into the darker stone.

As I entered the town, this impression grew, and it occurred to me that the entire town seemed somehow unreal—more like theatrical sets of an exaggeratedly pretty little village than a place anyone might actually live.

I saw the glint of the sun on the window of a nearby shop, and something about the character of that light troubled me. I searched the sky, and realized with a start that the sun had fallen quite low. I'd only departed the coastal road a short time before—no more than three quarters of an hour, I thought. But now, somehow, the sun was low on the horizon. It would not be very long before it began to sink into the Mediterranean.

This was not right. I took a step backward, studying the perfect stillness of the town. Two carriages stood on the street, abandoned. One had a broken

wheel and was tilted onto the road where that corner had collapsed.

I did not share the superstitious nature of the mourners I had spoken to on the roadside as the funeral passed by me, but this place made me uneasy, and night, it seemed, was not far off. I did not wish to be there after dark, superstition or not. I started back toward the woods.

I had gone as far as the cemetery when the music started again. Hardly louder than it had been when I heard it from the coast road, it lilted and danced in the air. When I turned, I saw a man at the top of the hill. He made his way down the road toward me, playing a flute, swaying with the music, which grew louder as he approached.

I stared a moment, and then laughed softly at myself for

falling under the spell cast upon me by the fears of the locals. Their superstitions had gotten to me, after all. Local lore might have kept most people away from Cicagne, but the town was not abandoned. The evidence swayed with the music as he came toward me, playing his flute; a thin, dark-haired man with sharp features.

So much for curses, I thought.

The man watched me as he played, a mischievous light in his eyes. He stopped just a few feet in front of me, blew one final note upon his flute, then bowed. He wore a grin and exuded such a friendly air that I could not help but offer him lonely applause.

"Thank you, *signore,*" he said as he stood, clutching his flute in one hand. In the fading light his face had a golden hue.

"You're very welcome," I replied. "You drew me back, my friend. I thought the town was empty. I was about to leave."

"As you can see, it is not. Though we get few visitors. The legends keep them away. We're cursed, you know."

He laughed as he said it, and I joined him, relieved to find that my nervousness had been foolish, after all. "So I've been told."

He bowed his head courteously. "I am Dante."

"Demetrius," I told him. "I saw your lovely town from the road and could not resist a closer look. I've never seen another quite like it."

Dante spread his arms. "There is no other like Cicagne. She's unique in all the world. Famous, once upon a time. Shall I tell you her story?"

"I'd be grateful," I replied.

A look of great concern crossed the man's face. He looked at the eastern sky, which had turned the deep blue of twilight. To the west, the sky was still light, but not for very long. Dusk had arrived.

"Where are you bound?" he asked.

"I'd hoped to be in Genoa tonight."

Dante looked at me with regret. "Genoa is still quite far. Even if you are determined to sleep there tonight, by the time you arrive, you won't find another soul awake to give you a meal. Come to my home. My wife, Caprice, will have supper ready soon."

I hesitated, glancing back at the road through the woods. In the shade of the trees it seemed to be night already, and the mention of dinner had started my stomach growling with hunger.

"We get so few travelers passing through, Demetrius. Share with us the tales of your journeys. It's a fair exchange for a plate of veal and eggplant and a glass of wine."

I hesitated only a moment. It would be full dark before I could even return to the coastal road, and—though I'd thought Genoa somewhat closer—if Dante was correct about the distance, the idea of arriving in the middle of the night did not appeal to me. Also, I felt like such a fool after my earlier anxiety that it seemed to me I would be giving in to superstition to decline. To do anything but accept would have been both insulting and foolish.

"My empty stomach would never forgive me if I said no," I confessed. "If you're certain your wife will not mind..."

"She'd be furious at me if I allowed you to leave," he said, with another lit-

tle laugh. "Come along, Demetrius, and you'll learn the sad history of Cicagne."

He put the flute to his lips and piped a few notes. Dante started off, playing his instrument, and I fell in beside him. My pack and bedroll had grown heavy after the long day of walking and I looked forward to being able to set it down, just for a while. As we strode together up the hill toward the center of town, in the twilight I got a closer look at the shops and homes that lined the road. There was still no sign of movement, but many of the second- and third-story apartments had their colorful shutters closed up tight, and a dim glow of candles or oil lamps flickered within.

I breathed easier. We weren't alone, after all.

A curious sight caught my attention. One of the buildings in the row on the left had a garish painting of a marionette on the door. But this was no grinning jester. Instead, the puppet was a figure of some martyred saint, with a sword in his chest and spikes driven through his skull, splashed in bloodred paint, with a halo above his head.

"What is the meaning of that?" I asked.

Dante lowered his flute and nodded. "Yes. My apologies. I'd promised you the tale of Cicagne. I enjoy the music so much, because it helps to wake this quiet place."

"You play very well," I said.

"Kind of you to say," Dante replied. "And, now, I owe you a story. It begins with once upon a time, as all the great and tragic stories do."

4

"Once upon a time," Dante said, "Cicagne was famous for its puppet theatres. Some of them showed the old stories, the comedies and ribald tales, but very few. The town looked down upon such things and preferred that the shows focus on Christian themes, stories of the Bible, of suffering and sacrifice and the punishment of sinners.

"In those days, the finest puppeteers in all of Europe gathered here to perform during Cicagne's annual festival. Sometimes, those who put on shows considered improper were driven from the festival, and from the town."

As he spoke, I gazed around in fascination. We had passed two other puppet theatres, abandoned and shuttered. One had a pair of intricately carved marionettes hanging in the front—a wooden Jesus, and another puppet that looked like a half-rotten dead man. *Lazarus,* I thought. I noticed at least two of the shops had many puppets hanging in the windows for sale. The artisans who had crafted such things had to be extraordinarily gifted. Even in the last bit of twilight, though I could see some of them only in silhouette, the skill that had gone into making them was obvious.

"Now I understand some of the talk of a curse upon the town," I said. "The sinners were driven off—"

Dante laughed. "That's a harsh way to put it."

I shrugged. "Just trying to understand how such legends are born."

"All right, then. Here is the true legend of Cicagne. At the edge of town there is a graveyard of criminals and suicides. The townspeople believed that the evil the sinners committed in their lives remained with their spirits after death. In the heart of the cemetery, they planted a tree it was said would draw all the evil from the dead buried there, so their spirits would not haunt the town.

"The tree grew quickly, strong and thick, so high that it dwarfed the forest around the town. And it worked all too well. It not only drew the evil spirits from the dead buried around its roots, but its power drew sinners to Cicagne from other towns, miles away."

Fascinated, I glanced at Dante. This, then, was the true beginning of the superstition I'd heard about. The stars had begun to come out in the deepening night sky. We arrived at the top of the hill. To one side of the town square was the church—a huge structure large enough to be a cathedral. Nothing in the quaint town could compare to the size and grandeur of that church. Both of the towers I had seen from the coast were a part of it—one at either end—and the colored marble used in its construction gave it a bright, glorious design that, in a strange way, fit with the rest of Cicagne. The towers made the church seem almost as though it was yet another puppet theatre—the largest and most elegant of all.

In the center of the town square, in front of the church, there was a huge stone platform that I presumed had once been a part of the puppet festival. The road split there, the left fork curving westward, back toward the sea, which I could not glimpse over the tops of the buildings. Dante turned down the right fork.

"Just along here," he said, gesturing with his flute. "Caprice will be waiting."

More of the shuttered windows were lit from within now, golden light slipping through the cracks. As I followed my host, I thought of the cemetery I had seen with its blank grave markers and the enormous tree stump. I had always believed that every legend must have a seed, and here was the evidence.

"One Sunday, a giant walked into Cicagne," Dante said, as he led me past several smaller puppet theatres and other buildings. "He went into the graveyard of sinners and cut down the tree. He carved it into a puppet twice again as big as a man. This giant figure was as beautifully crafted as any marionette had ever been, with every joint detailed and its face lovingly painted. He dressed it in finery and used thick rope for its strings, and then he built a puppet theatre in the town square. There was a stage of stone and a wooden box as big as a house, strung with curtains.

"While all of the faithful were inside the church, he took his place in the box and made his giant marionette perform. The puppet spoke in a sweet, alluring voice that the people could not resist. A crowd formed. In the midst of the puppetry, the sweet voice spouted all manner of blasphemy, and the people of Cicagne could only smile. Soon, people began to come out of the church to hear its voice, though the priest begged them not to go. But even the most faithful were lured from their prayers."

When Dante broke off telling his story, I blinked several times. It felt as though I were coming awake, so entranced had I been by this tale. As absurd as it was, I could imagine it happening all around me. I had seen the stump of that tree and the graves of those criminals and suicides. The stone base of the giant puppet theatre still stood in the town square in front of that pristine church.

In the darkness—for it was truly night now, and only the stars and sliver of moon and the glow between shutters in the faces of those buildings provided any light—I saw his sharp features pull into another grin. Dante put his flute to his thin lips and played a few happy notes, then bowed deeply.

"Here we are, my friend," he said, and with a flourish he gestured to the door of a building on the left side of the street.

This road was narrower than the one we had followed into the town square. The buildings seemed toppled together like fallen dominoes. Dante threw open the door and warm, golden light flooded out into the darkness.

"Caprice, we have a guest!" he called.

I paused a moment at the threshold. Though a fire burned in the hearth within and the lantern light tugged at me, still something clutched at my heart, making me hesitate.

Then his wife emerged from the kitchen, wiping her hands on her apron, a look of sweet happiness and curiosity upon her face. She wore her hair tied back beneath a scarf while cooking, but I could see that it was black as a raven's wings. Her eyes were wide and pretty and her cheeks were flushed from work.

"Dante? What do you mean—" she began, faltering when she saw me on the threshold. "Oh," she said. "Please, come in. It's been ages since we've had a guest."

Made so welcome, I could not refuse. I entered their home and immediately was grateful that I had. The night had grown chilly—the heat of the early-summer day only a memory now—and the warmth of the fire felt good.

"Caprice, this is Demetrius," Dante said as he placed his flute upon a shelf. "Demetrius, my lovely bride."

"Ma'am," I said, "it's a pleasure to meet you."

She put a hand to her mouth and gave a charming giggle, then laughed at herself for doing so.

"Please, Demetrius, set your things down. Rest with us a while. It looks as though you've come a long way."

Indeed, I had. I thanked the lady of the house, and as I slipped my pack and bedroll to the floor and eyed a chair at the dinner table, she went back into the kitchen. Dante called to her, telling her he'd promised me veal and eggplant, and hoped that she wouldn't make him a liar. Caprice poked her head around the corner to assure us that she had not changed the evening's menu. Once again I noticed the color in her cheeks and I wondered if it was truly exertion or embarrassment. It occurred to me that it might be rouge, but that seemed unlikely, given the religious nature of the town and the fact that Caprice had not known her husband would be bringing company for dinner.

The smells from the kitchen were enticing. My stomach growled so loudly that Dante joked the wolves were at the door. As we washed our hands and he poured three glasses of wine to go with dinner, he asked me a bit about my travels, all questions I dutifully answered. He had never left Cicagne, he said, and though I thought this quite sad, it would have been rude to say so.

"Enough of me for a moment, Dante," I said. "You never finished your story, though I must say it's sounding less and less like the tale of Cicagne and more like something from a storybook."

"The true legend, I promised you," he said, nodding. "All right, here's the rest. The giant had his puppet theatre in the town square, and his marionette sang and spoke to the people in its sweet, poisonous voice, speaking all manner of vile blasphemy. The priest could not restrain them. They gathered and listened."

Outside, rain began to fall, pelting the windows. Regret filled me. Though it had occurred to me that I might have no choice but to sleep somewhere in Cicagne that night—and that perhaps Dante and Caprice would invite me to spend the evening beneath their roof—I'd still hoped to push on to Genoa after supper. But the rain seemed determined to keep me from traveling farther. Genoa seemed suddenly quite far away.

Caprice came out of the kitchen and set a third place at the table, then returned a moment later, balancing an enormous platter. She served us both veal with mushrooms and capers and a thin gravy. It smelled extraordinary.

"The priest cried out to God," Dante said, fingers steepled under his chin as though preparing to say grace over his meal. "He called upon the Lord's wrath. The day had been perfect, the sky without a cloud. But now the heavens darkened and a terrible storm gathered above the town."

His wife appeared with a second platter, this one laden with stuffed eggplant. Again she served us, then she prepared her own plate. She sat across from her husband and both of them turned to look expectantly at me.

"Aren't you going to eat?" Caprice asked.

I smiled, a bit startled by her manner and her stare. Her husband was in the midst of telling a story and she'd only just sat down herself. But I picked up my fork politely.

"Go on, Dante."

A flash of lightning turned the darkness white and illuminated the inside of the house. Something caught my attention from the corner of my eye, but the lightning faded, and when I looked there were only shadows.

Thunder cracked open the sky and shook the timbers of the house.

"Demetrius," Dante said, far too jovially. "Eat."

Fork in hand, I looked at the plate. My stomach roared at me. The smells made my mouth begin to water. But in the back of my mind I began to recall folktales I had heard in my youth and in my travels, stories of fairies and roadside demons. In all of those stories, the traveler's mistake is accepting food from these creatures, leading to death or eternal imprisonment.

I began to cut my veal, slowly.

"And did God bring His wrath down upon the giant?" I asked.

"He did," Dante said. "The storm was terrible. Lightning struck the theatre, and it burned, all but that stone foundation. But that was only the beginning of the Lord's punishment."

Another flash of lightning lit the room, and this time the thunder came instantly, rattling the plates and knives and wineglasses.

"Aren't you going to eat?" Caprice asked again, her tone brittle, a frantic look in her eyes.

I glanced down at the fork and knife in my hand, at the bits of veal I had cut. "It's the oddest thing," I said. "I don't feel very hungry."

Dante jerked back from the table so that the legs of his chair scraped the floor.

Caprice stared at me. "But you *must* be," she insisted. "Such a long journey. You must eat."

Thunder crashed once again, shaking the house.

But there had been no lightning.

I dropped the fork and knife and slid back my chair, tensed to move. Again, the thunder pounded the sky outside. Then again. Still there was no more lightning, and I knew then that this was not thunder. It came again, that booming sound, with quickening rhythm, and as the pace increased, I knew what it was.

Footsteps.

"Good Lord," I whispered.

Caprice and Dante shrieked and put their hands over their ears, though from the crashing thunder of those footfalls or my invocation of God I will never know.

"He's coming!" Dante cried.

"Who?" I demanded. "Who is coming?"

His wife stared at me with terror etched into her face. "The giant. He haunts us...haunts all of Cicagne!"

With the next thunderous step, a crack splintered a pattern across the floor. I could not breathe. My heart clutched into a fist in my chest and I felt

a dread and terror unlike any I had ever known or imagined.

I stood, knocking my chair over, just as the door burst inward, torn from its hinges. The monstrosity that came through the door had to bend to enter, and the wooden frame cracked and tore away as the giant pushed into the house. It screamed something I could not understand, the roar shaking the walls. Twelve feet tall, it could not stand erect, so it bent like some lumbering beast as it pointed at me.

Trembling, I backed away. My foot caught on the chair I had knocked over and I stumbled. Falling, I felt myself caught by something soft and yielding. I tried to rise, to pull away, and found my arms tangled in a web of string. Panicked, I twisted round, trying to make sense of my surroundings. The gas lamps flickered and in their tremulous light I saw that nothing was as it had seemed.

This was no house, but the broken-down ruin of one of the town's puppet theatres, decorated with faded and dusty two-dimensional sets. The giant stumbled over seats once occupied by an audience, snapping wood as it crashed onto its knees, reaching for me.

I tried to tear myself free of the tangled strings. My breath came in hitching

gasps as I looked around for the source of those strings, and I saw Dante and Caprice, jerking with every moment of my struggle. They were wooden things with clacking joints, life-size marionettes. Her rosy cheeks had been painted on by some diabolical artisan generations ago. Their clothes were crumbling off, and the wood of Dante's face looked soft and damp with rot.

A scream echoed through the place—my own. I drove my feet against the floor, forcing myself away from them and from the giant, but only dragging Dante and Caprice closer. The puppets stared at me with wooden eyes and painted-on smiles, and as I tugged to free myself, they clawed at me. Caprice's sharply splintered fingers dug into my side, and my shirt was no protection. The scratches were deep, and blood trickled down.

I could not escape by trying to pull away from them. I reached for the Dante marionette and snapped off its head with a wet, rotten crack. Both of them sagged on their strings. I slipped my left arm free, loosening the web that I had tangled myself in. The Caprice puppet fell mournfully upon Dante with a clack of wood as I freed my legs.

Then the giant grabbed my arm and hoisted me from the ground as though I were some errant child. Silently, it pulled me toward it, squeezing the breath from me. Its mouth opened and it dragged me nearer. I felt one of my ribs crack; heard the snap in my ears.

My arms were free. Suffocating in its grip, I tore at its face. Its desiccated skin was like paper. Beneath, my fingers struck wood. I tore, exposing the carved face of a giant puppet, and at last I knew.

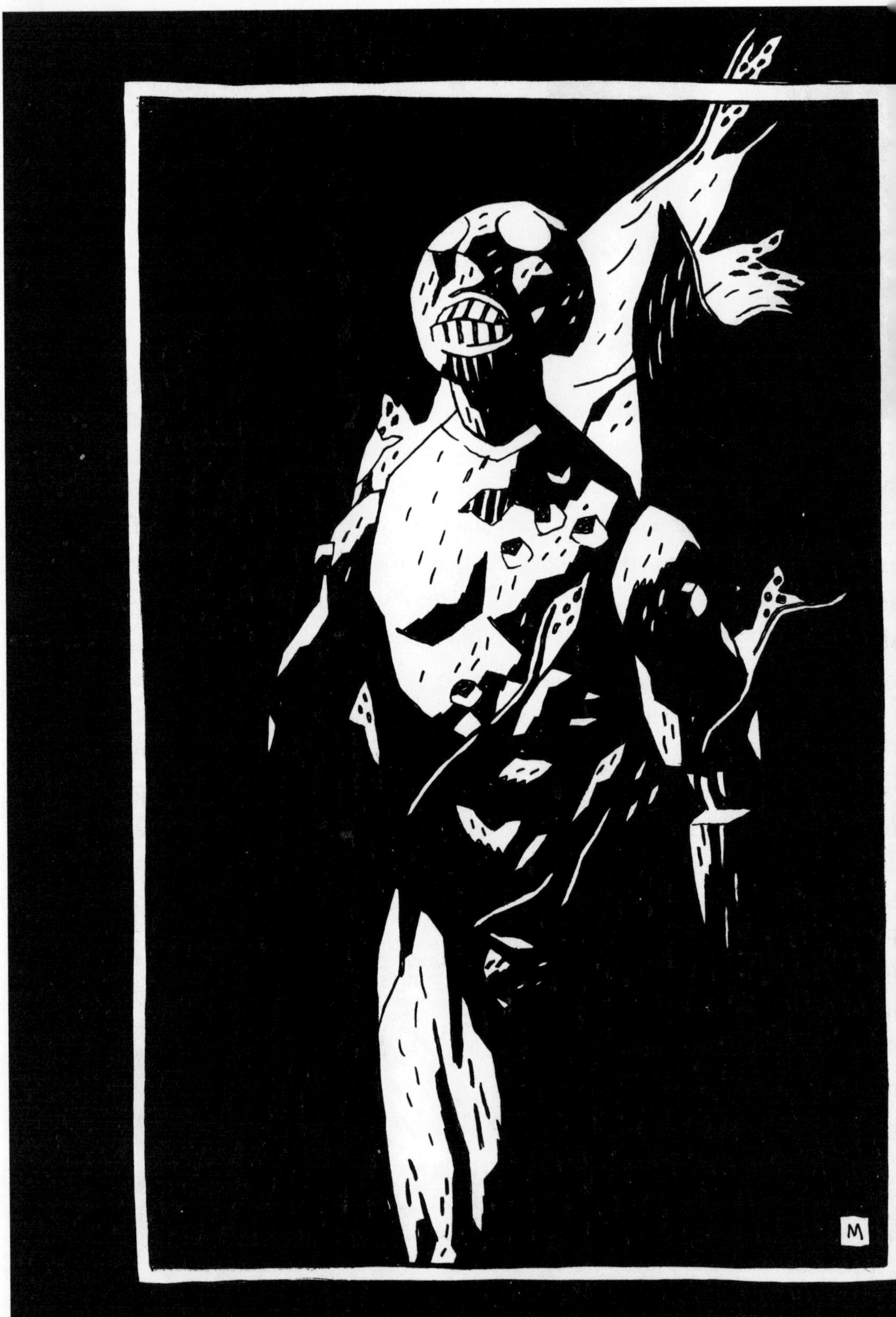

This was the blasphemous thing Dante had spoken of, carved from the tree of sins.

Again I beat at the monstrosity. With both hands, fingers hooked into claws, I tore away all of the mossy flesh of its face.

The giant roared and released me, bringing both massive hands to its head. It had shattered a dozen chairs beneath it as it crawled through the rotting theatre to reach me. I ran around it and through the gaping ruined doorway, and out into the road.

The rain pattered all around me and the sky rumbled low with real, distant thunder. Puddles had formed on the cobblestone road. I splashed and stumbled and fell, barking my knee. The fear racing through me made my skin feel as though it were on fire, and every raindrop seemed the prick of a pin.

A crash of glass and wood erupted behind me, and I knew the giant was free. I glanced over my shoulder as I lurched forward again, and I saw the lumbering puppet rise to its full height. Tatters of its false face hung down around its neck and the evil of its carved features glistened with rain.

I ran, one hand clutched to my side where the puppet had gashed me and blood had soaked my shirt. The ground shook as the giant pursued me. From the buildings on both sides of the road came the clatter of wood, and light splashed down onto the cobblestones. I looked up, even as more shutters swung wide.

Inside the open windows I saw flickering lights—candle flames the size of men—and they watched me pass by. Were they the ghosts of those murdered in Cicagne so long ago, or the spirits of the damned that had been drawn to the town over the years? I believe the latter, though I could not say why.

The sky flashed white with lightning, and thunder followed in its wake, joined by the concussive force of the giant's footfalls. I fled up the street,

stumbling again as I entered the town square, though I managed to stay on my feet. The stone platform in the square was no longer bare. Upon it there stood a translucent apparition, the ghost of a giant puppet house, ablaze with spectral fire.

I darted away from the sight. At the crest of the hill now, I could only think of retracing my steps down through the town and into the woods, and at last to the coast road. But I heard the wooden tread of the giant right behind me and I knew I had at best a dozen steps remaining before it had me.

The church loomed to my left. I turned and raced up the steps. A wooden fist struck the cobblestones behind me. The giant did not breathe and it no longer roared, but its joints clicked and its feet pounded the ground as it chased me up the stairs.

With both hands I grabbed hold of the door handle, and said a silent prayer. The door was heavy. Years of dust and grit spilled down as I dragged it open. As the giant lunged for me, I threw myself inside. When I hit the floor, all the breath was knocked out of me. Reaching after me, the giant's hand struck the door, slamming it closed.

I lay on the floor, just inside, gasping as I struggled to get my breath back. Outside, the giant began to howl. Its cries tore at my soul and stilled my heart with terror. This was the wail of anguished suffering from the pits of Hell itself. I scrambled away from the door, staring at it, waiting for it to be torn open and for the giant to crash through into the church. Yet nothing happened.

Warily, I rose. My heart battered at the inside of my chest and I feared it would burst. The pulse throbbing in my temples kept time with my shuddering breaths as I walked backward up the center aisle of the church, staring at the door. Still, the giant did not come.

Only as I reached the altar, bumped against it, and turned to glance around at the holy icons decorating the church, did I realize that the monstrous thing could not enter. It could not cross the threshold of the house of the Lord.

Nor could I leave, as long as it awaited me out there in the storm, howling with the wind and lightning and thunder.

I cowered in the shelter formed by the altar. As my heartbeat and my breathing slowed, the sounds of the storm diminished, and all I seemed to really hear was the wailing of the giant. But there was another sound in the church—one that had been there all along, beneath the others, subtly insinuating until at last I could hear it. At first I attributed the dripping noise to the rain that had soaked my hair and dampened my clothes, but then I realized it was coming not from me, but from a corner of the darkened church.

Without a sound, without drawing a breath, I turned.

Lightning flashed, and in the corner I saw the bones of a twenty-foot giant, contorted and bent, its skeletal legs drawn up beneath it. Gore was crusted to those bare bones and blood ran and dripped all over its frame.

The flash of lightning subsided. In the dim illumination that came through the stained-glass windows, I could just make out the giant skull turning toward me, staring at me with dark hollows.

This was the final horror. Shaking, I slid to the ground. Terror and blood loss overwhelmed me. With the sin-wood giant howling outside and its creator's quiet pleas whispering from the shadows, I surrendered to the black oblivion that swept over me. As I fell unconscious, I felt sure I should never awaken again.

Yet morning came, and I awoke in a heap of rubble. I lay twisted in the midst of piles of granite, and of pink and white marble. But this was an old ruin. Grass had begun to grow over some of the rubble, the land reclaiming the stone that had been removed from it.

Painfully, I dragged myself from the ruin. In the morning light I surveyed my surroundings. Around me was nothing but a wreckage of stone and overgrown beams and shattered terra-cotta. To the west was the ocean, perhaps half an hour's walk. To the east was sheer cliff, with a forest atop it.

I hesitated not another moment. As fast as I was able, I made my way to the coastal road and hurried north, glancing over my shoulder again and again, wondering what I would see. In two hours' time, I arrived in Genoa and went to the home of the sea captain I had traveled there to meet. I no longer had my pack or bedroll. I had no doubt they were somewhere in the ruins where I had awoken, but in the two hours I had walked from there it had never once occurred to me to return to fetch them.

The letter from the first mate of my former ship was in my pocket, and I gave it to the captain as an introduction. His wife doted on me, serving me a wonderful lunch and strong coffee, and kept staring at my eyes.

When they asked me what had happened to my things, and where I had gotten the cuts on my side that had soaked blood into my shirt, I told them the tale, just as I have told it to you. As I did, I removed my shirt and she cleaned my wounds and bandaged my side.

"A nightmare visited you last night, Demetrius," the captain's wife told me, as her husband looked on. "By all accounts, Cicagne was just as pretty as you describe it, and its puppet festival was renowned throughout Europe. But it has been gone for two hundred years or more. A storm destroyed the town, they say. The entire hill collapsed, sliding down onto the plain below, crumbling toward the sea."

The captain and his wife stared at the bandages on my side and at the torn, bloodstained shirt I had just removed, but they said nothing more, and neither did I. None of us ever mentioned it again, but I have never forgotten.

And that is why I never doubted a word that Lord Baltimore, or that desperate prophet of a monk, told me.

THE SOLDIER'S TALE:
AGNUS DEI

———

"Then he thought of the pretty little dancer,
whom he was never to see again,
and this refrain rang in his ears:—
'Onward! Onward! Soldier!
For death thou canst not shun.'"
—The Steadfast Tin Soldier
by Hans Christian Andersen

1

When Aischros had finished telling his story, the table fell silent. The murmur of voices in the bar around them had grown louder, as though the onset of evening had woken something in the pallid, spiritless patrons of the inn. Outside the window, dusk had turned nearly to night, and its color was a vivid cobalt blue more alive than the City seemed during the day or after dark. At sunrise and in those few moments of early evening, the world cast an illusion that it was not decrepit and tainted with disease.

Childress caught himself staring out the window, breath snared in his throat at the sight of that vibrant color. He forced himself to look away. There was nothing to be gained through illusion.

He'd finished the cigarette that Doctor Rose had given him, but did not ask for another. It had been the first he'd smoked in over a decade, and more a personal challenge than a pleasure.

The three men sat together for a minute or two without speaking or smoking or taking a drink. Aischros's tale had untethered something from its moorings inside Childress, and he suspected it had done the same to Doctor Rose. They were not here merely to recount the bizarre adventures of their younger days, or even to put together the puzzle pieces of Henry Baltimore's life. Whether it had been Henry's intent or not, they were here to discuss evil.

He opened his mouth to break the silence, to share those thoughts with his companions, but then the serving girl arrived to deliver their dinner. She brought some kind of small roasted birds for Doctor Rose and Aischros, with potatoes and mushrooms in a gravy the color of rust. When she brought his stew, Childress saw that it was the same color, and when he dipped his spoon into it, he dredged up bits of potato and mushroom and some kind of gray meat, and realized that he'd ended up with the same meal his friends had been served, only in a quickly coagulating broth.

Doctor Rose thanked the girl. Childress only smiled weakly at her.

Aischros put his fork to work instantly, hungry enough not to be picky. Doctor Rose poked at his potatoes doubtfully and then tore into his bird.

Childress stirred his stew. A thick film had begun to harden on its surface, which the spoon churned back into the concoction.

"That's an extraordinary story," he said, ignoring his meal. He glanced up at Aischros. "Even by the standards already set here this evening."

Aischros licked a dab of gravy from his lips. "It is true, and no dream, as some might suggest."

Childress nodded. "Oh, I'm certain it is. That makes it all the more troubling."

He forced himself to scoop a spoonful of broth and bring it to his lips, sipping just enough to get a taste. His nostrils flared with displeasure, more from the lack of any real flavor than disgust. Reluctantly he began to eat the stew, knowing that he needed sustenance—even from something as pitiful as this.

"Mister Childress," Doctor Rose said, his fork poised above his plate, "I believe you had a story for us as well. The history we've constructed thus far is grim and grows grimmer still, but I gather you've encountered Henry more recently than either Demetrius or I."

Childress gave up any pretense of interest in his stew. He set his spoon aside.

"I am the alpha and the omega, it seems," he said. There had seemed humor in the words when they occurred to him, but it was lost in the speaking. "I knew him as a boy. The last time I saw him was perhaps a year and a half after the death of his poor wife. I was still a soldier, but for all intents and purposes, the Great War was over. I suppose I could have been shot as a deserter when I walked away from my post, but by then, no one cared. So many had fled the battlefields to be with their families that it simply didn't matter anymore. The Hessians were still the enemy, but a war needs armies, and the plague had not discriminated between ally and enemy."

Childress trudged along the hard-packed road with his duffel bag slung over his shoulder. He'd twisted his ankle in a hole at the roadside that he felt sure was a snake den, and he limped a little as he walked. It did not trouble him much. Far better that than a snakebite.

Nothing moved around him except the stalks of wheat in the field just off the road. The withered, dying wheat should have been harvested months ago, and the wind made a dry rasp blowing through the field. If not for the distant bark of a dog, Childress would have thought the world had come to its whimpering end.

A pair of dead sparrows lay in the road. He stepped around them and tried not to wonder how two such birds could have died together. A bit of morning frost rimed their feathers. Winter had begun, though the sun still burned off much of the frigid air during the day. At night, the cold worked its way into his bones.

He longed for a warm bed, or at the least a decent blanket and a seat by the fireplace. But he had deserted his post, and could expect no such comforts until he had made it home at last.

Childress was not alone. Thousands of men had deserted. The truck he had stolen to make his way west to the Channel had been commandeered at gunpoint by a grizzled old sergeant who was taking his entire platoon home, and orders be damned. Childress had wished them luck and started walking.

That had been two days ago, and now

he gauged he was perhaps half a day's walk from the coast. He could practically smell the salt in the air.

For more than a mile he'd been traveling through the midst of an abandoned battlefield. The road was pitted with craters from shelling, but these were mere blemishes in comparison to the ravaged ground on the north side of the road. Trenches gouged in the earth lay open and empty, wounds that would never heal. The entire landscape was a pattern of holes—some left behind by mortar shelling and others dug by hand and surrounded by berms put in place to make them suitable bunkers.

Strewn across the battlefield was the wreckage of an army. An overturned truck had been burned, and its blackened frame made him think of the skeleton of some ancient beast. Here and there lay wooden boxes that had once held ammunition, some of them shattered but others neatly stacked as though someone might come back for them at any moment. But Childress knew that no one was coming back.

Perhaps not ever.

A small vehicle with a broken axle sat rusting, half vanished in the wheat field. Beyond that, he saw a tank. From the moment he spotted it, he could barely focus on anything else. It loomed ominously ahead, a silent sentry, and though he felt certain it must be unmanned, there was no visible damage. The idea that it was simply sleeping, waiting for someone to pass, crept up the back of his spine and insinuated itself into his brain. Irrational as such thoughts were, he could not tear his gaze from the tank as he passed.

Once beyond it, he saw that one of the tracks had broken and come loose, stranding the war wagon. Even then, he wondered how much damage—if any—had been done inside. He could imagine some farmer or wandering child climbing in to investigate someday.

His gut gave a sick twist as he realized how unlikely such a thing would be. By the time anyone returned to this ravaged ground to live, the tank would be a rusted hulk. There were few places to shelter after dark in the area, and not many people would be foolish enough to pass through here on foot, the way he was, for fear that they would fall prey to the unnatural things that now prowled the night. If it had been later in the day, he would have hidden away inside the tank until morning. It would have made a perfect bolt-hole. Unless, of course, something was already inside, using it as a shelter from the sun.

Childress glanced nervously at the tank and picked up his pace.

Yet there were other wrecked and abandoned vehicles to come. Soon he was weaving his way through a graveyard of ruined trucks and tanks, all of which had been destroyed in battle. Metal had been twisted and cracked and burned. Some of the vehicles lay on their sides and others had been turned over, exposing punctured underbellies. He moved swiftly through the silent, jagged wreckage, unwilling to spend a moment longer in that place than was necessary.

When he rounded a turn in the road and began to climb a gently sloping hill, it seemed he had left the battlefield behind. At the top of the slope he saw one final vehicle, off in the trees at the far end of the field of wilted wheat. Once, it had been a small airplane. The canopy of the cockpit was like a spiderweb that clung to the body of the plane. One wing and the tail had been torn off and were nowhere to be seen, as though a giant had snatched it out

of the sky and broken it up in his hands.

On the opposite side of the road, the earth was lined with rough-hewn grave markers, remembering soldiers who had been buried with little fanfare, as the plague had begun to spread through the ranks of the allies and Hessians alike. Some of the graves were disturbed, soil cast aside as though something had come up from within.

BALTIMORE   143

Childress kept his eyes on the road after that.

After he'd crested that hill, he saw a wide, churning river in the distance. On the bank of the river was a town that, before the war, had been on the verge of becoming a city. The road would lead him right through the town, alongside the rushing water. From the hilltop, the town looked almost deserted, but there were sure to be people there. Once upon a time he would not have hesitated to stop there and try to get lodging for the night, a hot meal, and a glass of ale. He was a man of some means, after all. But this was not his country and, despite the plague, many would not look kindly upon an army deserter.

He could have lied, of course, but they would see his duffel and his uniform, so his lies would hold little weight.

There were other reasons he did not wish to pass through the town. The population would have been diminished by war and plague, like every other place on the continent, and those who remained would be desperate and paranoid, perhaps hungry as well. And, as in other towns, there would be those infected with the plague. It was only mid-morning, so he did not worry about the dead...not with the sun still high in the sky. But the infected were a threat as well.

The mere thought of coming into contact with the plague, of becoming infected, skittered like a nest full of spiders across his skin.

Childress left the road and struck out northwest across open land. He would skirt the town entirely, make his way around it, and then follow the river out to the coast. Surely there would be a port at the river's mouth, where he could find a ship to carry him across the Channel, back to England.

Home.

He hiked across fields and through a spit of woods that seemed to separate two farms, crossed stone walls, and trekked up and down the hills above the river valley. From time to time he lost sight of the town, but was always aware of its presence. It lurked below, full of menace, much like the silent tank abandoned on the road.

The sun had passed its midpoint in the sky and it was early afternoon by the time he reached the river. The town lay a mile behind him and Childress was both relieved and dismayed. His stomach growled. He had had nothing to eat that day except moldy bread and cheese that an old man in a cottage had given him the day before. He filled his canteen from the river and took careful sips.

As he strode along the river for the rest of that short winter day, the sun grew weaker and the temperature dropped quickly. He rested several times, but only for a few minutes at each stop. The ocean would not be far now. Childress passed two small settlements, both on the opposite side of the river. The few houses he encountered on the northern bank were quiet; nothing stirred within.

When the sun was low in the west and the blue sky had gone winter pale, he saw the dark shape of a port city on the horizon, black smoke rising from its chimneys. Normally his nose would have wrinkled at the sight, but the smoke was a sign of life. Not all of the chimneys and smokestacks were churning their furnace breath into the air, but enough so that he felt less uneasy about approaching.

At dusk, he reached the city. Dull black eyes stared at him from alleys and windows as he followed the river. Gray, expressionless faces leered from the shadows.

He pulled his pistol from inside his duffel and thrust it into the waistband of his trousers so that it would be the first thing anyone would notice when they looked at him. He held the duffel over his shoulder with his left hand, keeping the right free to draw his gun.

Soon, he came upon a neighborhood where fires burned in metal barrels and people gathered in drunken revelry. They sang and danced and played whatever instruments they had to hand. The people were as ragged as the filthy, run-down buildings around them, but they were alive and vibrant. Most of the men looked like soldiers or sailors, now returned, but he also saw dockworkers and shopkeepers. Rough men with grizzled faces clutched bottles of liquor and pawed women so slatternly that if they were not whores, it was only because they did not take money for their services.

Childress had never been happier to see people in his life. As he passed through the street, a laughing man handed him a bottle and he gratefully took a long swig of vodka. A woman cozied up to him with promises in her eyes, but he only smiled at her and moved on. When another man approached, singing loudly, Childress joined in. He spoke French well enough, but the drunken man was slurring so badly he could barely make out the words.

"What are we celebrating?" he asked.

The man gave a bitter laugh. "The end of the world."

Childress's smile fractured, then vanished. He would not accept that. As ugly as the world had become, he had faith that society would rise again from this trial, just as it had risen from the terrible wars and plagues of the past.

The trick was to survive it.

The singing man was a burly, bearded fellow, gray-haired and flushed with drink and more exertion than was good for his heart. A twinkle in his eye might have been mischief, but Childress thought it must be panic instead. Now he understood the dancing and the fires and the whoring. The whole thing had an edge of desperation that could all turn violent at any moment.

Beneath the giddy revelry was a layer of madness.

Childress could only think of home.

"Excuse me, friend," he said, getting the man's attention again. "I'm trying to get home to England. Do you know anyone with a boat that could carry me across the Channel?"

The man nodded and grabbed Childress by the right wrist, dragging him through the revelers. His left hand went to the butt of the pistol sticking up from his waistband, fingers brushing it.

"Duvic!" the gray-bearded man called, waving to a lanky, unshaven man who was dancing with a blond woman. Her breasts seemed about to spill out of the top of her dress.

The lanky man, Duvic, turned with a smile, his hands all over the woman even when they stopped dancing.

"What is it?" Duvic asked. Then his eyes narrowed and he studied Childress closely. "Ah, another one, yes? Another Englishman sneaking home, thinking he can run from death? There's nowhere to run, soldier. The water won't stop the plague. It rides with the vermin on every ship that crosses the Channel, and with the men, too."

Childress stared at him. "But you can take me?"

"If you can pay," Duvic replied, glancing down at the pistol, perhaps wondering if he could take it—and Childress's money—without having to transport the man to England.

"I can pay," Childress told him. He did not reach for his gun, but he tensed, prepared to defend himself if need be.

Duvic hesitated a moment and then nodded. "Then I will take you home."

"When?"

The man looked longingly at the whore upon his arm, then kissed her deeply, laughing as he did so. His hands reached down and cupped her buttocks as he pressed her to him. Then he sighed and pulled away from her.

"Pay me enough, and I'll take you now."

Childress swallowed. "Is it safe on the docks after dark?"

"Safe as anywhere," Duvic said, tossing off the words like a spent cigarette. "The rats scurry if you make enough noise. Most of the time."

"All right. Let's go, then."

The man spared his woman a regretful glance and then they started off. The gray-bearded fellow who'd introduced them called after Duvic, insisting that he receive a fee for his part in the bargain. Duvic waved at him, though Childress did not know if that was a dismissal or an agreement.

They did not walk along the river. Duvic led him on a circuitous route through the city that included well-lit streets where gas lamps burned. Along these affluent streets, it was almost possible to believe that the war and the plague had never happened. But then they entered an area far more deteriorated, and soon were beside the river again.

The docks were ahead.

"Just a bit farther," Duvic told him.

They passed a bridge that spanned the river, which was narrower here than at any other point since Childress had followed it. Things shifted in the shadows along the bank of the river and he kept one hand on the grip of his pistol, glancing warily back toward the bridge and into the pit of darkness beneath it. The water was black.

A shape emerged from beneath the bridge—a barge, piled high with plague victims, their gray limbs twined together, bodies withered and faces gaping and grotesque. Atop this mountain of corpses stood a thin, skeletal figure in a black cloak that flapped about it like wings. And it *saw* him.

Childress cried out to God and drew his pistol. He fumbled with it and the gun dropped to the ground. He flinched as it struck the road, afraid it would discharge, but it spun and then lay there, useless. A cold chill passed through him, the icy pressure of the bargeman's regard, and even as Duvic called to him in alarm, Childress turned back toward the bridge.

There was nothing there.

2

The innkeeper had lit a fire that raged in the hearth, but Childress felt sure it had grown colder instead of warmer. The flames provided no heat to the lifeless, soulless void within that room.

He stared at his companions.

"This vision," Aischros asked, his voice curiously flat, "you're certain you did not imagine it?"

"Quite certain."

Aischros frowned, and drew a hand across his face. His palm came away damp with cold sweat.

"Why? What is it, Demetrius?" Doctor Rose asked.

Aischros glanced at him and then stared at Childress. "I saw something similar—or thought I did—just today, on my way into the City."

The three men were silent for a moment. Doctor Rose shuddered. Childress shook his head, not in denial but rejection. He did not want to know such things.

"You made it home, obviously," Doctor Rose said. He smiled thinly as he ran a hand through his red hair. It picked up the firelight, providing the only real color in the place. The doctor had a dandy's concern for his appearance, despite his mangled right hand. Childress wondered why an opium addict would care so much about how he looked; surely little pride could remain in the man. Yet perhaps his vanity was some strange compensation for his failures.

"You crossed the Channel," the doctor went on.

Childress nodded. "It cost me dearly, both what money I had and a pocket watch my grandfather had given me. But yes. I made it to England. By then I could think of nothing but home. It was mere days before I arrived at Boscastle Harbor. My family had left Trevelyan Island and relocated in the town, and my homecoming was joyous. A young man fools himself into believing he no longer needs to be held in his mother's arms or to hear the gruff approval of his father's voice. But to find them alive and well was the finest hour of my life.

"It was tainted by the news of what had driven them off the island. I learned then of the death of Henry's parents and sister, and the murder of his wife. No one knew where Henry had gone, or when he might return. Only a handful still lived on the island, they told me. My parents longed to return to our home there, and intended to do so, once they were certain the plague had passed.

"I had to tell them that it would get worse before it passed, and that we would be safer on the island than the mainland. I determined to investigate the state of things on Trevelyan Island, particularly my family home, and persuaded a fisherman to carry me out there.

"And that was where I last saw Henry Baltimore. The last any of us saw of him, I believe."

Despite the pall of fear that hung across the rest of the country, the captain of the fishing boat that carried Childress toward Trevelyan Island was a man of high spirits. He shouted orders to the two men who crewed his boat and stood at the wheel, calling back to Childress in amiable tones. The captain, whose name was Williams, had only recently settled in Boscastle, chasing rumors of better fishing in these waters than those of his home on the Welsh coast. He wanted to hear stories of the war—glorious tales of battle with the Hessians—and invited his passenger to confirm his suspicions that the rumors of the plague had been exaggerated out of all proportion.

Childress felt himself an entirely different species from Williams. He felt sure that such lightness of heart had been possible for him once upon a time, in his boyhood, but that part of him had since been shriveled to nothing. Still, he ventured to share a tale or two of the war before the plague, of the greatest accomplishments of the allied efforts against the Hessians. Only one of the stories was his own; others were borrowed accounts of the triumphs of grim, courageous men.

On the subject of the plague, however, he could not pretend.

"The sickness is as bad as you've heard, I'm afraid," he told the fisherman. "It's brought the rest of Europe to her knees. Already, infection rages here in England. In another age, there was the Black Death. Now the Red Death is upon us."

Williams tried to laugh it off, but his voice sounded hollow and his smile faded. He kept his gaze forward from then on, focused on their destination. The boat rolled on the waves and sliced the wind. Childress went to starboard and peered ahead through the salty spray, shivering with each gust of winter air. The sky hung low and heavy with the promise of snow.

He saw smoke rising from Trevelyan Island.

"What is that?" Williams asked, pointing ahead. "Do you see it, Mister Childress? Something's on fire up on the island."

"I see it," Childress replied, heavy dread settling upon him.

"What is it?"

"The Baltimore estate."

Williams glanced at him, a stricken expression on his face. "What, them that died of the plague?"

Simplified as this was—Henry's wife had been murdered and many others on the island had died of plague, not just the Baltimores—Childress nodded.

"Perhaps it's best, then," Williams said. "Fire purifies, Mister Childress. Perhaps it's best."

Anger simmered in him, but Childress did not reply, for he was not sure where to direct his anger. He'd intended to make a visit to the estate of Lord

Baltimore while on the island, but his primary reason for coming had been to examine the state of his own home. If no one else on the island seemed touched by the plague, he wanted his family to move back here before the sickness began to consume England as entirely as it had the rest of Europe.

Now, though, he would go directly to the island's peak. The black smoke churned into the air—mixing with the dark storm clouds—and as the boat sailed closer he could see the peak of the manse in flames. No lightning had started that fire. Someone had set a torch to the place.

Childress had his service pistol in the deep pocket of his thick coat. The weight was a comfort to him. He'd been unsure what he might encounter out here and thought it best to be prepared for anything.

When Williams and his crew brought the ship around and eased her up to the long dock, Childress did not wait for them to tie her to the pilings. He leaped down onto the dock and started striding away instantly.

"Two hours, remember. That's what you told me," Williams called after him. "The storm's coming."

Childress paused and turned, his hand already sliding into his pocket to grip the gun. Somehow the winter wind felt even colder and more bitter on the island than it had been out on the open water.

"It may be longer," he admitted. "But wait for me, Mister Williams, if you hope to be paid."

The fisherman's high spirits vanished. He scowled and seemed about to argue, then obviously thought better of it. Childress did not wait to discover what he would do, but glanced up at the black smoke rising from the lord's manor and hurried up the long path toward the burning house.

When he reached the estate, he could only stand and watch the conflagration. Flames gouted from shattered windows. Half of the roof had already buckled and he saw blackened beams on fire, jutting toward the sky. As he watched, one stone wall crumbled and the entire house seemed to collapse on that side, like a wounded soldier going down on one knee.

Childress stared at the burning house, the infernal heat tightening the skin of his face, for several long minutes. He had played in the attic with

Henry on hundreds of rainy afternoons. Together they had run through the hallways, climbed trees and played soldier on the grounds, hidden in the garden from any adults who had come to search for them, and had their first taste of wine. A thousand thousand memories were burning with that house.

"Good-bye," he whispered.

Only when he turned away from the house did he see that it had begun to snow. The heat from the fire was such that the thick, heavy flakes melted and evaporated before they reached the blaze. Now he saw the snow coming down, the wind gusting, fluttering a white veil of storm before his eyes. He remembered Williams's reservations, but spared them little thought. If the fire had been set, the culprit might still be here.

Childress walked the perimeter of the grounds as the snow began to accumulate beyond the heat of the fire. Twenty minutes of this turned up not another living soul, and at last he relaxed his grip on the pistol in his coat pocket. He gazed at the burning house again. The fire had begun to diminish, much of the place reduced to charred stone and embers, but the plume of black smoke had grown even thicker, an ebony swath across the ivory sky.

At last he turned and began to make his way back down the path. Childress would not leave without visiting his family's home to complete the task that had brought him back to Trevelyan Island, but first he would go and speak with Captain Williams. He wanted to assure the man that if he did not want to sail back to the harbor in the storm, all three fishermen would be welcome to sleep in the Childress home for the evening, and they could all return to Boscastle in the morning, when the storm had passed. There might be little in the larder, but there would be water, and wood for the fireplace.

When he reached the bottom of the path, he was relieved to find that Williams had not departed. The snow had accumulated quickly and it crunched underfoot as he started toward the dock. Childress looked up and saw the flakes swirling and dancing against the white sky, seemingly endless. The snow had laid a quiet upon the island even more complete than what had been before. Somewhere out on the water, a buoy clanged.

He glanced out toward the sound. Through the thick curtain of the storm, he saw a shape coming across the bay. He blinked and stepped away from the dock, moving along the shore to get a better look. It was a sailboat large enough for only two or three men. A single, stark figure sailed her toward Trevelyan Island.

A feeling of suspicion and curiosity passed over him. Who was this man? The arsonist, perhaps?

The wind battered the small craft, tilting it so severely that it nearly succumbed. Somehow, the man kept its sail from dipping into the surf. With the power of the storm caught in its sail, the boat arrowed toward shore. Childress realized with a start that the man intended to beach the craft.

"What in God's name?" he whispered, the words stolen by the wind, carried away with the snow.

Williams and his crew forgotten, Childress raced along the shore to intercept the small boat. When it skipped across the waves and hit the beach, hull shushing over sand and ice and snow, he felt certain it would tip instantly. But the black-clad figure on its deck lowered the sail so swiftly

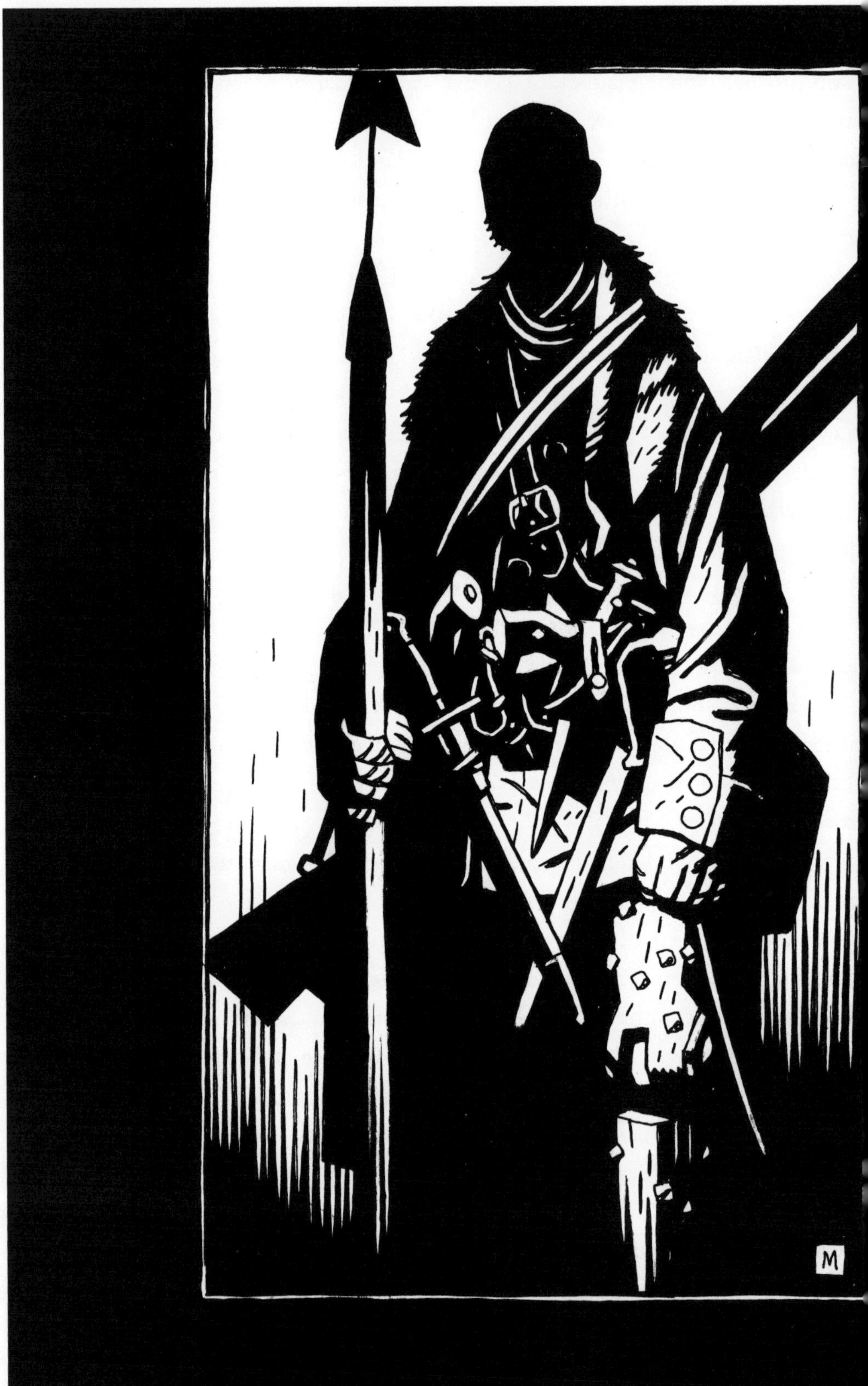

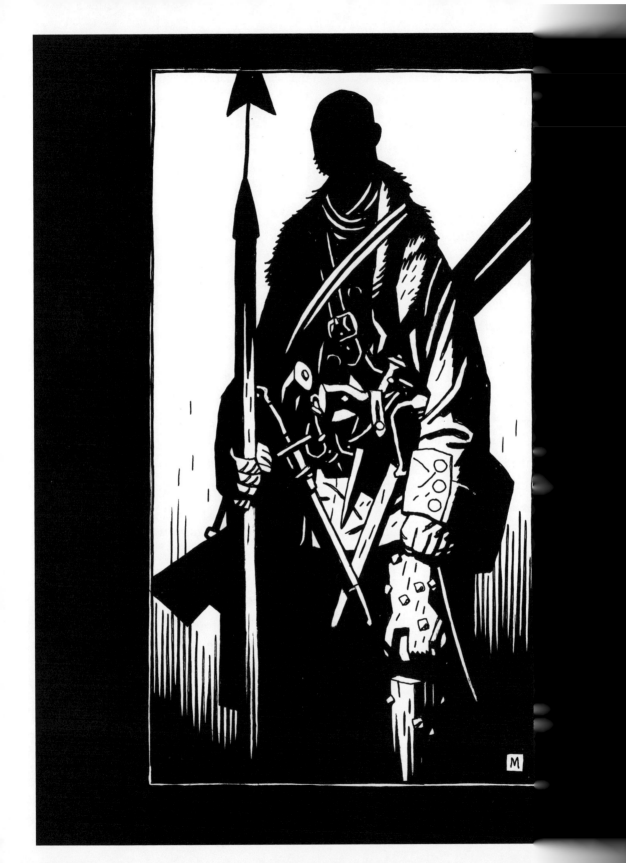

and with such skill that the boat rocked slightly and then came to rest at an angle on the sand, snow and ice crusting its mast and prow.

The sailor dropped down to the frozen shore. In the storm, Childress could see him only as a dark silhouette. In one hand, he carried a harpoon taller than he was, and a rattle of metal and clank of wood accompanied his every step, echoing off the snow.

Childress stood upon a rocky stretch of shore, watching the man approach. With a gust of wind the storm seemed to lessen, as though it were parting to allow him passage. He wore a long black coat with a fur collar, similar to the heavy winter greatcoats worn by Hessian officers in the war. His clothing was a combination of the uniforms of various armies. A pair of rifles hung from his back and other weapons were belted all over his body. Dagger handles and pistol butts jutted from their holsters and scabbards.

As he walked, Childress saw the shapes of other weapons hidden beneath his long coat, one of them a small axe. An army saber hung at his side, clanging against the man's wooden leg. Yet this was no stump or peg. The knee was fully jointed and squeaked with every step. A shudder of revulsion and horror went through Childress as he stared at that wooden leg, so much like the clacking, carved limbs of a puppet.

The newcomer limped slightly, and his wooden left leg dragged somewhat as he walked. As the man drew within a dozen feet, Childress could see that scores of nails had been driven into that wood, gleaming with the moisture of sea and storm.

The man stopped, ignoring Childress completely. He let his harpoon fall into the snow. From a pouch he withdrew a handful of nails, and then drew the small axe from its sheath. He dropped to his right knee and used the blunt end of the axe blade to hammer the nails into his leg. The wood shrieked as the nails were driven home. Each strike of the axe clapped against the stormy sky.

Childress stared at him. So fascinated had he been by the weaponry and that nail-studded leg that he had scarcely noticed his features. The man was bald, head shaved to the scalp, but he had a bristle of beard. He did not look up even for a moment, but Childress saw something familiar in his profile.

"Oh, my Lord," he whispered. "Henry?"

The man set another nail against the wood of his leg and swung the axe.

"It is you, isn't it? What are you doing?"

"One nail for each of them," Baltimore said. With a final blow, he hammered the last nail so that its head was flush with the wood. Most of them protruded a quarter inch or more, but this last he had hammered all the way in.

He hung his head, and Childress could hear him murmuring a prayer. Then Baltimore retrieved his harpoon and rose. He stood half a dozen feet away now, and made no move to approach.

"They're at peace now, Thomas," he said. "When I put the first nail in, for Elowen, I was a fool not to realize what had happened. I had seen what the demon had done to her. How could I not have realized that the Red Death and the Red King were one and the same? I saw the plague begin, old friend. I helped bring it into the world, and now I do penance for my part in it. But before I surrender to my fate, I will find the monster that has caused me such agony, and see it burn."

Childress hesitated a moment, but Baltimore stared at him with such intensity that it was clear he expected some kind of response. The loneliness in those eyes cut him deeply. They were cold and vacant. Vengeance had become some infernal engine within Baltimore, and its blazing fire had seared away everything else.

"I don't understand" was all that Childress could say.

"I should have seen it then, but I did not. I set out on my quest to destroy the devil, the master vampire, unaware that he had wrought his misery not only upon me, but upon the world. I didn't realize at first that the plague and the vampires were one and the same. I sought only my enemy, and when my pursuit of him led me to other vampires, I exterminated them. But that was not my purpose. I destroyed them because they were his kin, and because their evil tainted everything they touched. I hoped to hurt him.

"At first, the vampires were few. But soon there were more and more, and

I understood at last that the sickness was not mere disease. The plague breeds vampires. It is their infection. And when I understood, I realized that I had to return home. The plague victims are being burned for a reason. The priests and doctors conspire in whispers, telling the people it is to keep the sickness from spreading. Yet only a fool would not see that it's to keep them from rising.

"I didn't burn them, Thomas. Mother, Father, and Helen. I didn't know, in those early days. I came home to bring peace to them, and the others who were not at rest here on the island. One by one, I caught them as they prowled the island or hunted for blood on the mainland. I chained poor, sweet Helen in the room where she once slept so innocently. Her shrieks were terrible, but I kept her there while I hunted my father and mother, and brought them back to the house as well. When I had them all, I brought them in chains to the cemetery, to the crypt where they ought to have rested for eternity. There, I burned them, rendering them to ashes."

Childress took a step toward him, thinking to comfort him in some way. It would have been easy to think him a madman, but Childress had seen too much not to hear the truth amidst the ravings of his old friend.

Baltimore turned and looked out to sea. "I gathered their ashes in a vase my mother had loved. Then I returned to the house and set fire to it. I stood with that vase for several minutes, watching to make sure that the flames would spread, and then I took the ashes of my family out into the bay. Mother loved the bay, you know. I scattered their ashes across the waves, thinking that somehow the ocean would cleanse the stain from them.

"They were my responsibility, Thomas. Not merely my family, but all of those on the island, whose families had been loyal to the Lords Baltimore for generation upon generation."

The scent of smoke still lingered in the air, drifting with the falling snow.

"You could never have known what was to come," Childress said.

Baltimore met his gaze, unflinching. "I must go and say a final farewell to my Elowen—to everything I might ever have been—for I will never return here again. Trust no one, my old friend. The stain is not upon you yet. Find a place to wall yourself away from the hell that creeps across the land. Stay safe. Stay well."

He marched past Childress and started up the path toward the dying blaze that was all that remained of his home and, beyond, the empty crypt where the bones of his family ought to have rested. Childress almost called after him, but fear and a terrible foreboding made him hesitate.

Baltimore seemed almost a ghost to him. The mere presence of his old friend had deeply unsettled him. A kind of communion existed now between Baltimore and the dead, and Childress wished to have no part in that relationship. The plague had raised dead men from the earth, and though Baltimore was no vampire, he seemed somehow not unlike them, a man whose heart and soul were dead, and yet who somehow continued onward.

As he watched Baltimore disappear into the falling snow, Childress knew he ought to follow him, to hear the tale of his travels and the horrors he had seen, to offer whatever small help he might provide. But he could not escape the thought that his old friend went now to that empty crypt to find his own final rest. Trevelyan Island itself seemed to have become some kind of No Man's Land between the living and the dead, and Childress could not abide spending another moment on that abandoned rock. He could not force himself even to call out to Baltimore. Instead, he hurried back to the dock, raising Williams and his two crewmen with a shout, and climbed aboard the fishing boat.

Childress promised the men three times what they'd agreed if they would cross the bay in the storm. Greed trumped caution, as ever, and they set off at once, sailing over rough seas, half-blind with the snow.

On the deck, Childress drew his coat tightly around him and did not spare a single glance back toward Trevelyan Island.

3

Childress rested his fingers on the spoon he'd been given to eat his stew—which he'd barely touched—as though the metal tool were some strange, protective charm. It felt warm to the touch.

"The war never ended for Baltimore," Doctor Rose said, pushing his plate away, his meal only half-eaten. "Only the enemy has changed."

"The rest of us surrendered without a fight," Childress replied. "When I should have joined him, stood by his side, I retreated as quickly as I could."

"He asked all three of us here," Aischros said, gnawing the last bits of meat from the leg of the small bird he'd eaten. "Perhaps you'll have another chance to stand with him."

"I've hoped for that every day since I watched him vanish into that snowstorm."

Doctor Rose glanced out the window. "It's quite dark now. I hope nothing's happened to him. What dreadful irony, after all that he's endured."

Aischros wiped his mouth with a threadbare napkin. "He'll be here."

"I know he will," Doctor Rose admitted. "And I confess that I fear his coming."

Childress stared at him, feelings of both shock and kinship welling up within him. A glance at Aischros told him that they were all frightened of what the night might still hold.

"Mister Childress," Aischros said, dark eyes narrowed. "You've told us of your last meeting with Lord Baltimore. But I know you've got another story.

The doctor and I both had experiences that made it easy for us to believe the things we learned of Baltimore's life."

Doctor Rose arched an eyebrow.

Childress splayed his hands upon the table, steadying himself. "As did I," he said. "You're correct in that assumption, Demetrius. Like yourself, I traveled by sea a great deal as a young man. My father was an importer and I frequently journeyed on his behalf to distant shores. One such venture took me as far as Chile, in South America.

"It was the last journey I ever undertook for my father."

First, I must confess to you that my father's business was not always entirely lawful. In addition to copper, fruit, herbs, and clothing woven in the local customs, he conducted a trade for many years with Chilean locals who provided him with artifacts from the centuries of Incan rule in their country. There were weapons and armor pieces as well as statuettes, masks, and other icons.

When he was a young man, my father had arrangements with the Chilean government, but by the time I was old enough to become involved—to travel as his representative—such relationships had crumbled. The Chilean people had begun to insist that their heritage be preserved. As importers—and as Englishmen—we'd seen it happen many times before.

Egypt had turned into a similar quagmire. Laws were being passed to prevent locals from selling such artifacts, and foreigners from buying.

I regret now my involvement with such transactions. But at the time I did not recognize the finer points of the argument or understand the complaints of the Chileans. If there were those in possession of such artifacts and they wished to sell them, and we were willing to buy, it seemed to me that the law should not intrude upon honest business.

We steamed southwest aboard the *Sarah Jane,* which my father had named for his mother. During that journey—my second to South America—I reached my twenty-first birthday while navigating the Strait of Magellan. The sun rose orange beyond a thin layer of clouds and the water rippled only lightly with the breeze. Had we been under sail instead of powered by steam, we would have been becalmed. It was a rare, peaceful day. When I think of all of the things I have seen and learned in the years since then that I wish I could unsee and unlearn, it is that orange sunrise that I recall. Would that I could return to that day, turn that ship around, and choose another path.

But we cannot go back. None of us can.

We made port in Valparaiso. Beyond the city was hilly country, and past that, nothing but infinite blue sky. Aside from the beauty of the place, I was astonished by the ethnic mix of its population. Immigration had transformed it into a veritable Babel. Just on the docks alone I saw Englishmen, Spaniards, Germans, Italians, and Frenchmen, in addition to locals whose origins were as diverse as those of their visitors. What I loved most about Valparaiso was the sheer industry of the place. The docks buzzed like a hive of bees, so many men at work loading and unloading ships, backs bent to their tasks. There was a joie de vivre in those men that I still recall with admiration; a great camaraderie and optimism that seem all but extinct now.

Though I represented my father's interests, a man named Geoffrey Hoskins was the true leader of the expedition, bearing the title of Importation Manager. He was a grim creature, given to dark rumination, and though he deferred to me I could see that he had little regard for me aside from my heritage.

Hoskins and I left the crew to provision the ship for her return journey and ventured into Valparaiso, where we spent two solid days conducting our business for Childress Importers. In addition to the fruits and herbs, we purchased copper sheeting and various linens and wool, as well as small trinkets from artisans, objects that would provide an entire season's worth of curiosity to the well-to-do Londoners who would buy such things merely to show others that they had them.

On the second night, we were to be visited by a man named Matteo, who had been the primary source of Incan artifacts for Childress Importers for many years. When, by morning, Matteo had not appeared, Hoskins gathered half a dozen members of the crew and went out into the port in search of him. While they were gone, I sat in my cabin aboard the ship and composed a long letter to my father, reporting to him all that had transpired thus far. Whatever irregularity had interrupted our plans, still it seemed all business to me.

I never could have imagined what strange ugliness would soon arise.

Early in the afternoon, Hoskins returned with Matteo in tow. Of the six crewmen who'd accompanied him on his search, one of them—a lad no older than I was—did not return. A knife wound, I was told. When I inquired how the stabbing had occurred, I received only blank stares, or, worse, a roll of the eyes that suggested I was deliberately obtuse. And perhaps I was. You see, Hoskins had blood on his hands and bruised knuckles, and Matteo had been beaten so badly that his eyes were swollen shut and his split lip produced a fresh trickle of blood every time he tried to speak. Though he must have been nearly forty, he looked to have been handsome once. Now he would be scarred and his nose would never be straight, and there were teeth missing from his mouth.

I took Hoskins aside and made it perfectly clear to him what I thought of such behavior, and how it would reflect upon Childress Importers. Until that moment, I had considered Geoff Hoskins an unpleasant man, but not a cruel one. Yet he grinned as I spoke, flexing his bruised knuckles and studying them with a disquieting appreciation.

"Here's a bit of news for you, young Tom," he said. "Your da's going to be a fair bit angrier if we return without them Incan trinkets than if word gets round that the men from Childress Importers ain't the sort to cross."

I felt the truth in those words. I would have liked to argue, but could not. Even so, the death of one of our own crew surely ought to have elicited more worry from Hoskins than he'd shown. I said as much, and he nodded in grave sympathy.

"Sad turn, that is. But this sort of thing's dangerous business, sir. Exotic locations, storms at sea, rough customers in port. That snake Matteo led us a merry chase through the filthiest dives in Valparaiso. The lad who didn't make it back died doing his job. He had a hand on Matteo and got stabbed by one of his mates, who took exception to our wanting to have a private chat with him.

"It's the way of things, young Tom."

The way of things. For the rest of my life, I'll never forget those words. They troubled me deeply at the time, and frightened me as well. But over the years they've come to be a melancholy sort of comfort.

I stared at his bruised knuckles a moment and then glanced toward the hold, where the crew had disappeared, dragging Matteo along with them, tightly bound in rope.

"I presume your bludgeoning has produced some word of the artifacts?" I asked, at pains to use my tone to remind him who was truly in charge of our expedition—that he might be the leader, but I was the employer. I could replace him on a whim, as long as I was willing to explain my actions to my father.

Perhaps he did not think that much of a threat.

Hoskins grinned. "Oh, he told me what I wanted to know after the third blow. The rest were just to teach him a lesson."

My stomach roiled in revulsion. I'm sure he could see it in me, and it only amused him. The ship creaked beneath our feet as it rolled upon the water. A long moment passed as I fought the urge to confront him further about his behavior, but no matter my own feelings, I knew that Hoskins was doing my father's work.

"The way of things," I said grimly.

"Now you've got it, lad," he replied, no trace of humor on his face.

I nodded, more in agreement with myself than acceptance of the unpleasant truths I had learned. "All right," I said. "What did he tell you? Do you know where the artifacts are located?"

Even as I spoke, several members of the crew came out onto the deck with packs they had prepared for a trip inland. I stepped toward them, emerging from cool afternoon shadows into the heat of the sun. Then I turned back to Hoskins.

"What is this?"

Hoskins gestured to the crewmen as they did an inventory on the contents of their packs.

"Matteo is going to take us to the place where he and his men have been digging up the artifacts. It's an Incan ruin on a mountainside above a lake. There's a village there. Matteo says the people were willing to let him dig in trade for things he brought from the city. The authorities have not caught up with him yet."

"No?" I asked. "Then why didn't he show up to meet with us? Why did it take a beating to learn the truth from him?"

A shadow passed across Hoskins's face at that and his brows knitted as he

took a step nearer to me. I thought he might strike me, but he did not.

"He's frightened," Hoskins said. "Matteo has a daughter, nine years old. The fool took her with him last time they were digging, and she vanished. The villagers claim some kind of demon snatched her, but Matteo worries they killed the girl themselves. Either way, he's afraid to go back."

That brutal smile blossomed again. "Of course, we're going to bring him back. We'll get some horses and Matteo will lead the way."

Intimidated by his nearness, I had to force myself to meet his eyes. "I'm not sure we ought to risk it."

Hoskins snorted derisively. "The village is fairly remote, and the existence of this ruin is not public knowledge. As soon as the authorities learn of it, we'll never get so much as a piss pot from the place. So we're going to go up into the mountains and make our own deal."

Having just been schooled in what sort of deal Hoskins might be likely to make, I determined to accompany him.

"You'll stay here, young Master Childress. It isn't the sort of work your father would approve of," Hoskins said.

Though I was nearly as broad and an inch taller, the man's physical presence was ominous. Hoskins's intimidation came from the grim bent of his mind and the blood on his fists—from his obvious willingness to inflict pain and his skill at doing so.

There were seven or eight members of the crew on the deck at the moment—four who were preparing to trek inland and several others who were going about their duties, seeing that the ship would be ready to depart when the time came. All of these men watched as I stood up to Hoskins, surprise etched upon their features. None were as stunned as Hoskins and myself, however.

"I'm going to accompany you, Geoff," I said. "I insist. That leaves you with only two choices. You must accede to my wishes, or kill me. You've left me with no doubt that you are indeed the killing kind, but I don't believe you'll take my life. My father might brush off the death of a deckhand as a tragic accident, but I wager you'd pay a terrible price should any harm befall me."

Hoskins glared at me for several seconds. His nostrils flared. And then he laughed.

"All right, Tom, all right," he said. Then he strode over to a deckhand. "Mister Kirk! Put together a pack for Mister Childress. We leave within the hour!"

* * *

Hoskins was as good as his word. By mid-afternoon, a group of seven set off from Valparaiso on horses I had arranged through a merchant in the port with whom we had conducted some of our lawful business. Aside from Hoskins and myself, there were four members of the ship's crew. All of us kept a watchful eye on the last of our companions—Matteo himself.

We traveled northeast with Matteo as our unwilling guide. The journey took us into the hills through long valleys. Reluctant as he was, Matteo never wavered in our course and made no attempt to slip away, even during the first long night when we made camp beside a swift, narrow river. By the following morning, he seemed a different man. The swelling on his face had gone down and his lip had begun to heal, but that could not account for the new rigidity of his spine or the iron set of his jaw.

His daughter had vanished or been killed in that mountain village, and he had fled. The men thought him a coward, and I was no exception. His little girl had been taken from him, and the man had run away.

Now, though, I saw a different side to Matteo. Forced to return, he had adopted an air of grim resignation. When we slowed, it was Matteo who spurred us on. As we rode up from a green valley and into the more difficult mountain terrain, the anguished man had desperation in his eyes. I presumed that he was ashamed and hoped that his return would bring him some kind of

redemption, even in his own heart. Yet I wondered why he had fled in the first place. How could he have left without knowing the truth of his daughter's fate and attempting to find justice for her?

The second night of our journey, we camped beneath an overhanging ledge to shelter us from the rain, which poured down with such power that I can still recall the sound. Late at night, I shared a

watch with Kirk, one of the sailors in our party. Matteo lay awake, his dark eyes gleaming in the night. By now there seemed an almost religious fervor in him. I felt compelled to speak to him.

Kirk was out of earshot, and so I sat down beside Matteo.

"I don't understand," I said. "You were terrified. What's changed?"

"Nothing," Matteo replied. "I am still terrified. But I am also angry. If I must return, then I bring my anger with me. The people of the village do not have the courage to kill El Cuero, but that is because they do not wish to die. I do not want to die, but I cannot live, knowing that the demon still waits there in the lake."

The rain punished the ground. It was so loud that I knew no one else could hear us. I stared at Matteo's brutalized features, but all I could see was the zeal in his eyes.

"So, you believe there really is a demon?" I asked him.

"I have seen it, my young friend. And so will you."

The certainty in his voice shook me. I stared at him. "What do you mean? This creature—El Cuero, you called it—what is that?"

He gave a dismissive snort and turned away. "You would not believe me now. But perhaps when you see it with your own eyes."

After that, he would say nothing more.

4

Early the next morning, we rode into the village, which was not at all what I'd expected. We passed several farms on our way in, and the main street was intersected with several others, all of which seemed to turn in upon themselves. As remote as the location was, there were dozens of homes built up around the central square. On the northern end of town, almost as though it had been an afterthought, there stood a little white church, with a bell tower that rose above the rest of the village. The bells were ringing as we rode down the street. People stopped on the dusty road to watch us pass. Some of them, upon seeing Matteo, turned away and crossed themselves.

The village was set in a valley between two peaks. We had come through the pass and into the valley, and farther to the north, the remains of an Incan settlement lay half-revealed on the face of the mountain, as though a landslide had either buried part of the ancient city or uncovered the rest.

To the east, behind the village, was the lake. The water seemed a darker, richer blue than the sky, and it was larger than I had imagined, covering miles of the valley floor. When we dismounted our horses in front of the church, I stared at the water, searching for some sign that there was anything at all out of the ordinary about it. Yet I saw nothing.

Several older men strode down the street toward us. A skinny yellow dog barked and ran in circles around them. I'd expected them to be guarded, at least, perhaps even angry to see Matteo back in their village. Instead, they wore expressions of grief and sympathy.

Hoskins seemed not to have noticed.

"Tell them we want to start digging again," he told Matteo. "Ask them how much they want."

I frowned and stared at Hoskins. The ugly man spoke better Spanish than I did, by far, and I didn't understand why he wanted Matteo to speak for him. Years later, it occurred to me that Hoskins wanted to be able to hear what the villagers would say if they believed he did not understand them. Not that it mattered. Now that we'd brought him there, Matteo had no intention of being our guide any longer.

"Look around, idiot. You think they need your money up here? They raise cattle and sheep; they fish in the lake; they grow their own crops. Your money's worthless to them. But you do what they want, and they'll let you take whatever you like out of the ruins," he said, gesturing angrily toward the mountain.

"Yeah?" Hoskins said. "What is it they want, then?"

Matteo grinned, and I saw madness in him. "They want what I promised them, when they let me dig in those ruins. They want El Cuero dead."

Hoskins shouted at Matteo, demanding to know what he was talking about, but Matteo ignored him. The three village men shot disdainful glances at the rest of us as they spoke to Matteo. They spoke so rapidly that I understood only a few words, but it was clear that they were offering their condolences on the loss of his daughter.

"What the bloody hell are you talking about?" Hoskins demanded. "What's this El Cuero?"

He looked around for an answer, glancing at the villagers, at Kirk and the other sailors, and then at me.

"It's the demon," I told him. "The demon that's supposed to live in the lake. The thing that took his daughter."

Hoskins stared at me in open disbelief. He handed the reins of his horse to Kirk and went to stand by Matteo and the village men, listening carefully. They behaved as though he wasn't there. I heard something about a dog, and then a boy, and the mention of El Cuero time and again, but otherwise it was gibberish to me.

"What is it?" I asked Hoskins, no longer able to contain myself. "What's going on?"

He held the back of his head with both hands, as though afraid his skull would split open. Laughing, eyes wide, he turned to look at me.

"This little bastard's been lying to us all along. He had a deal with them; get rid of the demon and they'd let him take whatever he wanted, which he then sold to us. Clever prick. He strung them along for a good long while, had his whole crew up here, went about the motions of trying to catch this monster—whatever it is. Had his whole family up here, he did. Little girl wandered off. Had a little ribbon in her hair, far as I can translate it, and they found it by the lake. Matteo did a runner."

"Jesus," one of the sailors whispered.

Then there was silence in the street. You couldn't have asked for a more beautiful day, or a more serene spot. But underneath it all, the place was rotten. I could feel it. While Hoskins was talking, Matteo and the village men had fallen silent and they were staring from him to me.

Matteo sneered at Hoskins, then turned from him, like he didn't matter at all. Geoff wasn't the sort to stand for that kind of thing, but he took it, that day. I think he was just so confounded that he didn't know how to react to anything.

"Mister Childress," Matteo said, "there are dozens—maybe hundreds— of Incan artifacts up in those ruins. Things my friends and I had gathered or uncovered before my greed and lies cost my daughter her life. In the time since I left, El Cuero has taken another child, a little boy whose dog went too close to the water. The boy was only seven years old, but already he knew better. But El Cuero dragged his dog into the water, Mister Childress, you see? You know how boys are with dogs, yes? He had to go after his dog.

"These men grieve for my daughter, just as they grieve for that boy. And they would both be alive if I had done as I promised. So, now I will do it, at last."

Hoskins looked at the three village men. Their skinny yellow dog barked at him, and he flinched. The animal began to pant and circle his masters again, even as the three men spoke softly amongst themselves, watching us all from the corners of their eyes.

"Let's say I believe there's something in the lake—" Hoskins began.

Matteo interrupted him with a snort. "Believe it or not, as you wish. It is there, and my daughter with it, down at the bottom of the lake."

His eyes were so full of despair and his voice so haunted that all of the sailors who had traveled with us shuffled their feet and looked away. Even Hoskins—brutal, bloody Hoskins—seemed affected.

"I'm sorry for that," he said. "But we've a job to do. Now, are you saying that if you kill this thing, we can just cart off everything up there in the ruins?"

Matteo said something in rapid-fire Spanish to the village men. One of them looked over at Hoskins with his upper lip curled in disgust. He looked at me, and he nodded.

I would like to think that what I did next, I would have done regardless of any benefit to myself or to my father's company. Still holding the reins of my horse, I went to Matteo and stared at the three men. A wind picked up, strong enough to blow dust up from the road and make the bells in the church tower ring weakly, though it wasn't the hour.

"*Dígame sobre El Cuero,*" I said.

Hoskins glared at me. "You're just as mad as the rest of them."

"Perhaps," I allowed.

They were hesitant at first, but slowly, with Matteo translating, they told me the tale of the demon they called El Cuero. They did not know the demon's real name. It had been christened El Cuero because of its peculiar nature, which, when I heard the tale, I did not believe any more than Hoskins.

In a time remembered only by the oldest living soul in the village—a woman as brown and weathered as an old saddle—a demon possessed a young man of the village. With the evil inside him, the young man became a cannibal. He would snatch small children and young girls from the village and drag them to the lake, where he drowned them before drinking their blood and eating their raw flesh. He weighted their corpses down with stones, but not all of the bodies stayed down.

He was captured, and in punishment, the villagers first stoned him and then they drowned him just as he had drowned his victims. They weighted him down and sank him into the lake, and for a time, they believed his evil had been cleansed from the village, and only the grief remained for those he had murdered.

But one day, a leather maker went to the lakeshore to cure the hide of a donkey, and the hide was lost in the water.

Soon, it began to happen again. Girls sent to get water from the lake began to disappear. Children playing on the shore, wading in the water, vanished beneath the surface. Horses grazing on the grass, drinking from the lake, were dragged under. Many people saw the demon in the lake. Flat and leathery, it floated on the water, edges rimmed with a hundred eyes and as many claws. It would drift on the surface toward those who did not suspect

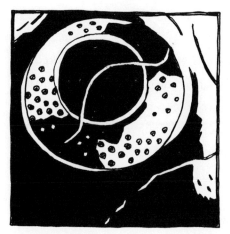

its true nature, luring them in with curiosity. Others simply did not see it until its claws snagged them. El Cuero wrapped around them and dragged them to the bottom of the lake.

As Matteo translated the words of the three village men, Hoskins became aggravated. His face red, he stared at them, then turned to me.

"Come, young Tom," he sputtered. "You can't possibly believe any of this shite!"

I fixed him with a hard look that silenced him. A queer confidence had come upon me and for perhaps the first time in all the days we had worked together, I became the leader of our expedition in more than name.

"Mister Kirk," I said, turning to the sailors, "return to Valparaiso. Take two men. Engage the services of locals and secure us two large wagons with which to transport the artifacts from the ruins back to port."

"Yessir, Mister Childress," Kirk replied. He hesitated a moment and glanced worriedly at Hoskins, who only scowled. Then he spoke quickly to two of the others, and they were off.

Many other people had come out of their homes, and now they began to move warily toward us. They were ordinary people with troubled eyes, not the monsters I had imagined when I'd first heard the story of the vanishing of Matteo's daughter. The yellow dog began to whine and sniff at my feet, glancing back and forth between me and its masters. The wind brought the delicious aroma of something cooking nearby. Despite the Incan ruin and the remoteness of the place, despite the demon in the lake, it was a village like any other. These were people, like any others.

"Matteo," I said, though I kept my gaze upon the three village men, "tell them to bring a sheep or a pony and meet us by the lake. Tell them we'll need rope, and every man with strong arms and a brave heart."

The bereft, grieving father looked at me, his eyes and face still bruised from Hoskins's beating. He nodded in approval and then turned and began rattling off instructions to the villagers.

I mounted my horse, snapped the reins, and headed past the church, even as the bell rang for the half hour. With Kirk and the others already departed for the long ride back to Valparaiso, only two men remained—Hoskins, and a burly, bearded sailor called Nick Forrester, who looked as though he had been the offspring of an unfortunate coupling between wolf and ogre.

"What do you think you're doing?" Hoskins demanded as he and Forrester caught up with me.

"Don't be dense, Geoff," I replied. "We need those artifacts. We're here, and these people will be happy to let us take them, as long as we take care of their problem first. Matteo doesn't even want his payment anymore. All he wants is to see El Cuero dead."

Hoskins spurred his horse and used the animal to block my way. Its hooves pounded the ground, its coat glistening in the sunshine. The man sneered at me as though I were some kind of beast myself. My horse snorted with frustration when I pulled it to a halt.

"You don't honestly believe all of this," Hoskins said, and it wasn't a question.

I stared at him. "Not the legend that goes with it, perhaps, but let me ask you something. If there's no creature in the lake—demon or otherwise—can you explain what happened to Matteo's daughter and all of the others?"

The troll-like Forrester, normally quiet and gruff, sniffed. "Got to be sumfin' in the lake, Mister Hoskins."

With a shudder, Hoskins gave him a withering stare that promised retribution. Forrester smirked, as though the threat had come from a small child and not his superior. It seemed to me a mistake for Hoskins to presume he could intimidate the man. Even if he could have hurt Forrester, the grizzled sailor seemed not to care.

I guided my horse around him, and Hoskins and Forrester fell in behind me without another word. When we reached the water, I turned north and rode a short way along the shore until we came to a stand of trees that offered some shade. I dismounted and tethered my horse to the tree farthest from the water, and both of the sailors did the same. The beasts could linger in the shade and graze on the short grass there.

In the quiet of the mountains, I stood and stared out across the lake. The water rippled a bit on the shore, and I told myself it was only the wind, not something stirring underneath.

Only minutes passed before we saw Matteo leading a crowd of men and women from the village. The yellow dog trotted along behind a woman, yipping and jumping to try to get her attention. It stayed away from the water.

A young man—little more than a boy, really—walked next to Matteo, carrying a lamb in his arms like a baby. The boy's features were pinched as though he fought against tears. The faces of the men who walked with him were cold and grave, but some of those villagers who straggled behind seemed curious, almost excited. There was no place here for spectators, but how was I to tell them that? It gave my gut a twist to see the fascination flicker in their eyes, so I tried not to look at them.

A low muttering accompanied them, like the buzz of swarming bees.

At the instruction of one of the three men I'd spoken to by the church, the boy set the lamb down. Several others approached with lengths of rope spooled over their shoulders and let it spill to the ground.

"All right," I said, motioning toward Matteo. "Let's get to it."

Hoskins and Forrester stood by and watched as Matteo and I tied ropes around the lamb's neck and torso, and one to each of its legs. As we held it still to bind its limbs, the little creature uttered loud, panicked bleats that carried out over the lake.

The villagers moved back from the water, farther away than we'd tethered the horses. We were inviting the demon to come for a feast, and no one wanted to be near if it answered our invitation.

Six ropes were tied to that single pitiful lamb, and three men held each rope. Hoskins stood back with his arms crossed, watching as though the entire proceedings were beneath him. Matteo, Forrester, and I held on to the rope that had been tied to the lamb's torso, with Matteo in the front.

We could only wait then. Even the buzzing of the spectators ceased. Aside from the wind and the lapping of the water upon the shore, the only sound was the plaintive bleating of the lamb. The animal's voice began to fail. Behind me, Hoskins muttered something about wasting our time, but I barely heard him. My attention was focused on a broad, round patch of water that seemed calmer than the rest of the lake, flat and undisturbed by the wind.

It moved closer, floating on the surface.

The sun shone brightly and there were dozens of people nearby, yet in that moment I felt like a small child, sitting up late at night and listening to all of the creaks and groans of my house, and wondering what really lay beneath my bed or hung just outside my window. I had never seen a demon, and I told myself that El Cuero was just a strange animal, the sort of thing that legends always spoke of, but few had ever seen. Something rare, but natural.

As it floated nearer, slowly, stalking the lamb, I saw the dull eyes that gazed out from thick folds of dark brown rawhide, and the long spiny claws that protruded from its edges. I knew then that there was nothing natural about the thing. A foul stench floated from it, and even its smell was nothing I had ever encountered before. It was sulfur and rot and blood. The thing stank of evil.

Every man and woman on the shore of the lake stood unmoving, holding their breath, as El Cuero glided across the water, billowing on the surface. The lamb tried to walk toward Matteo. One of the village men hauled on

the rope holding a foreleg and the lamb fell, bleating more loudly.

"Holy Christ," Hoskins whispered behind me.

The demon flowed up from the water like a wave and fell upon the lamb. The silver prongs of its claws sank into the animal's flesh, and the lamb began to scream as the demon wrapped around it, dragging it into the water with such speed that at last I understood how so many had been taken.

The surface of the lake rippled as El Cuero sank beneath the water. Its hide pulsed with the struggles of the lamb.

Matteo shouted in Spanish and then in English, screaming for us to pull. As one, all of the men hauled on their ropes, throwing their weight into the effort. I knew the lamb was dead already—we had sacrificed it as bait—but the thought of the ropes snapping its neck and legs sickened me. Still, we pulled with all of our strength, and dragged the demon toward us. El Cuero's hide surfaced again and it slid toward the shore. We felt resistance as its bulk, wrapped around the lamb, hit the shallows.

Then, El Cuero pulled back.

It thrust away from the shore so abruptly and with such strength that several of the men stumbled to their knees. One of the villagers splashed into the water, still holding on to his rope. A flap of the demon's hide unfurled, claws snatching the man, and it dragged him under, cradled with the lamb.

Matteo screamed in fury and called out to God, repeating the name of his daughter—Beatriz—over and over again.

The demon plunged into the lake. The rope burned my palms and I had to wrap it around my body, trying to anchor myself. In front of me, Forrester swore and twisted the rope around his forearm, digging his feet into the dirt. Still, we staggered forward. This was the strength of the devil. I knew it then, as certain as I felt the ground beneath my feet. El Cuero had no fins that I could see, no limbs, yet somehow it propelled itself away from us.

Matteo staggered into the lake, refusing to let go, even as he was dragged in up to his waist. Other men let the rope slide to avoid going into the water.

Hoskins ran past me and Forrester, toward Matteo. He roared at the villagers in Spanish, commanding them to help, to join in. This, he told them, would be their only chance to kill the demon. If they did not stop it now, it would prey on them forever, and on their children and grandchildren. First two, then five, then a horde of men and women came forward and joined the others at the ropes.

Matteo began to scream. He stared down into the water at his legs.

"Hoskins!" I shouted. "Get him out of there!"

I would have run forward myself, but I anchored the rope that was attached to the lamb's torso. Villagers were grabbing hold to help Forrester and me, but not quickly enough.

Hoskins reached Matteo just in time to take the man's hand as El Cuero pulled him down. Matteo screamed, not in fear, but fury, as his fingers were pulled from Hoskins's grip. He beat at it with his bare hands as it snagged him with those claws.

Once again it thrust away from the shore, dragging the lamb and two men with it. Feet slid on grass and earth, and several others slipped into the shallow water at the edge of the lake.

"Pull!" I screamed.

El Cuero was powerful, but there were too many of us now. Working together, we dragged it back to the shallows. Its hide pulsed, squeezing its victims. Hoskins and I exhorted the villagers to pull harder. The rope had cut Forrester's skin, but the man was still pulling.

With the next massive effort, we hauled the demon onto the shore. Something still moved inside it—one of the men it had enveloped, I imag-ined—but it tightened around the poor soul. Now out of the water, it did not try to lash out, but clutched its prey as if in fear that it might be taken away. The eyes on its hide stared at us.

El Cuero was completely out of the water, but still, something tugged back.

"Jesus Christ, Tom!" Hoskins shouted. "Have a look at this!"

Seven or eight men had joined me

and Forrester on our line, and so I let go and raced up to Hoskins. We were off to one side of the creature. The stink of the thing made me cover my mouth and nose. When I reached Hoskins and saw what had made him cry out to God, I stood and stared, slack-jawed as an idiot.

A thick cord of damp muscle, black and crimson, stretched from the bottom of the thing back into the lake. It seemed to comprise dozens of tendrils, all twined together. For a moment, I considered simply cutting the cord—if it anchored the demon to the lake bottom, that seemed the swiftest solution—but as I stood there, I saw it pulse, and *pull.* I knew then that there was more to this abomination than what we had seen. What we had dragged from the water was the thing that had taken so many victims into the lake, but it was not the entirety of the demon. It was tethered to something by that disgusting throbbing length of twined cables.

"Pull!" I screamed, revulsion and hatred burning in me now. My stomach roiled with the urge to vomit, but I quelled the feeling by sheer will. "Pull!"

Whatever was on the other end of that horrible umbilical, it fought Hoskins and Forrester and the villagers. But there were too many of them. They dragged El Cuero across the valley toward the slope of the mountain, and as they did, more and more of that black and crimson cord was exposed, torn up out of the lake . . . along with the things that were tangled in its tendrils.

First to come was the corpse of a little boy, bloated and blue, his eyes missing from their sockets. Several of the village women screamed and wailed and I glanced over and saw a man fall to his knees—the man whose son had been taken. After that, twisted and knotted in tendrils that had pulled away from the twined mass of the thick cord, was the body of a dog, and then a little girl who could only have been Matteo's Beatriz. I thought, seeing the condition of her body, that it was perhaps better that he had died than live to see her.

There were others. So many others. Animals and children, girls, some of them preserved by the lake. But as El Cuero was dragged farther and farther from the water and more of the dead emerged, the remains were rotten

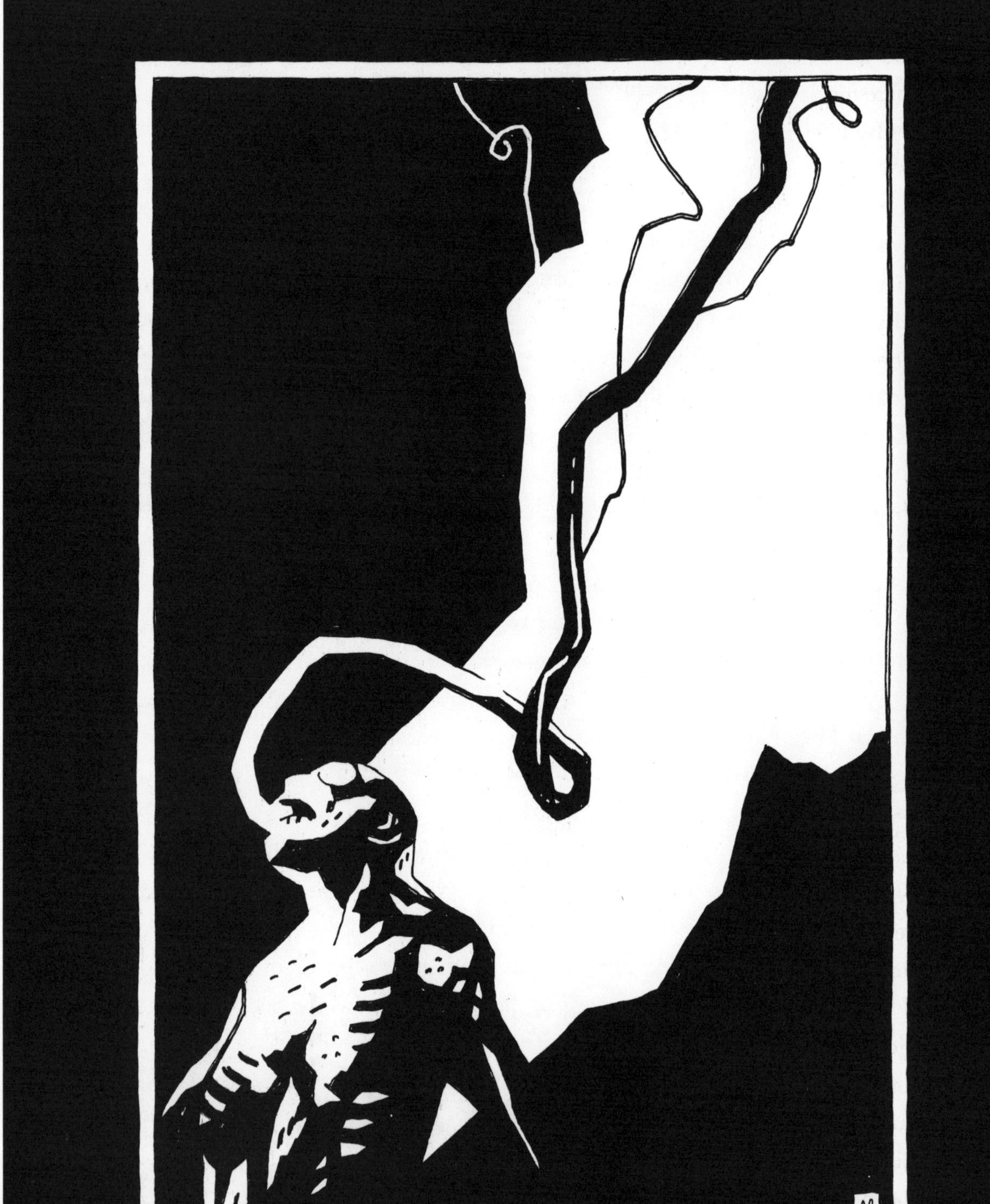

and indistinguishable from one another. Some of them had been down there for decades.

By now, I was the only one still on the shore of the lake.

Something splashed in the water, and I shouted, shaken from the hypnotic effect of that abominable trail of corpses. In the shallows, something twisted and flopped and struggled, fighting against the inexorable pull on that cord. Its skin was bleached white and tinted blue, and it quivered like jelly. Its eyes stared, pale and blind from so long at the bottom of the lake. The twined mass of tendrils disappeared into its open jaws, and I knew, looking at it, that it was the source. This was the true demon, lurking at the bottom of the lake. El Cuero had only been the lure...the net.

It hissed through nostril slits and dug its claws into the soft bottom of the lake, trying to stay under water.

Once, it had been a man.

I thought of the tale Matteo had told of the demon-possessed murderer who had been drowned in the lake, and I knew it was the truth.

Cries of disgust and horror rose from the villagers as the thing was torn from the water. The stink struck me like a putrid sewer fog and I turned and vomited what little I'd eaten that morning. Then I ran for my horse and retrieved my machete from its sheath.

I intended to behead the thing. I believe in that moment I would have hacked it to pieces and kept cutting until exhaustion crippled my arms. But as I ran toward it, the putrid, jellied flesh hissed and began to burn and smoke in the sun.

In seconds, it crumbled to ash. As it did so, one by one, its victims followed suit, the burning racing along that disgusting cord as though it were a fuse. Cinder and ash swirled on the breeze off the lake, and soon nothing was left, save an ordinary brown animal hide, wrapped like a blanket around a dead lamb, and two drowned men. Matteo's face, in death, seemed strangely peaceful. Whatever evil had infested El Cuero, it had departed.

Even so, the villagers took the animal hide and the bodies of Matteo and the other man, and the sacrificial lamb, to a rocky place at the base of the mountain, and burned them.

You wished to know, gentlemen, how it was that I did not hesitate to believe the things that Baltimore told me. I trust no further explanation is required.

THE SAVIOR'S TALE:

BENEDICTUS

---

*"The only two who did not move were the tin soldier
and the little dancer. She stood as stiff as ever on
tiptoe, with her arms spread out; he was equally
firm on his one leg, and he did not take his eyes
off her for a moment."*

—The Steadfast Tin Soldier
by Hans Christian Andersen

1

As Childress finished his tale, Aischros could only sit silently regarding his two companions. Their dinners were half eaten. Doctor Rose tapped frequently on his wooden matchbox. Around them, the susurrus of voices and activity in the inn's barroom had diminished to a creak and whisper. Many of the inn's guests had already retired to their rooms upstairs and some of the local patrons had departed. There were perhaps twenty people remaining— themselves and the innkeeper included. A pair of elderly men played darts with dreadful inaccuracy that did not seem to distress them at all. Even the dim light from the gas lamps around the room seemed gray.

His glass was still half full, but Aischros did not reach for it. There wasn't anything in this place he wanted now, not even to pass the time. The stories had insinuated themselves under his skin and crawled there, as if the taint of all of the evils they had discussed had infected him, simply in the telling. A desire to depart rose in him, abrupt and powerful.

"It's getting late," he said, glancing from Childress to Doctor Rose. "We still don't know why we're here, or if Lord Baltimore will join us. It's been hours."

Childress cast an eye toward the door, then frowned. "Are you suggesting we leave? Where would we go, Demetrius? I, for one, will not be able to sleep tonight without knowing why Henry summoned us."

Doctor Rose laughed softly. "I never sleep."

Aischros considered a moment, then shook his head. "I couldn't leave either. Though this place troubles me. But what do we do if, when they close for the night, Lord Baltimore still has not arrived?"

Neither of his companions had a reply for that.

The door opened and a breeze slid, serpentine, through the inn. All three of them turned to appraise the newcomer. Aischros saw that the man had two intact legs and felt a rush of disappointment. Yet there was something odd about him. The new arrival wore a bright blue cap in a place that did not welcome vivid color. His clothes were not expensive but they were impeccably neat, and he did not have the air of surrender around him that seemed imbued in the rest of the inn's patrons. He glanced around as though searching for a familiar face, and a moment later, he seemed to settle upon the three companions.

The man approached them with military stiffness and stood before them almost at attention.

"Good evening, gentlemen." He kept his voice low, but it was obvious he was a man unused to quiet or inconspicuousness. "Might you be Doctor Lemuel Rose, Mister Thomas Childress, Junior, and Captain Demetrius Aischros?"

Aischros blinked as though clearing a hallucination from his mind. He frowned and stared at the man. "Who the hell are you?"

Doctor Rose cast a hard look at him and then stood. "I'm Doctor Rose. You have us at a disadvantage, sir."

The man bowed his head. "My apologies, gentlemen. It was not my intention to trouble you. I'm a courier, and I have a packet that I've been instructed to deliver to this address, on this day and hour, to you three gentlemen."

Disappointment washed over Aischros. He glanced at Childress and saw the same dismay in his eyes. They both understood what the arrival of the courier must mean: Baltimore wasn't coming.

"All right, then," Doctor Rose said. "Let's have it."

The courier nodded and reached inside his jacket. He withdrew a leather pouch tied with dark string and handed it to Doctor Rose. If he had any

reaction at all to the scars and missing fingers of the doctor's hand, it did not show on his face.

The courier stood by as Doctor Rose untied the pouch. The doctor frowned and looked up at the man. Aischros began to reach into his pocket for some coins—the courier obviously expected a tip and certainly deserved it for having braved the City at night.

"Right, sorry. I've got it, Demetrius," Childress said, and he stood and crossed the courier's palm with several heavy coins.

The courier thanked them, glanced once around the inn, then retreated. As he disappeared into the darkness outside, the door swung closed behind him. Aischros was unsettled by the fact that the courier would rather be out on the streets after dark than inside the walls of the inn, with its dimly crackling fire and plentiful whiskey and ale.

Doctor Rose reached into the pouch and withdrew a small book—a journal of some kind—and a sheaf of yellowed pages scrawled with writing. Aischros held on to the arms of his chair and studied Doctor Rose as he examined the documents. Childress seemed frozen in place, one hand on the back of his chair, unable to return to his seat.

"It's not from Baltimore," Doctor Rose said, studying the first yellowed page that had accompanied the journal.

The chair creaked beneath Aischros as he shifted forward. "What? How could it be from anyone else?"

The doctor looked up. "It's from a man named Iancu Vulpes, of a village called Korzha, in Romania. He claims to have sent this journal at the behest of Baltimore, whom he met—" Doctor Rose glanced down and read aloud from the letter. "'Korzha had been almost emptied by the plague. There are more of her people in the cemetery than walking her streets. The village was already a ghost of herself by the time Lord Baltimore passed through. He gave us life again, and in return, he asked only that I see to it that this journal, written in Baltimore's own hand, reached you at the appointed time. The rest of this letter will make little sense to you until you have read his journal. Please do so now and then return to my letter.'"

Aischros shook his head. "What in hell is going on here? Has he summoned us here only for this, to read his journal?"

"We're here, Demetrius. There's only one way to find out what Henry had in mind, and that's to forge ahead," Childress said. He slid back into his chair and gestured to Doctor Rose. "Would you do the honors?"

The doctor glanced around as though concerned they might have drawn attention to themselves, but the patrons who remained in the room were like sleepwalkers. Doctor Rose turned back around and stared at the journal in his hands, running his thumbs over the leather cover as though he could feel some kind of resonance in that book. Aischros wondered what he was thinking in that moment, but would not intrude so far as to ask.

After a long moment, Doctor Rose took a deep breath, opened the journal, and began to read.

The Journal of Lord Henry Baltimore
June 10, 19___

And so I begin the fifth volume in the series of journals I have kept since I set off for the war. It seems like several lifetimes ago, and perhaps it is. For the benefit of anyone discovering or otherwise receiving this journal, should you have come into possession of it without also possessing my previous ramblings, you may seek out the first two volumes within the tomb of my family on Trevelyan Island, off the coast of Cornwall, in Britain. The third and fourth volumes I have recently deposited in a locked box in the Bank of the People in the Romanian city of Brasov.

Seek them out, if you wish. They tell the story of my transformation, and the rise of evil across the land, and the spread of the plague. If you, reading these words, are ignorant of their meaning, then you have no need of the information contained herein, and I have been victorious in my quest. If, however, you know the evil of which I speak, you will have no need to read the previous volumes, and perhaps you shall find some vital bit of knowledge within these pages to aid you in your own struggles with the darkness that has descended upon Europe and the world.

From Brasov, I headed east. Word had reached me of an infestation in Odessa and I intended to make my way there, but as always I intended to make the journey by foot—or by cart or horse, should some gentle soul offer a ride. Such kindness is rare in these times, and who can blame those who close their shutters tight, or urge their horses on a bit faster when they see a stranger approach? It matters not to me. On foot, I am more likely to encounter other travelers who bring word of the taint of evil, requiring my intervention. This is my purpose. It is why I was chosen.

I am the scourge of the vampire. I am the one they whisper about, and go about in fear of, the way that all of humanity now goes about in fear of them. I am the hunter.

I've traveled two days' walk to the east of Brasov. This morning, the third day of my journey to Odessa, I followed a road that was little more than a wide, wooded path. Once, I felt sure, many carriages had rattled along this road, and surely there must be travelers' inns along the wayside, though many such establishments no longer welcome visitors. Even those that still operate will not accept a guest who arrives after sunset.

The morning was cool, but as I made my way along the road, the sun began to break through the branches above and it warmed my hands and the back of my neck. Such warmth never reaches deeper than my skin. The chill inside me will never disappear.

I carried the harpoon I have used as a walking stick since first setting out on this quest. Once, the burden of the weaponry I wear would have driven me to the ground, but now it seems weightless to me.

The scent of something burning reached me and I peered along the road ahead. Through the trees, I could see the chimneys rising from the roofs of a town. Smoke rose from one—a cooking fire, I presumed, since the night had not been very cold. The other chimneys were all dormant.

I had dried smoked beef, bread, cheese, and several apples in my pack—and I am more than capable of hunting and foraging for food if necessary—but when the opportunity presents itself, I welcome a real meal. If there was a place in this town to find hospitality, I intended to take advantage of it before moving on. I would not stay long, for my destination lay far ahead on the northern shore of the Black Sea.

Still, I imagine that I picked up my pace as I neared the town.

I sensed the presence in the trees to my right even before I heard the movement there, among the branches. I turned, my left hand dropping to the butt of my pistol, only to see a withered old woman standing at the edge of the road.

Her hair was a dull gray and her face wrinkled, jaundiced, and pale. She wore a black shawl over a brown sack of a dress. Her eyes were bright blue, and so full of life that I shuddered to see her, thinking of folktales I had heard about young men and women who'd had their youth stolen by witchcraft. Outwardly, she herself looked like a witch. But the hag's blue eyes seemed so much younger that, had she told me a tale of black magic wrought upon her, I'd have believed her.

Instead, she hissed at me and crooked a finger, beckoning me toward her. My hand came away from the pistol but I kept a tight grip upon my walking stick. This skeletal hag was no vampire, but I had no way to know if she wished me good or ill.

"Beware," she said, in her own language. "Beware the town."

I speak precious little Romanian, but I understood enough of it to interpret her warning. She continued to rattle on, gesturing back along the road, indicating that I should retreat and find another path; one that did not take me through this place.

I set my jaw and turned toward the town again. The hag cried out in surprise, hissing again and calling after me. Her warnings grew frantic. She deemed me an idiot, another word I knew in Romanian, and cursed at me. Her warnings and curses only hurried me along. My blood raced and I felt a grim strength rising in me.

If there was such a shadow upon this place that that bright-eyed old woman warned travelers away, I knew I belonged here. The chimney smoke still drifted on the air as I approached, but now I caught another scent rising from the town—decay. Death had been here, and the hag's warning made it clear that it had not yet departed.

One of those creatures I had first seen when I lay near death in the Ardennes had visited this quiet place. The Red Death—the plague—had followed, and created revenants in its wake. The true vampires—the carrion-eaters I had first perceived as kites—spread their disease, and its victims were transformed into pale shades of the devils that had spawned them.

It had happened all across the continent. Why should this tiny hamlet be any exception?

Whatever evil lingered in the town, I felt it stir and shift at my approach. But the June sun shone down, warm and bright, and so the darkness could not rise to flee or to fight. Not yet. But I am certain that it felt my arrival, just as I felt its presence. I've been chosen to give the darkness something to fear.

As I emerged from the woods, I passed a stable where a single skinny black horse grazed in a pen. It flinched and wandered away from me without raising its head. Cottages and larger houses stood beyond the stable, and then the larger buildings at the center of the town. Even before the evil had arrived, there must have been little to the place save for the hard work and good intentions of those who had built it.

Hammer strikes echoed from within one of the buildings I passed.

Through the windows I saw a man pounding nails into a length of wood. I'd seen such work before, and even if I had not seen other examples of his craftsmanship in the place, I would have known he was building a coffin.

Only a scattering of people were out on the street: men and women with deathly pallor, trudging through their day's activity like sleepwalkers. A woman stood by a pump, drawing water into a metal bucket. In a nearby basket, a baby squalled, arms flailing free of its blanket. She seemed not even to hear her infant's cry.

There were no congregations upon the street, none of the gossip that I've encountered in nearly every place I've ever visited. The people in this town wandered past one another as though each of them were lost in a dream and did not recognize, or even notice, the others. And that was how they treated me as well. One old man crossed himself when he caught sight of me and diverted along a path between two buildings that led to a cow pasture I could see beyond the town. To all of the others, I might as well not have existed at all. They gave no sign of having noticed my arrival, which, given my appearance and the fact that I was a stranger to them in a time when they must have feared strangers, was quite odd indeed.

Some of the houses and buildings were so silent I felt sure they were empty and abandoned, either because the occupants were dead or because they had fled from the town. Black sashes had been tied around the door handles and front posts of several homes, and I did not have to wonder about their significance. I have seen similar expressions of mourning far too often in recent years. I could have told them that the sashes ought to have been red, but it was not my place.

I came upon a dwelling with its own stable and a large carriage house. Once, it had been beautiful. There were flower gardens in the front and on both sides, but no one had tended to them this spring, and now weeds strangled the flowers.

This was precisely the sort of travelers' inn I had hoped to encounter. No black sash ordained its porch or door. In my journeys I have found that innkeepers are the most reliable source of information about the goings-on in any town. They hold the town secrets, and the news about those who have passed through.

An old man sat in a small chair in front of the place. The chair looked as though it had been made from kindling and might snap at any moment, as did the man himself. When I went up to the door, he watched me with rheumy eyes. His jaws moved as though he were chewing, but from what I could see, there was nothing in his mouth. His stare was vacant, as though nothing remained of the mind that I presumed had once thrived there. My shadow fell across him as I passed, and he gave a small whimper in the instant that he was deprived of the sun.

When I entered, I found the inn deserted. The sunlight did not reach very far into the rooms, and though the place had clearly been well cared for, a thin layer of dust covered everything.

I called into the gray emptiness of the place, prepared to depart in search of some other source of information about the darkness that had fallen upon that town. Before I could leave, however, I heard a creak upon the stairs and I called out again.

Slowly, wiping tears from his red eyes as he came, a man descended toward me. He got control of himself, sniffling and wiping the last wetness from his eyes, and studied me with the same anxious curiosity that I often encountered.

He spoke to me in Romanian. I hoped he understood at least as much English as I did of his language. Either that, or we would have to converse in Hessian, and I hated the feel of those words on my tongue.

"A room," I said.

He blinked, but I knew that any innkeeper in Europe understood at least that one word in English.

"You . . . stay here?" he asked, in dubious, halting words.

I nodded.

"Plague is here," he said, eyes narrowing as he stared at me, wondering what sort of lunatic would want to sleep a night in this godforsaken town.

Once again, I nodded. I reached inside my jacket and showed him the silver cross that hung from the chain around my neck. His eyes lit up with a flickering hope.

"You . . . a priest?"

"No," I told him. "I'm a soldier."

He frowned, and though I wasn't sure he understood me, he beckoned for me to follow him as he went to the desk. In Romanian, he rattled off the cost of a room. I could see he still could not understand my presence there, but he would not argue it, either. I spilled a few coins on the desk and he nodded.

Then he paused, unable to continue.

It was as though, for a moment, he simply froze. His control shattered and tears began to fall. Then he shook his head, embarrassed and angry with himself, and wiped the tears away again.

"*Imi pare rău!*" he said. "*Fiică a mea.*"

I'm sorry. My daughter.

"What is it?" I asked. "She's sick?"

He shook his head. The grief in his eyes told me all that I needed to know. His daughter was not sick. She was dead, and her death had been all too recent. So few travelers were on the road in these days of sickness and shadows that he had stumbled downstairs in response to my summons out of habit, but the man was in no condition to put up guests.

Yet I am no ordinary guest.

I stared at him, and I felt sure that he could feel the cold that emanated from within me. My coat hung open, but I drew it back so that he could see the weapons arrayed upon me, and the red sash tied to the scabbard of my saber. I clutched the silver cross in my hand and stared at him.

"Where is she?" I asked.

Fear caught his breath. He shook his head, confused, and I could not blame him. Like all fathers, he had never expected to bury his daughter, but it was about to come to that.

Unless I could stop him.

"Vampires," I said.

His eyes widened, and then glanced downward. The folklore of the region had been rife with tales of vampires long before the plague had come, long before the evil had begun to infect the land. Once they had been content to prey upon the dead and dying, and occasionally on the lost and wandering. Now the taint was everywhere. Yet he refused to believe it, despite all he must already have seen.

"*Se va naştere,*" I said.

With a cry of anguish and denial, he swiped at the coins I had placed upon his desk, scattering them onto the floor.

I stared at him. "*Unde?*"

He shuddered, but I saw that his eyes were dry. For the moment, sorrow and revulsion had eclipsed his grief. He could not save his daughter's life, but there was something he could still do for her, so that she could rest, free of the taint of the Red Death.

"What's your name?" I asked, in English.

"Vulpes," he replied.

I held out my hand and told him mine, and we clasped each other's wrists, and a pact was made. He led the way upstairs, along an empty hall. No sound came from any of the rooms. The dust on the floor eddied in the drafts that swept through the old inn.

At the end of the corridor a door led into another part of the inn. Here, there was not a speck of dust. Vulpes had kept the place clean during his daughter's decline. These were the family's living quarters. From along the hall, I heard a softly singing voice, and when we arrived at the open door to his daughter's bedroom, I saw that a young man sat in a chair beside the bed. I can only presume that he was singing to himself, for his sister's corpse was covered by a sheet. I wonder, though, if he thought perhaps that her spirit still lingered there, somehow, and he was hoping to bring her peace.

The young man rose. In a stilted exchange of English and Romanian words, Vulpes introduced me to his son, an olive-skinned boy with long dark hair, nearly black eyes, and almost feminine features. Fortunately, the boy spoke far better English than his father. His name was Iancu, and he claimed to speak better English than anyone in Korzha. This was the first time I had heard the name of the town and I repeated the word, perfecting my pronunciation.

Vulpes spoke to his son in a rush of Romanian that I could not follow. What few words I could decipher confirmed that the innkeeper was explaining to his son that I had come to safeguard the dead girl's spirit. When Vulpes mentioned vampires, Iancu scoffed and turned to stare at me. I stared back. He seemed a serious young man, and his love for his sister—and grief at her passing—were palpable. Still, he was young, and did not believe the old legends.

"What will you do with her?" he asked, his stare becoming accusatory.

"The only thing that can be done," I replied. "To purify her soul, we must burn her remains."

It was as though I'd struck him. He reeled backward three steps and put a hand against the wall to steady himself. Hatred blazed in his eyes, and then he turned his fury upon his father and shouted at him in Romanian.

The argument raged for only a few moments before Vulpes began to weep and collapsed into the chair where his son had been sitting only moments before. Though his daughter's lifeless body lay only inches away, he seemed incapable of looking at her. When he looked at Iancu again, his eyes were pleading.

The boy spun on me. "I do not believe in vampires!"

I remained impassive. "Then you are a fool. I have never been to Korzha before, but even I can see that the town is a ghost of itself. It is being drained of its lifeblood, just as your sister was. You know I speak the truth, even if you wish to deny it. You've seen it with your own eyes. Tonight, or perhaps tomorrow night, they will come to claim her and she will rise. Would you leave her soul with the stain of such evil upon it? You love her enough to sing sweet songs to ease her soul upon its journey, but that journey will never begin as long as the taint of the Red Death is in her. I've told you what must be done to free her from the shadow of evil. Do you love her enough to do that for her, Iancu?"

The boy's eyes blazed. "Why should I believe you? Who are you to say such things?"

"Who am I? I am the only one they fear," I replied.

Iancu shook his head. "I cannot let you burn her."

Vulpes spoke his son's name, quietly and with a father's love.

I looked at the corpse covered with that white sheet, and then at the tall, westward-facing windows. Sunlight streamed in, but later, they would be first to see the night fall.

"Sit with me tonight," I said to Iancu. "You and I, we'll keep her company. See with your own eyes, and in the morning, we will discuss what is to be done."

His eyes were cold with pain and doubt, but he agreed.

And now we wait. Vulpes has given me a room, and a hot meal. His son has avoided me since our introduction in the dead girl's bedroom. I sit, and write this, and await the dark.

2

The Journal of Lord Henry Baltimore
June 10, 19__, Evening

Vulpes was kind enough to prepare an evening meal. The man is an excellent cook. The venison was tender, and the stuffed cabbage filled with delicious flavors. The boy sat and stared at his plate in almost total silence, lacking any appetite. His father ate only a little. Not wishing the effort or the food to go to waste, I helped myself to a second and third portion. I could not know how long it would be before I had another such meal.

Vulpes wished to join Iancu and myself in his daughter's room, but I refused to allow it. The room was not large, and we needed to wait quietly in the dark. I doubted the man could sit close by his daughter's corpse without lapsing once more into tears. Also, when the moment arrived—no matter that he had agreed with me—I worried that he would not wish to see her burned, and that he might interfere. It was best that he stay out of the room. I told him that someone had to see to it that no one else entered the inn, and that we weren't disturbed. He salvaged his pride by accepting this as his purpose.

At dusk, I entered the dead girl's room. Her name, I had discovered, was Mircea. Iancu had once again taken up his post in the chair by her bed. I had tied her corpse to the mattress with thick rope earlier in the day, with only her father to watch over me. Iancu refused to take part. Now he glanced at me, dark eyes full of love for his sister and something like hatred for me. I ignored that look and went to the foot of the bed. For a moment, I gazed at the sheet that covered her corpse. The last of the daylight filtered out of the room and I watched Mircea's shroud turn darker gray, and then lighten slightly, as the night came on in earnest and it picked up a glow from the moon and stars outside the window.

Cloaked in darkness, Iancu stared at me. I spared him only a glance, and then I retreated into the far corner of the room, where the shadows were darkest. One by one, I touched the grips and handles of every gun and blade that rested in their holsters, sheaths, and scabbards upon me. In my left hand, I carried a lantern, but its light was completely dimmed by the iron hood that covered it. I controlled my breathing so that metal would not rattle and leather would not creak. My wooden leg, heavy with iron nails, I kept motionless and silent. I disappeared into the shadows of that corner.

I could feel the boy's anxiety, and I watched as he shifted position in the chair, first sitting up and then leaning forward with his elbows on his knees. He mostly stared at the familiar shape beneath the shroud, but from time to time he glanced out the windows at the moonlit night. After a while he seemed almost to have forgotten I was there, but that was only illusion. His body was coiled with tension.

Hours passed, and as the night crept on, his anger at me deepened. At first he had refused to allow himself to believe what I had told him, but in his heart he had suspected it was true. As the clock ticked past midnight, I sensed the change in him. He was no longer frustrated only with me, but with himself, for entertaining the thought that I could be right, and for allowing the horrific image of burning his sister's corpse to even enter his mind.

My fingers caressed the metal hood over my lantern, and the warmth of the iron told me that the flame still burned within. A distant church bell rang once—one o'clock in the morning. I heard Iancu sigh heavily.

"That's enough," he said, his accent making the words nearly a growl.

202   *Mike Mignola & Christopher Golden*

Iancu rose and crossed the room toward the corner where I stood. In the moonlight, I watched him take the glass off an oil lamp atop the girl's bureau. A box of matches lay beside the lamp.

"Stop," I whispered, as he slid a match from the box.

His face was hidden by the curtain of his dark hair, but he froze at the sound of my voice.

"In the morning," he said, "you will go, and trouble my father no more."

Iancu did not notice the way the darkness seemed to shift in the room or the dimming of the moonlight. Something flapped outside the window, like a war banner whipped by the wind.

It struck the glass, and Iancu turned.

A winged blackness battered the window, a large avian shape, far darker than the night. The creature slapped its wings against the glass and the sound was like the rasp of sandpaper.

"What in hell is—" Iancu began to whisper.

I held the lantern in my left hand, so it was with my right that I reached out and clapped a hand over his mouth, dragging him back against me and pinning him there. He began to struggle, unused to being handled so roughly.

"Be still," I commanded him, my voice low. "Watch."

The boy ceased any effort to fight me, but I did not remove my hand from his mouth. Together, we watched the window. Then, from the bed, there came a sigh like the whisper of cloth, and we looked to see the dead girl trying to rise up from her mattress. The sheet had slipped down to reveal her face and right shoulder, and her legs had moved enough to emerge as well. But the rope held Mircea there, and the ember of evil that had brought her to life moaned with quiet despair to find itself held captive.

Iancu shrank back in horror. I lowered my hand, but he kept silent, staring at the shifting corpse that had once been his sister.

At the window, the creature flattened its wings against the glass, obscuring all light from outside for a moment. Then a sliver of moon and starlight was revealed at the top of the upper panes. An inky shadow began to slip into the room through the crease between the window and its frame. I placed a steadying hand on Iancu's shoulder to remind him of the need for silence.

The shadow slid into the room and flowed along the wall, until the last of the black bird was gone from outside. Evil had worn that shape, but it had never been a bird. The shadow spilled toward the ceiling and glided across the room until it hung above the bed where the dead girl struggled against her bonds with a quiet whimper. The sound was like a child's sadness, and my grip on Iancu's shoulder grew tighter to make certain he did not respond with pity, and unwittingly surrender his life. His sister's flesh was gray, but mottled with bruises of settled blood. Her eyes were dull and black and dead.

Gently, I nudged Iancu out of my way. He had the presence of mind, at least, to be quiet about it. I took a breath and stepped forward. In my left hand, I raised the iron lantern high, and with the right, I slid open the hood to reveal the cross aperture cut into the metal. A beam of lantern light shone across the room in the shape of the cross, striking Mircea and the living shadow above her.

The girl hissed and bucked against her restraints. But the piercing scream that tore through the room came not from the corpse, but from the writhing shadow that fell from the ceiling and crashed to the floor, splintering the wooden chair where Iancu had sat vigil for so long.

The room filled with the stench of burning flesh. The shadow pulsed and stretched and took form. It appeared for a moment to be almost human, but then that fluid blackness crouched and its silhouette seemed more akin to a wolf than a man. It arched its back and again it shifted. Wings spread out behind it and its head swiveled toward us. Its eyes glowed a dark crimson and I took a step closer, the light from that lantern—with its blessed flame—searing its flesh. Its eyes blistered and with a snarl of defiance it turned away.

It lunged for the window. Glass shattered and the wooden frame splintered as it crashed out into the night, and then it was gone. I went to the broken window to be certain, but nothing lurked outside. Those black wings would descend upon another home in Korzha tonight, I had no doubt. But it would not return to the inn.

When I turned, I saw that Iancu had gone to stand over his sister's bed.

He stared down at the thing that lay there. The corpse was motionless, frozen in death, but its upper lip had curled into a bestial snarl. Once, she had been beautiful. Now she was damned.

I made no attempt to comfort the boy. His grief and sorrow are his own. Tomorrow, we will burn her.

3

The Journal of Lord Henry Baltimore
June 11, 19___

We burned Mircea Vulpes shortly after dawn, in a cemetery just beyond the town. Her father and brother wept, but I saw that there was a kind of peace in their eyes, along with their grief.

"Fire purifies," I told them.

They said a prayer over her ashes and bones, but I did not join them. The fire was enough.

Vulpes told me that I was welcome at the inn for as long as I remained in the town. I nodded, but said nothing. How to explain to him that his town was nearly dead, that only fate would decide if it would recover from the evil that had been wrought there? Iancu had told me that more than half of the town's people had died of the plague or were still suffering from the illness.

The news did not surprise me. The previous evening's visitation had already proven there was at least one vampire still preying upon Korzha. If I could kill it, they would likely recover. If I did not, they would die, and rise again, their souls stained crimson and black. The thing in the girl's room the night before had not been the fiend I had sought for so long, the demon that had taken my family from me and murdered my sweet Elowen. Yet I felt its presence like a prickling of the skin on the back of my neck. I have sought it for so long, vengeance churning like an engine within me, that perhaps I feel it everywhere. So I would seek it out here, and I would destroy every vampire I could find, whether or not it was the one I sought . . . the one who had forged me in the fires of Hell and set me upon this crusade.

The day was warm, though a thin layer of clouds cast a gray pall across the town. Rain would have been welcome, but did not come. The smoke from Mircea's burning bones rose and disappeared in that gray shroud of a sky.

"Our thanks, Lord Baltimore," Vulpes said, sniffling and trying to maintain his dignity as he wiped at his eyes.

Iancu stood stiffly and forced himself to watch his sister burn. The stench of her roasting flesh was hideous, but he reacted to it not at all. His tears were silent and he made no attempt to wipe them away, as though he was not even aware that he was weeping.

The residents of Korzha had become sleepwalkers. Those who had risen early did not come near the cemetery to inquire what transpired there. The black smoke rising from the burning corpse might once have drawn

curiosity, but now it had the opposite effect.

The cemetery was not large, but it was well kept. The stone markers were mostly intact, even those of great age. On the opposite end of the cemetery, the stones marched up a low hill, where a tiny church overlooked the boneyard. Unlike the rest of the cemetery, the church had fallen into ruin. Weeds and vines grew rampant around it. The windows were shattered and shutters hung loosely or had been torn away completely. It appeared long abandoned, a hollow place, forgotten.

As we stood, watching the fire burn low on those charred bones, one spectator did arrive. I saw him out of the corner of my eye and wrapped my hand around the butt of the pistol I had carried back from the war. All of the people of Korzha had the gray pallor of plague victims, but this was grief and shock and exhaustion. They were not all tainted. Still, I was wary, and I watched the man approach with the comforting weight of the pistol grip in my hand.

"Do you know him?" I asked, glancing at the grieving father and son.

Vulpes nodded. "He is Tibor."

"The gravedigger," Iancu said. He closed his eyes tightly and turned away at last from his sister's remains.

I watched as the gravedigger approached. His hair was little more than white wisps and despite his thin, rangy body, he had a perfectly rounded potbelly, like a scrawny girl six months pregnant. His countenance was that of a skull, the skin of his eyes sunken and his teeth bared in a perpetual death grin. Yet he was neither dead nor infected with the plague.

His head tilted to the left. At first I thought this an affectation, that he was studying the burning bones of Mircea Vulpes. But soon I realized that it was some affliction that kept his neck thusly bent. He tutted and shook his head, but I saw only mad amusement and fascination in his eyes, not the sympathy that his tutting implied.

Vulpes and Tibor exchanged words in their own tongue, while Iancu nodded solemnly. I wondered if they were only talking about the girl's tragic death, or if they shared with the gravedigger the circumstances. Yet I found myself distracted, my mind wandering. A frisson of uneasiness passed through me.

"Ask him—" I began, abruptly. Then I paused and turned to regard Iancu. All three men were looking at me. "Ask him how many have died of the plague."

Iancu rattled off the question. The gravedigger glanced around, threw up his hands, and raised his eyes so that his unruly eyebrows arched. He spoke in a dialect so thick I could not decipher a single word. But when he was through, the boy stared at him.

"You're certain?" the boy asked, in Romanian. That much, I understood.

The gravedigger nodded and spread his hands wide, head tilted painfully as he gestured to the cemetery all around us. Iancu shook his head. I studied him, and then looked at his father.

"It is full," Vulpes told me. "Tibor says it is full."

I studied the place, the freshly turned soil, the vast spaces where there were no headstones—yet—but many recent graves.

Tibor grinned, showing only a few yellowed teeth. He proudly raised one arm to show his muscles and said something in his garbled tongue, congratulating himself on the strength and fortitude required for the job of digging graves for dozens—perhaps hundreds—in the space of months.

"He says they will have to make the cemetery larger if we keep dying,"

Iancu said, watching me curiously. "He doesn't include himself. If the plague has not taken him yet, he says it never will."

I only half listened to the boy, striking out across the cemetery. I paused at a patch of recently turned earth and plunged my hand into it, letting it sift through my fingers. Then I rose, striding twenty or thirty feet away, my wooden leg sinking deep into the soft ground, and repeating the process. This time, I inhaled the scent of the dirt. Three more times I paused to touch and smell the earth in that cemetery, until a dreadful certainty formed in my mind.

I stood and turned to face the three men, who still stood around the now smoldering bones of the dead girl.

"There are no bodies here," I said. "Not one, save for Mircea."

Iancu sputtered. "That's impossible."

"Nevertheless, it's true."

Vulpes shook his head in confusion and then said something to the gravedigger that caused Tibor to begin shouting at him. The man shook his head, gesticulating wildly at the graves around him.

I ignored his raving and glanced around. My attention was drawn back to the ruined little church on the hilltop at the far end of the cemetery.

"Why has the church been left to rot?" I asked.

Vulpes and Tibor continued to argue, but Iancu moved around his sister's remains and came to stand beside me.

"The priest, Father Silvestru, abandoned Korzha and his church. He sold it to a nobleman who was passing through. The man claimed he wished it to be his private chapel and, in time, his tomb."

I started away without another word, striding toward that hollow place, that former house of God. Iancu kept up with me, though with some difficulty, despite that he had the use of two good legs, and I only a replica for my left. We'd gone no more than a dozen steps when I heard the mad, potbellied gravedigger shout something in a frantic tone.

"What does he want?" I asked, without turning.

"He's calling for us to stop. He says the air in the church is poisoned. Tibor and my father are both coming after us."

I nodded and kept on. At the base of the small hill, I paused and studied the scarred, rotting face of that little church. Once, it had been beautiful, but I suspected the same could have been said of the town of Korzha, and of the young girl we had set ablaze only a little while earlier.

Beyond the church I saw only trees. With the gray skies, the woods were dark and forbidding. To the left of that crumbling place, half hidden amongst the trees, I saw an old coach, overgrown with weeds. On its door was a noble family's crest, but it was obscured by mold.

The innkeeper and the gravedigger caught up to us. Tibor shouted at me, his words guttural, without any of the elegance that the Romanian language usually held. Vulpes tried to interrupt him, I imagine to explain that I did not speak enough Romanian to understand, but the crook-necked old man stared at me with wide eyes and prattled on.

"Silence!" I said, and though he might not have known the word in English, he must have seen the warning in my eyes, for he complied.

"Iancu," I said, "what became of the priest?"

The boy shook his head. "I do not know."

I nodded toward the gravedigger. "Ask him."

Quickly, Iancu rattled off the question in his own tongue. Tibor glared first at him and then at me. The old man pushed the white wisps of his hair back and stood defiantly, as though the muscles he was so proud of could have stopped my bullets or blades.

At length, he relented, lowering his gaze. He answered quietly, brushing the words away with a shaking hand, as though they meant nothing.

"Father Silvestru has become a hermit, he says," Iancu told me. "He has retired to a little cottage in the woods that he keeps as a chapel, only for himself. No one goes there."

I turned to study the face of his father. The old innkeeper still seemed confused, but a glint of iron showed in his eyes now. I had saved his daughter's soul, and he trusted my intentions. I wondered if that trust would cost him his life, as it had cost others theirs.

"The plague," I said, "it came after the sale of the church? It arrived with the nobleman?"

Vulpes nodded.

"And this nobleman, did he have a scar on his face?" I reached up and traced a line upon my own features. "Here?"

"I never see him. Never saw," the innkeeper replied.

The gravedigger gestured to the woods and spoke again, his words insistent.

"Tibor says that Father Silvestru keeps to himself, in his chapel, because he prays now for all of the souls of Korzha," Iancu said.

I sneered at the gravedigger. "He's not doing a very good job, then, is he?"

The cold dread inside me grew heavier. I turned toward the church once more. "Vulpes," I said, "go into the woods. Fetch the priest and bring him here to me. Take other men with you—people you can trust—in case he does not wish to accompany you. But bring him."

The innkeeper hurried away. His son watched him depart with grave concern etched upon his features.

"What is it, Iancu?" I asked.

He shuddered visibly. "No one goes to the chapel. Not only because Father Silvestru wishes to be alone, but because the place is haunted."

"Haunted by what?" I asked.

The boy shook his head. "I do not know."

I glanced at the church and then at the position of the sun in the sky. I had no idea how long it would be before Vulpes returned with the priest. My only certainty was that the man who owed me so much would not return without this Father Silvestru, who had turned his back on the souls of Korzha.

There was time.

"What of him?" I asked, pointing at Tibor. "I'd wager he knows the tale."

Iancu spoke to him, and the gravedigger gave me a solemn glance and began to speak. His voice was quieter now, almost as though he feared to tell the tale, even during the daylight hours. Iancu translated as Tibor spoke, and this is the story he told.

"I knew Father Silvestru well," he said. "When he was young, and I was not quite so old, we saw each other every day, when he walked through the graveyard, or when I stopped in the church to pray. We often said that we were partners, that he attended to the disposition of the spirit, and I the disposal of the flesh. Partners in death, we were.

"As the years passed, we did not meet quite as often. I prayed less, after a lifetime without any answers to those prayers. And Father Silvestru did not come down amongst the dead unless he had funeral rites to perform. Still, it saddened me when he sold the church and disappeared into the woods. He loved his church, and I never would have thought him capable of abandoning it.

"When I learned that he had taken the little chapel in the woods as his home, that ancient place of stone and old wood, it troubled me even more. All my life I had heard that it was haunted, that pagans had worshipped there before some traveling monks had repaired the place and dedicated it to the one God, and made it a chapel.

"After the plague began to spread, and I spent my days burying its victims, I knew that we needed the priest back in his church, or at least in the town, where he could see to the souls of the departed. One day, I finished burying a family—mother, father, and little boy—all of whom I had watched grow since birth, and I washed the grave dust off my hands, put aside my shovel, and went into the woods to find the chapel. I would bring Father Silvestru back, whether he wished to come or not. I would shame him into coming, if I had to.

"I went into the woods, in search of the chapel. Hours slipped by, and it grew dark, though it seemed to me dusk should still be far off. I stopped at a stream to refill the water skin that I had brought with me, and when I looked up, I saw an unearthly light in the deep woods, moving toward me. Unable to move or speak, I could only stand and watch as a parade of flickering golden lights passed by, floating above the ground, though not adrift. They moved with purpose; with direction.

"Studying them, I saw that each had the hint of a face. Some, I recognized. I had known at once that they were spirits, and now I saw that they were the ghosts of all those who had died of the plague since it had come to Korzha. I had dug their graves, and now they floated past me in a line, slipping deeper into the woods."

Iancu had been translating the story without interruption, but as Tibor spoke of ghosts, his eyes had widened and he had glanced back at the charred bones of his sister, perhaps thinking her spirit might rise at any moment.

The boy interrupted the gravedigger with a question, and Tibor answered, brow furrowed, with an offended air.

"What did you say?" I asked.

Iancu shrugged. "I've never seen such a thing. There are stories about the woods here, about the magic and evil that lurks in the trees. But they are only stories. I have never heard one of them from someone who claims to have witnessed the events himself."

"Ghost lights," I told the boy. "There are such legends all over the world. Where I was raised, we call them will-o'-the-wisps. Now, ask Tibor to continue."

The young man brooded a moment, then nodded to the gravedigger and bade him go on. Once again, Tibor spoke, and Iancu translated.

"I was frightened, but also full of wonder," the gravedigger said. "When the last of those ghost lights had almost vanished in the woods ahead of me, I followed. I had made no decision to do so, but my legs carried me, as though I had been enchanted. I drifted along behind them, mesmerized as the spirits swayed in the air.

"Soon, I saw a clearing in the trees. The sky above was dark. I thought at first it was the gray of a coming storm, but perhaps it was night already. I cannot say.

"In the clearing was the chapel, which had stood on that place longer than there had been a town here. It seemed built of stone and shadows, with a wooden frame for the door and windows, and a roof made of timbers as old as the tallest trees in the forest. The ghost lights swayed and danced across the clearing and, one by one, drifted through the wall and into the chapel. I went to that window and peered inside.

"Father Silvestru knelt at the altar in the chapel, his eyes closed, and his hands clasped around a small black wooden box. He seemed entranced

himself, or even asleep. I wanted to rap on the glass or call out, but I could not raise my hand or my voice. I could barely draw breath.

"Against one wall was a table where once there had been row upon row of candles that worshippers would light in remembrance of their dead. All that remained now was a thick layer of dust, and the hardened wax pools where the candles had melted down and never been replaced. One by one, the shimmering spirits went to that table and reached out to light a candle. One by one, they vanished, until all of them had gone.

"But invisible candles burned, their flames flickering in the gray gloom of the chapel. The flames hung in the air above the dust and wax hardened on the table.

"As though released from some invisible grasp, I fell back from the window, struggling to catch my breath. I could have gone to Father Silvestru then, but I did not want to speak with him any longer. I did not want to enter that chapel ever again. I have not gone back into the woods since that day."

The gravedigger paused. As he'd spoken, his body had seemed to curl in upon itself, his head tilting farther until it bent him to one side. Even though Iancu had translated the words, I had watched Tibor's face during the telling, and felt as though I could see the memory unfolding in his eyes. The fear and wonder he had spoken of were writ upon his features.

For long moments, we three stood together in silence. I stared into the shadows of the ruined church at the edge of the graveyard and then I looked back across the field of stone markers toward the town. I knew it might be quite some time before Vulpes returned with the priest, and already, most of the morning had passed.

"Iancu," I said, turning to the boy. "Take Tibor and give your sister the

BALTIMORE   *217*

burial she deserves. Your father will thank you for it. When that is finished, if he has not returned, go and seek him out, with whatever men of Korzha are willing to assist you."

The boy frowned. "And if evil has touched Father Silvestru?" he asked.

"Then perhaps you will die," I replied. "But the source of the horror that has befallen you is here, and I must stay to see that it does not escape. You will be in far less danger while seeking out the priest than you would be if you were to remain here."

Iancu nodded. "All right," he said. "We will find you here when we return?"

"Yes," I said, gesturing toward the ruined church. "I will be waiting."

And so I entered this wretched place, and drew my journal from the deep pocket within my coat, where I carry it always. The statues of the saints and the Mother of God have been toppled from their pediments, and the cross behind the altar shattered as though a hammer had been brought to bear upon it. Every surface is covered in cobwebs and dust, and I can hear the rats as they scrabble through the filth and shadows. There are two darkened passages, one that must lead to the priest's sanctum, and the other to the crypt beneath the church.

Now I sit on a dusty pew, in the gray light of day that washes through the westward-facing window beside me, and I write these words. By now, the earthly remains of Mircea Vulpes are in the ground, and Iancu has gone to aid his father in the search for Father Silvestru. Tibor, the gravedigger, has not returned, and I doubt I shall see him again. He will not enter the church, I am sure.

I wait for the shadows to rise. I do not fear the evil ones here, only that the leering, scarred demon that haunts my dreams and memories will not be among them.

4

The Journal of Lord Henry Baltimore
June 11, 19__, Later

The afternoon wore on toward evening as I sat in the ruined church, in the fading gray light, merely waiting. I had nothing to eat or to drink, but I have grown so used to hunger and thirst that the tightening of my belly and dry rasp of my throat were not unusual, or unwelcome. A sliver of hunger sharpens the mind.

Light rain had fallen, spattering the floor. With the windows broken, the church has been open to the elements, and in some places, rot and mold have begun to eat away at the timbers. When the shower passed, the sky lightened for a time, then began to dim with the afternoon's slow creep toward evening.

I heard the priest screaming; that was the first sign I had that Vulpes and his son had returned. An hour or two before dusk, his cries drifted across the cemetery, echoing from stone to stone. I went to the door, the floor sounding hollow beneath the thump of my wooden leg. From there, I saw a mob coming; men and women of Korzha, perhaps thirty of them, all told. Vulpes and his son led the way. From the hilltop I could see beyond them, where several men escorted the priest, one on either arm, and one propelling him from behind. Father Silvestru walked a few steps, then tried to tear himself away, screaming obscenities and crying out to God, his mother, and his former flock for mercy. They ignored him, dragging and pushing him onward. He complied again, but only for a few more steps, before he began his struggles and protests anew.

Yet all the while, he held a small box of black wood clutched to his chest in both hands. The man's vestments were filthy and torn. His hair was wild and matted, and he wore a rat's nest of a beard. As they forced him up the hill toward the church, he sank down to his knees, the box still clutched in front of him, and the men were forced to half carry him, whimpering, up to the door, where I stood waiting.

"Father Silvestru," I said in Romanian, my heart unmoved by his pleas. "Welcome home."

His eyes went wide and I saw that he was half-mad, at least. It came as no surprise.

"Bring him in," I said to the townspeople in their own tongue. I knew little Romanian, and spoke it horribly, but they understood.

When they dragged him across the threshold, the priest screamed as if they were cutting out his heart, but he never loosened his grip on that wooden box. It drew my eyes, that elegantly carved thing. Upon it was the same noble crest I had seen on the coach that sat rotting in the trees outside the church.

"What does he have in there?" I said, reverting to English as I turned to Iancu.

The boy scowled at the priest. "He says it is the gold that the nobleman paid him for the church. We tried to open the box, but we could not pry it from his hands. He thought we were trying to steal it," Iancu said.

Vulpes raised his hand to show me the strip of cloth wrapped around it. Blood had stained the cloth and he unraveled it to show me a ragged wound.

"He bite me," the old man said, shaking his head in dismay.

The priest guarded the box jealously, gaze darting around, wary of each and every one of us. I took his arm and he screamed and kicked at me. But he made no attempt to strike me with his hands. That would have required him to take his hands from the box, and he would not do that.

I clutched his arm so tightly that he whimpered and for a moment the terror in his gaze receded. A fragment of sanity appeared there, and he grew docile. I stared down at the box, and saw that his long yellow fingernails were sunk into the black wood; not dug into the surface, but *grown* into the wood.

Every man in the church felt it. I could see the way they shifted uneasily when they looked at the priest, and at the wretched box in his hands. A dreadful malevolence emanated from the wood.

A shudder went through me.

I shook the filthy, ragged priest by the arm and glared into those desperate eyes. "You damned fool," I whispered.

Revolted, I flung him to the floor. He landed on his belly, like vermin, with the box held out across the floor in front of him. Father Silvestru tried to draw it toward him, but I planted my boot upon his wrist.

"Blestemat prost," I sneered, cursing him again, now in his own language.

I drew my army issue Webley, cocked the revolver, and fired at the box. The bullet shattered the black wood and its contents spilled to the floor. The box contained a few blackened coins—upon which were engraved curious symbols, barely visible—a scattering of stained human teeth and finger bones, and a great quantity of spiders, which scurried away.

That was the price Father Silvestru had been paid for his church, and for his soul.

5

The Journal of Lord Henry Baltimore
June 11, 19__

Father Silvestru screamed like a wounded animal and crawled about on the floor, sweeping up the remnants of the box and its contents with his arms. A terrible rage came over me. If this was the courage and humanity the world could expect from men of the cloth, there was no hope against the darkness.

"Judas!" I called him. *"Traducător!"*

The priest only whimpered and guarded his prize as though he could not perceive that it was not the gold he had been promised. I seized up my walking stick, which I had laid aside upon entering the church, and I dealt him a blow across the back. Something cracked inside him, and I cared not.

Some of the men shouted at me in Romanian. A young woman who had come to stand in the doorway of the church, and witnessed that blow, cried out in alarm and turned to flee back outside.

"Lord Baltimore," Vulpes began carefully, his accent thicker with the exertion of the day.

"Do not seek mercy for him now, sir!" I replied, fixing each of those men with a look. "He has betrayed his flock and his home and his God for a handful of bones and dust. That he thought it gold only makes him more a coward. This priest knew that he had given evil the keys to the house of

222   *Mike Mignola & Christopher Golden*

God, and he went to hide in the woods and pray for forgiveness, even as he clutched his prize."

I glared at Iancu. "Tell them!" I commanded, gesturing to the others. "Tell them. And then pick up the pitiful wretch and bind him to the defiled Saint Peter."

Vulpes sputtered. Iancu stared, mouth agape.

"Do it," I warned, "or all of Korzha will soon be dust, and her people with her. Tell them that their mothers and sisters and daughters will join Mircea in the ground. Tell them that the Red Death will claim bodies and souls. The darkness is here, my friends. And this *bazaconie* gave it a place to nest, and then ran away and let it feast upon you all.

"Tell them," I demanded.

Vulpes nodded gravely and put a hand on his son's shoulder. It was he who turned and began to speak to the men. The priest still lay whimpering on the ground. From time to time, as the men began to argue and shout at one another, Father Silvestru raised his eyes to make sure none of them would attempt to take his treasure. Yet he listened to their words, and I could see doubt flicker in his gaze. He was not completely mad. He knew what they discussed.

Iancu stood by his father and sided with him.

Outside, the shadows grew long. The light had begun to fade.

"*Nu!*" the priest said softly.

The argument ceased, and the men all turned to see the filthy, bedraggled priest struggling to rise, hands cupped around what little of his treasure he could carry. He stared out the front doors of the church with terror in his eyes.

"*Apus de soare,*" he said, glancing around at them in mounting panic. "*Apus de soare!*"

Sunset.

He was premature. Perhaps half an hour remained before dusk, but the sky had taken on a deep blue tint beyond the doors, and within the church itself, the shadows had deepened almost to darkness.

"Bind him," I said, glaring at the townsmen. "Bind him, and go to your homes, and hold your families close. Hurry! *Grăbeşte-te!*"

Iancu spun on them and repeated my exhortations. Three of the men turned and retreated. They had helped to force the priest to return to his church, but they would not bind him.

Vulpes and Iancu grabbed hold of Father Silvestru. The priest fought them, screaming, and tried to claw the old innkeeper with one hand while clutching his treasure against his chest. He spilled the finger bones and teeth and moldy coins to the floor again and tried to drop to his knees in pursuit of them. By then, the remaining men had joined in to help Vulpes and his son, and together they dragged and carried the shrieking priest over to a statue of Saint Peter, its face mutilated, the stone shattered as if by a hammer. They wrapped the priest's arms around the statue and bound his hands with a belt. One of the men fetched rope from the cottage of Tibor the gravedigger, and they tied it tightly round the priest.

When they had finished their task, I dismissed the men. Iancu wanted to remain with me for his sister's sake. Despite what he had seen, the boy had courage. I would not allow it. He seemed both disappointed and relieved as his father guided him away.

I watched from the doorway of the church as they walked across the cemetery toward their homes, the dusk gathering at their heels. The sun had begun to set.

The priest wept. I turned to find him sagging against the statue of Saint Peter, his face scraped by the ruined features of the apostle. I walked to him and leaned in close to stare into his terrified eyes.

He began to beg.

"No vampire should ever be able to set foot in a church, Father Silvestru," I said. "And no vampire should ever

be able to lay hands on a man of God. But you invited the Devil in, Priest. You defiled your church, and yourself. Pray, and you may yet be saved. Ask Saint Peter for forgiveness, for you will never have mine."

I left him there, pleading with the encroaching darkness and muttering what I took to be some half-remembered prayer. The door to the left of the altar hung ajar and within the gloom beyond it, I could see the stairs that led down to the crypt beneath the church. As I reached that door, I paused to study the shifting shadows behind the altar. The jagged pieces of the shattered cross lay in a pile of rubble. The image of the Son of God had been demolished, limbs snapped off, torso crushed; but a fragment of his face seemed to watch me with a single, remaining eye.

I glared back. "Damn you," I whispered to that broken savior. "Damn you for choosing me."

As ever, the Lord made no response.

I entered that stairwell, and descended into darkness. The stale smell of the withered, ancient dead enveloped me. I wondered how many of Korzha's people had been laid to rest here over the years. How many mayors and wealthy families? Certainly the poor would not have found themselves rotting in a place of such honor.

The darkness was near complete. The only illumination was the wan gray light that outlined the doorway behind me. It was just enough to show me the dark, low rectangle of a tomb upon the floor; perhaps that of the church's founder or first priest, I thought.

I waded through the darkness, disliking the yielding softness of the earthen floor under my tread.

The darkness became complete. Night had fallen.

In that black void, my mind drifted, as it so often had since the

Ardennes. At rest, my mind recalled once more the soldiers I had played with as a boy, the certainty I'd had that I had become one of them, and the children's story of the steadfast tin soldier.

Am I the vengeful creature fashioned by the predations of the evil that had dawned upon humanity before my very eyes, dreaming of a boyhood from another life? Or is all of this merely the nightmare of a boy trapped in fever, twisting in fitful sleep? Am I the tin soldier himself?

My eyes closed and I listened to the scurrying of rats in the crypt around me. Yet in the same breath I was in my bedroom on Trevelyan Island, and upon a shelf in my room sat a black wooden box that at once contained moldy coins and human teeth, and a Jack-in-the-Box devil, whose wooden head knocked upon the walls, insisting upon his release.

The Jack. The devil. The goblin laughed his machine gun laugh, and I could see upon the battlefield of my mind the flash of gunfire and the hideous dance of the men in my command, jerking like puppets as the bullets tore through them.

"A shudder ran through the tin soldier, but he remained undaunted. All at once the boat drifted under a long wooden tunnel, and it became as dark as it was in his box," I whispered in the darkness of the crypt.

The tale has been with me all my life, and I remember it still.

"It is all the fault of that goblin," I said, my voice a rasp. "If only the little maiden were with me, it might be twice as dark as this for all I should care."

But the maiden—my sweet Elowen—could never be with me. I burned her, just as we had burned young Iancu's sister.

Another rustling came in the darkness of the crypt. Rats. Of course there were rats. Just like in the story of that tin soldier, who descended into the darkness of the sewers only to be set

226   *Mike Mignola & Christopher Golden*

upon by the vermin. The rats had been sent by the goblin, by the Jack-in-the-Box, of that I felt sure. Agents of the Devil himself, surrounding the soldier, doing the Jack's work, with the echo of that knocking in their ears.

A sound came from the church above; the flap of heavy wings. The timbers above my head creaked. The priest's prayers had been muffled, but now a scream tore through the church, and every defiled stone and beam soaked it in.

My eyes opened.

I knew who I was. I *know* who I am. That boy. The tin soldier. The hunter. I am all of these things.

The red eyes of rats gleamed with their own light in the darkness all around me. They shifted upon the floor, a carpet of undulating rats, hungry and diseased.

My hands are as swift as the black wings of death, swift as the touch of the Red King. From beneath my long coat I drew the hooded lantern I had used the night before. I slid the hood from the base and struck a match, and a golden spectral light spread across the ceiling, and a cruciform glow shone through the cross-shape cut in the iron lantern.

Hissing forms darted away from that light, swift and primal.

They were not rats.

The earthen floor of the crypt had been turned like a freshly plowed field. The red eyes that had watched me were those of the men, women, and children of Korzha who had fallen victim to the plague. Their flesh was pale, save for the blue-black crescents beneath their eyes, and grave dirt clung to their clothing and hair. Their fingers were splintered and torn. They had tunneled from their graves, these dead things, into the safety of the crypt, the womb their maker had created for them.

And they would protect him.

As one, they rose. Some rushed into the searing holy light of that blessed lantern and began to burn, hissing and turning away. But they were dozens, and I merely one.

I laid my staff and the lantern on the top of the tomb and rose with them, drawing my Webley in one hand and my cavalry saber in the other. The true vampires—the carrion-eaters I had first seen that horrid dawn in the Ardennes—are difficult to kill. But these plague creatures were pale imitations, the foot soldiers of the Red King, and all that was required to stop them was a stalwart disposition and an utter ruthlessness. They had to be rendered down to parts—utterly destroyed—and later burned, to prevent their repair.

I was more than willing.

On they came.

Hands clawed at me, some of the fingers stripped to bare bone. In the blessed light of that lantern I saw not mothers and daughters, fathers and sons, but vermin. A little girl raked claws down my left shoulder and I shot her through the eye. Like six-armed Kali, I performed a dance of death, twisting and firing the Webley, even as I swept the saber down to hack through an arm or a neck.

I thrust the blade between the ribs of a woman who had once been beautiful, making her monstrousness all the more grotesque. Bullets caved in faces. I trod the ravaged corpses underfoot, breaking bones and crushing skulls. Their skin tore like parchment, and their bones snapped like kindling.

The Webley clicked on an empty chamber and I dropped it in the dirt and drew the huge Mauser semiautomatic I had recently acquired. Gunshots echoed like thunder across the crypt.

Smoke reached my nostrils, a mix of burning flesh from the leeches touched by the lantern's light and the copper scent of the red ash that rose like dust from the wounds I made. That was all the blood they had—a crimson sand that spilled from their veins and the hollows in their bodies as I hacked and slit them open, as the bullets tore through them.

They fell all around me, a shapeless red ruin of rotted flesh, dust, and bones. I climbed over a heap of ravaged dead and swung the saber to make room to fight. A tall white-haired vampire leaped at me, mouth agape in a silent scream. Two others lunged behind him. I drove the saber into his chest, twisted the blade in his heart, and it lodged in bone and was pulled from my grasp.

The twitching corpse careened into me. I took the impact on my right shoulder and knocked it away, and a leech in the shape of a little boy stumbled over it and fell. I shot him through the back of the head, a cloud of red dust rising from the shattered skull. I fired the Mauser to clear the space in front of me, but then the magazine was empty, and I did not have time to reload.

I dropped the Mauser onto the dead boy. Hissing, a female whose withered pale flesh had been laid obscenely bare by her torn burial gown ran at me. My fingers found the hatchet I carried on my hip and I threw it at her. It flew, end over end, and cleaved her skull in twain.

My hands reached into the cloaked shadows of my jacket and emerged once more with the instruments of death. I clutched a Scottish dirk in my right hand, and in my left, an antique two-shot Frank Wesson dagger-pistol. In seconds I had fired both bullets, bursting the dusty, desiccated skulls of the two nearest leeches, and then I put the dagger to use. A blade in either hand, I settled into the business of close-quarters killing.

They swarmed me then, clawing and snapping, tearing at my clothes, trying to get to my bare flesh with their teeth. One forced my head back, exposing my neck. His jaws opened and he darted toward my throat like a python. With a wrench of my arms and a twist, I thrust the Scottish dirk into his open mouth and the point emerged from the base of his neck, severing the spine.

Silently, I moved amongst them. It would have been simpler to have taken them on open ground from some protective cover, torn them apart with rifle rounds or even mortar fire, but the stench of their searing flesh and the red blood-dust that rose from their corpses gave me a moment's peace. Every time they wounded me, every gash and scrape that drew my blood, allowed me to feel for just that instant that I was still alive; that I was not one of them.

Another fell at my feet, twitching, and I drove my wooden leg through her chest, stilling her death throes. I turned, teeth grinding, nearly as feral as the monsters themselves, but nothing else stirred in that crypt. The red gleam in their eyes had dimmed. It was only carnage and dust and pale bones now. The corpses that lay within the cruciform glow of that slot in the lantern's iron hood were blackened with fire.

Still, I had not seen their maker.

I began to retrieve my other discarded weapons, returning them to holsters and sheaths. Then I heard a rustle of wings, followed by soft footsteps upon the stone stairs.

My walking staff lay upon the lid of the tomb at the center of the crypt. I made a path through the fast-decaying remains and snatched it up. My back was to the stairs. The golden glow of the lantern light still spread across the ceiling of the crypt, and the aperture in its iron hood cast that cross-shaped light upon the wall. I could have raised the lantern high, used it to ward off the vampire.

But I did not want to ward it off. I wanted it to come down under the hill with me. Close as a whisper.

When I heard the thing step into the crypt, I felt a prickle like a thousand spiders upon my skin. I turned to see the tall, slightly bent figure standing in the dark outline of the door. The lean, bony creature stood naked, there in the crypt, and I saw upon its pale chest a scorched path of flesh in the shape of the cross. Its eyes were the flat, dull black of the plague; hollow eyes, and so familiar. Yet they were familiar only in that I had seen

their like before. This creature still had two eyes, and upon its face there was no scar akin to the one I had slashed in the carrion thing that had stalked me on the battlefield. I sought the vampire that had poisoned my flesh with its breath and cost me my leg, had murdered my wife, and destroyed my family.

This was not he.

Yet, tonight, like so many others of its kind, it would die in his place.

"I see that the priest's prayers went unanswered," I said.

The vampire smiled. "His screams as well." A shiver went up my spine at the sound of its voice. I could not place the accent; the remnant, I presumed, of some ancient tongue, and some ancient land.

They were an arrogant breed. This one spoke as though I was some lowly serf, and it my master.

"You are trespassing, sir," it said, voice soft, but so low that it seemed to shake the stone walls of the crypt. "This place belongs to me. I have the documents that name me owner. Everything within these walls belongs to me."

As it said this last, it gestured toward the once-human refuse strewn about the turned-earth floor. We had conspired, this vampire and I, to make that old church little more than one enormous grave.

"I will forgive your intrusion," he went on, and a cruel smile lifted the corners of his mouth, but did not reach his dead eyes. "I will forgive your . . . trespasses . . . if you leave at once."

From within a leather pocket sewn into my long coat, I drew the head of the harpoon I had used to slice out the heart of the fiend that had risen from the dead in my mother's corpse. I screwed the harpoon onto the staff, as I had done so many times before.

The vampire watched me curiously, though not without, I thought, a certain disquiet.

"I have heard tales of you, Lord Baltimore," the vermin said. "You are formidable. Leave here, now. Leave this church, and Korzha, to me, and I will tell you where you will find the creature you seek, the one you have pursued these many years."

The temptation was momentary. Its kind could speak nothing but lies.

"I will find him. Have no doubt," I replied. "And when I do, you will be only memory."

It may have been that the thing trembled. It shifted, and took a step toward me.

"Unfortunate," it whispered.

"Such is my lot."

It leaped, black wings unfurling, hideous face elongating, and in my mind I could still see the way the creatures had torn at the corpses of the soldiers who had served under my command, snouts painted with their blood.

The vampire lunged for my throat, and I did not turn away.

CRESCENDO:
LUX ET AETERNUM

"One of the little boys took up the tin soldier, and without rime or reason, threw him into the fire."
—The Steadfast Tin Soldier
by Hans Christian Andersen

1

Doctor Rose faltered in his reading and began to flip the pages of Baltimore's journal.

"What is it?" Aischros asked, his voice a tired rasp. "Why have you stopped?"

Despite the gloom of the lantern light illuminating the inn, Childress could see what the ugly mariner apparently could not. The pages that the doctor riffled through were blank. He caught himself holding his breath, and slowly exhaled, but it did not ease the tension that coiled inside of him. From their expressions, he could see that his companions were equally on edge.

"The letter," Childress said. Like Aischros, he had been silent for so long while Doctor Rose read that his throat was dry, his voice gravelly. "The letter from the innkeeper's son . . . he said to return to it when we'd read through the journal."

Doctor Rose blinked as though coming awake and looked up from the book. He seemed puzzled for a moment, but then his gaze cleared and he nodded.

"Yes. Of course."

He closed the journal and slid it onto the table, and all three of them stared at it a moment as though it were some ancient artifact. Then Doctor Rose glanced around warily, having second thoughts about leaving it out in the open, and plucked it up from the scarred wooden surface once more. The doctor slipped the journal into the inside pocket of his jacket, alongside his cigarette case. Childress understood both Doctor Rose's concern about leaving the journal lying about, and his obvious reluctance to pick it up again.

Only a few people remained in the inn's barroom now. The lamplight cast a waxy yellow pall upon them all. Even the innkeeper had the appearance of a jaundiced, melting candle. One man sat at the bar, half-turned in his chair, lost in shadow so that he, at least, still appeared to be gray. The innkeeper paid him no attention at all, and the serving girl had gone home, or gone to bed, or gone off with one of her customers. Or, perhaps, all three.

Childress felt warm, almost feverish. The air in the room had grown close as the hour grew later.

"It wasn't the right one," Aischros said.

Doctor Rose flinched. He and Childress both looked at the scarred face of the mariner. All three of them had bent forward into a circle of privacy as the doctor had quietly read Baltimore's journal entries. Now Aischros leaned back and settled again into his creaking chair, gripping the arms once more as though afraid it might shift beneath him like the sea.

"What do you mean?" Childress asked.

Aischros knitted his brows. "The vampire," he whispered. "It wasn't the creature he calls the Red King. Not the one that destroyed his family and rotted his leg, the one he scarred on the battlefield. Has he not found the fiend, after all this time?"

"Apparently not," Doctor Rose replied, sipping from his flat ale, perhaps just to moisten his lips.

"Only one way to find out," Childress said. He sensed that the doctor was delaying the reading of the rest of Iancu Vulpes's letter, and wanted to get on with it. "Read on, Doctor. What does the boy have to say?"

Doctor Rose placed his truncated hand on top of the thick sheaf of ivory pages that lay half-folded on the table before him. He tapped twice on the letter with his knuckles and the stumps of his missing fingers, as though for luck, and then picked up the pages, and began to read.

* * *

"If you have seen all that is written in Lord Baltimore's journal, and you believe his words," wrote Iancu Vulpes, "then I am sure that you will wish to know the end of the tale, for his journal reveals nothing further of his time in our town before his departure. What he might have learned from the devil he encountered within the walls of the old church, what the monster told him that sent him off so quickly, I cannot say. I know only that he instructed me to send the journal as I have done, to three men who would gather at a certain place and time. I can only hope that it has been delivered.

"Perhaps now you will wish to burn the journal, to keep the evil it speaks of from spreading beyond its pages. This, I think, would be a very good idea. But I live in a place full of superstition and fear. If you are men with courage enough to be called friend by a creature such as Lord Baltimore, perhaps you do not fear the darkness. Perhaps the Red Death has not touched you yet. Or perhaps it has, and your scars have forged you into something other than men. You who are friends of Baltimore will understand my meaning.

"The hunter—for I can think of him no other way—had commanded my father and me, and the others who had come to the church, to leave the cemetery. I should be ashamed to confess that we did so, going back to the town and hiding away in our homes all through the long night. I could not sleep, and I feel sure there were many restless souls in Korzha that night, waiting for the sun to rise.

"My father also could not seem to rest. He laid a fire in the fireplace on the first floor of the inn, feeding it all night, though it seemed barely able to burn. When I had given up all hope of sleeping, I joined him there, and we watched the sluggish flames slowly consuming the wood. When at last the dawn arrived, we threw wide the door. I had just set foot over the threshold, into the street, when my father caught my arm.

"'Did you notice, Iancu?' he asked me. I did not understand what he meant, and he smiled. 'The quiet,' he said. 'There were no screams last night.'

"And he was right. Not a single dog had howled, and we had heard none of the grief-and-terror-stricken wailing that had seemed to accompany each night since the priest had first sold the church in the cemetery to that nobleman.

"My father and I hurried—as best he could hurry—back to the church. Never had I thought of him as an old man, but I had to force myself not to run through the cemetery, leaving him behind. The sun rose like fire on the horizon, a strange orange color I had never seen at dawn before. By the time we reached the little church, many other people had come from the town. They had all been touched by the infection in Korzha, watched their husbands and wives, their children, their brothers and sisters, rot from the plague. These were the survivors.

"Near the bottom of the hill, upon which sat that crumbling church, a patch of grass had begun to grow. I cannot say for certain that it had not been there the day before, but it was the first bit of color I had noticed anywhere in Korzha for a very long time. As my father and I climbed the hill with the others who had come to see what had become of Baltimore, I saw the crooked form of Tibor, the gravedigger, just ahead. My father urged me on, and I hurried to catch up to Tibor. It pained me to speak to him, for I could not look at him without remembering the sight of my sister's burnt remains as he dug her grave. Still, I had to speak with him.

"'What happened during the night?' I asked.

"Tibor shrugged. He had watched the church from his window. In the moonlight, he said, his view had been good. But though he, too, had remained awake all through the night, he had seen nothing leaving the church.

"Dozens of us gathered around the front of the church. The broken doors yawned wide, but the dawn's light did not reach into the darkness within. At first there was a lot of talking as the survivors of Korzha asked one another how they'd spent the night and if they'd seen anything coming from the cemetery or heard anything unusual. Like my father, the only strange thing they'd heard had been silence. Others asked Tibor the same question I had, and received the same answers.

"Quiet enveloped us then, and a painful impatience. Minutes passed in restless silence. My father broke from the crowd and went to the bottom step, looking up at the decrepit face of the church. I called to him to stop,

and several people backed away from the building when they heard the fear in my voice. If something still lurked in the darkness of the ruined house of God, I did not want my father to enter.

"He turned to reassure me, but then we heard several people gasp. Fingers pointed and whispers slipped amongst the crowd. In the shadowy doorway of the church, something stirred. Though the warmth of the daylight had always given us a sense of safety, in that moment I did not feel at all safe. Despite the sun, I was filled with a fear more appropriate to the dark of night.

"A shape appeared in the doorway. I knew it was Baltimore even before he stepped out from the shadows, for I heard the heavy knock of his wooden leg upon the threshold of the church. He held something in front of him—something that fluttered in his hands. I thought it must be a bat or some kind of bird that had become trapped in the rafters of the church. But the moment he came out into the sunlight, the thing stopped moving.

"Pale and grim and tired, Baltimore held out his hands so that we all could see the thing he clutched in them. It was neither bird nor bat. There were no wings at all, merely a black and twisted lump with a tangle of sprouts growing off of it, like some poison root freshly dug from the ground.

"'The sickness is gone from Korzha,' he said, staring at the crowd as though he accused us of something. 'The plague will trouble you no more. This is the vampire's heart. It must be boiled in clear water and a broth made from it, to be fed to all those who are still ill. Korzha is free, but not yet healed. The damned coward of a priest who betrayed his faith is inside, dead, repaid tenfold for his sins. You must take him out and burn him, and then tear the church down and burn every board, every splinter.

"'Find another priest, and rebuild,' Lord Baltimore instructed us. 'But not on this spot. Nothing should ever be built upon this hill, and nothing will grow here . . . faith, least of all.'

"An old midwife called Reveka took the heart from him. She was so ancient that she had been there to help my grandmother give birth to my father. That night, after she had done as Baltimore instructed and the broth of that dark root had been served to all those still ailing, Reveka retired to her bed and died in her sleep. The touch of that dark heart had killed her. Yet the next morning, as Baltimore had promised, all who had been sick were well again. In their joy, few in Korzha mourned Reveka. She had been very old, and had seen much. My father and I helped Tibor dig her grave.

"As for Lord Baltimore, after giving Reveka the vampire's heart, he returned to the inn with us. The devil that had tainted Korzha was not the one he had been searching for, but I sensed a new peace in him. He would say nothing of what had transpired in that church, but he entrusted me with his journal, and gave instructions as to when and where it was to be delivered.

"If this letter and the journal have arrived safely in your hands, I have done as the hunter asked. All that remains is for me to wish you well, friends of Baltimore. I would pray to God to watch over you, but I do not believe that He listens.

"Respectfully yours,

"Iancu Vulpes."

2

The innkeeper had begun to move about the room, snuffing the flames that burned within the hanging lanterns. Doctor Rose clutched the letter in his trembling hands, staring at its final sentiment. He wished he could believe that Iancu Vulpes was wrong, but he feared there was far too much truth in those words. The ravages of the plague had spread unabated across the land. If God existed, He was either deaf or cruel, for the chorus of prayers that had gone up from Europe in these past few years should have shattered the gates of Heaven itself.

With his ruined hand, Doctor Rose retrieved his cigarette case from his pocket, fumbling it open, and his remaining cigarettes showered down onto his lap and to the filthy floor of the inn. As the single survivor began to slip from his lap, he snatched it up.

He did not light the cigarette. Instead, he set it on the table beside the wooden box of matches and covered them protectively with his hand. It was a comfort just to have them there. There was no way he would put anything to his lips that had touched the floor of this place, and he might need the cigarette more later.

Childress said something. Doctor Rose was only vaguely aware that he had spoken. After a moment, the man reached across the table and gripped his wrist. Only then did the doctor tear his gaze from the letter in his hands. He looked up and met Childress's eyes.

"Where is he?" the doctor asked.

The tiny lines around those eyes crinkled as Childress frowned. He had no answer to the question. Doctor Rose glanced at Aischros, but the sailor seemed equally troubled. They had been sitting in this room, around this damnable table, since midday—twelve hours—and Baltimore had not appeared to explain the purpose of their gathering.

"At some point," Childress ventured, "we're going to have to admit the possibility that he may not be able to join us."

Doctor Rose tapped the wooden box and matches rattled inside. Something about the sound troubled him and he pulled his hand away and frowned down at the box and his sole cigarette.

Aischros scraped a heavy paw across his bristly chin. Dark circles sagged beneath his eyes. "You think he's dead?"

"I have trouble imagining it," Childress replied.

Doctor Rose scoffed and stared at them. "Baltimore isn't dead, gentlemen. All of this," he said, gesturing around them, then shaking the thick pages of the letter in his grasp, "it's too well orchestrated. If he'd been killed in the days since he scrawled the summons he sent to each of us, I feel quite certain we would know it."

A flash of anger crossed Childress's face. "Well, then, where the hell is he?"

Grim Aischros gave a dark laugh. "I think maybe you've answered your own question."

"So, we wait, then?" Doctor Rose asked.

Childress let out a long breath, and waved a hand in surrender. "What else can we do?"

In silence, they stared at one another. Doctor Rose noticed that none of them so much as glanced at the door now. He'd thought that the closeness of the air had come from the lateness of the hour, but the very atmosphere of the inn had changed. Its weight was oppressive. The hairs on the back of his neck rose like the hackles of a dog, and the scarred stumps of his missing fingers itched.

Whatever was going to happen, it would be soon. All of the numbness that lay upon the place like an anesthetic had been dispersed with the departure of

the inn's gray, failed patrons. Their pres-
ence had somehow deadened any current
of emotion or sentiment that might have
existed beneath that roof, but now, with
them gone, Doctor Rose could feel
malevolence around him, as though it
seethed in the very boards of this place.
His skin prickled with it.

All save one of the stragglers in the
barroom had retired for the night. A single patron sat at the bar as the innkeeper
moved from lantern to lantern, the shadows deepening as the lights went out,
one after another. It was quite late now, and there was no sign of Baltimore.

The innkeeper paused in his task and came toward them, hitching up his
pants. He seemed reluctant to approach.

"Sorry, gents, but you'll have to shove off now. We're shuttering up for
the night." He glanced over his shoulder at the lone patron still at the bar.
"That means you, too, Bentley. Toddle off to bed like a nice bloke, would you?"

Doctor Rose saw a wary light in the innkeeper's eyes, but the man at the
bar only laughed softly and rose from his stool.

"You don't have to speak to me as though I were some errant child,
Herbert. When have I ever left before you've thrown me out? And when
have I given you trouble when the time comes? Never, on both counts."

Aischros rose from his chair, its legs scraping the wood floor. Childress
stood and straightened his jacket, then smoothed his hair. Midnight or no,
the handsome son of good fortune wanted to look his best. Doctor Rose felt
a trace of amusement breeze through him, but it did not alleviate the
uneasiness he felt, or banish the growing sense of menace in the room.

"And now what?" Aischros asked.

Doctor Rose looked to Childress, some silent communication passing
between them.

"You can afford it, Thomas," the doctor said, arching an eyebrow.

The thin, gray-complexioned man at the bar—Bentley, the innkeeper had called him—paused to watch them a moment, his hands thrust into his pockets.

Childress nodded slowly, then turned to the innkeeper. "Herbert, was it? I presume you've a vacant room or two you could spare, so that we might wait for a friend who's meant to be meeting us here."

The barrel-chested man grumbled a bit. "Awfully late, sir. You've nowhere else to go?"

Aischros shouldered the knapsack he traveled with. "Nowhere."

Doctor Rose sighed, wishing the sailor hadn't said as much. He saw the innkeeper's expression change as the man calculated how severely he might be able to overcharge them. It wouldn't cost Rose at all—he hadn't enough money to pay for his meal, never mind a room. Childress would pay their way. But the greed that lit the innkeeper's eyes was more vivid than any color or emotion they'd encountered in this place, and it dredged a disdain up from within him.

"I suppose I could accommodate you—" the innkeeper began.

The man he'd called Bentley interrupted. "No need for that, gentlemen," he said. He hadn't moved. Only stood there with his hands in his pockets. For the first time, Doctor Rose noticed the spatters of paint that dotted his jacket and trousers. "If you're sure your friend will still be along this evening, you're welcome to join me in my studio until he arrives."

Herbert the innkeeper blinked, seeing the money slipping through his hands. "That's not necessary, Bentley. These gents'd like to get a good night's sleep, I'm sure."

Aischros stood mostly in shadow, now that most of the lanterns had been put out. The scars on his face seemed to glow ghostly pale. He shot an intimidating glare at Herbert.

"I don't think I could sleep," the mariner said. "Not here. Not tonight."

"Your studio, sir?" Childress asked. "You're an artist?"

Bentley offered a slanted, wan smile, though it was amiable enough.

"Painter. Sometimes sculptor. I've maintained rooms on the third floor here for my studio and apartment for years."

"You're certain we wouldn't be disturbing you?" Doctor Rose asked. "It's awfully late."

"Ah, yes. The hour," Bentley said, offering an awkward shrug. "I sleep very little, actually. A few hours in the early morning. I don't like the dark, you see. I find it unsettling. Makes it difficult to surrender myself to sleep until I see the sun on the horizon. I paint in the hours when most are sleeping."

"Stumbles down here in time for afternoon tea, most days," the innkeeper said with a desultory sniff.

"If you're certain?" Childress said, ignoring Herbert.

Bentley executed a tiny bow. "Quite."

Introductions were made all around, and then the artist gestured toward a doorway on the other side of the room. "The stairs are just through there. Perhaps a brandy to warm you, and a fire. There's a draft down here, I find, that never lets the heat accumulate."

Doctor Rose thought that the absence of warmth at the inn had nothing to do with a draft, but he said nothing of those suspicions.

The three men followed the artist as he led them out of the bar, through a parlor, and into the main foyer of the inn. Travelers who wished only a room would enter through a heavy wooden door, a separate entrance from the one that led into the bar. From the water stains on the wall and the warped wood of the door, Doctor Rose surmised that the bar received a great many more visitors than the guest rooms of the inn. The dust and the faded, peeling wallpaper here made the inn's original purpose seem almost an afterthought.

The entire foyer seemed off-kilter, every angle slightly wrong. The stairs were crooked and slanted. When they began to ascend, the doctor expected every one to creak loudly, but no matter how much the building had settled, the construction was solid. Not a single squeak rose underfoot as they climbed to the second-floor landing, then proceeded upward toward the third.

In his life, Doctor Rose had stayed in dozens of inns and hotels. Never had he walked the stairs and corridors of a place so silent. It was late, certainly, and that must have accounted for a portion of the quietude, but still, should there not be some laughter or argument coming from behind a door, or the grunting, sighing, creaking-bedspring chorus of lovemaking?

A shudder went through him as they followed the artist along the third-floor corridor. *How foolish of you, Lemuel, to think that anyone could make love in a sepulcher like this,* he thought. Even whores would hesitate to do their business here. The plague had turned all of Europe into a funeral. Those still in mourning were the fortunate ones. This place had the claustrophobic air of a tomb.

Baltimore must have had a reason for summoning them to this address in particular, but Doctor Rose could not fathom it. Even as he, Childress, and Aischros paused at the end of the corridor—with its dimly flickering sconces and tilted picture frames on the walls—and waited for Bentley to unlock the door to his rooms, he wished he were anywhere else.

"Here we are, gentlemen," Bentley said, opening the door and entering. "Let's see what we can do about that brandy."

He stood aside so that they could pass. A tall man, he bent toward them as he spoke, as though he feared that words uttered from a greater height might not reach them. His thin brown hair was tangled and unruly, as though it had not made the acquaintance of a comb in several weeks. For the first time, Doctor Rose noticed several dark paint spots dappling his left cheek—black, or red, perhaps.

Bentley closed the door.

They stood in a high-ceilinged room on the topmost floor of the inn. A skylight in the roof let in a shaft of moonlight that illuminated an easel in the center of the studio. A canvas perhaps four feet square was propped on the easel, and still-damp paint glistened moistly in the light of the moon.

Doctor Rose's gaze only drifted over the painting as he attempted to make out the rest of the room in the darkened studio. There were several small tables with what appeared to be statuary upon them—Bentley's sculptures, he supposed—as well as shelves, and the square and rectangular shapes of other paintings on the walls. But the corners of the studio were lost in shadows without definition, and some of the walls were decorated in uneven shapes that he imagined must be other ambitious sculptures.

"It's marvelous," Childress said, glancing around at the expansive studio. "I'd never have imagined there was anything back here but cold little rooms with cots like torture racks, storage closets, and clanking pipes."

The artist laughed softly. "Those are in the back. The studio is my life, really. The other rooms, for sleeping and eating only, are practically a dungeon."

Bentley struck a match and lit a single oil lamp. The yellow light flickered and cast new ugly shadows into the corners, where something lay piled like pale kindling.

As the artist moved across the room, the light fell on the large canvas upon the easel, and Doctor Rose drew a sharp breath, frozen to the spot. He felt himself sway in the grip of memory and despair.

In gruesome detail, the painting depicted an enormous bear with burning eyes, its fur matted with blood and snout crusted with gore, as it stretched wide the jaws of a sheath of human skin that lay on the forest floor, preparing to slip back into the body of the Nordic soldier it wore in its obscene masquerade.

The young Norseman's face was precisely as the doctor remembered it. Bentley had painted the curse of Private Harbard.

Aischros made a low, choking noise in his throat. Even as Doctor Rose turned to look at him, the mariner's ugly face twisted, eyes narrowing, and he turned a haunted gaze upon the doctor.

"What do you see?" Aischros asked.

Doctor Rose wiped the back of his truncated hand across his dry lips, wishing for a drink. Or his last cigarette.

"The demon-bear," he whispered, staring at Aischros. "And you?"

"The giant," the mariner replied. "The sin-wood puppet."

Childress passed between them as though entranced. He said nothing as he approached that canvas, but Doctor Rose felt sure he must be seeing the creature he had encountered in the mountains of Chile; El Cuero, and the demon at the bottom of the lake. The thing had appeared to each of them as the devils of their own personal nightmares.

"Thomas," Doctor Rose said.

The artist had paused and turned to regard them, a dreamlike smile on his narrow features, yellow lamplight flickering shadows onto his face.

Childress turned away from the canvas with a hand over his mouth as though he might retch. With wide eyes, he stared at Doctor Rose.

"Doctor," Aischros said. "Look again."

The painting had changed. They all stared at it now. Whatever sinister intention had been smeared upon that canvas, it had given each of them a horrific vision. But the artist's true vision was apparent now, and upon its revelation, Doctor Rose shrank back a step, slowly shaking his head, mouth working but unable to speak. Or to scream. For this wretched portrait was far worse than what they had first perceived.

Bentley had painted a figure striding out of a bleeding sunset. Upon its gray corpse head sat a crown of red flame, and in its right hand it held a gold scepter. Under its left arm, it carried a poorly made wooden coffin. The crimson light of the setting sun stained the land. The Red King wore a scarlet cloak that spread behind it like the wings of a raven, and in the shadow of that cloak, corpses and gray wraiths rose from the ruined earth to fall in behind the king, the army of the Red Death.

"The monk," Aischros said.

Childress whispered the name of God, but as Doctor Rose expected, Heaven gave no reply. It was, indeed, precisely the vision that the monk had described to Demetrius when they had met in the cemetery on Trevelyan Island, the vampire master that Baltimore had been hunting all along.

"What in hell is this, Bentley?" Childress demanded, turning on the artist

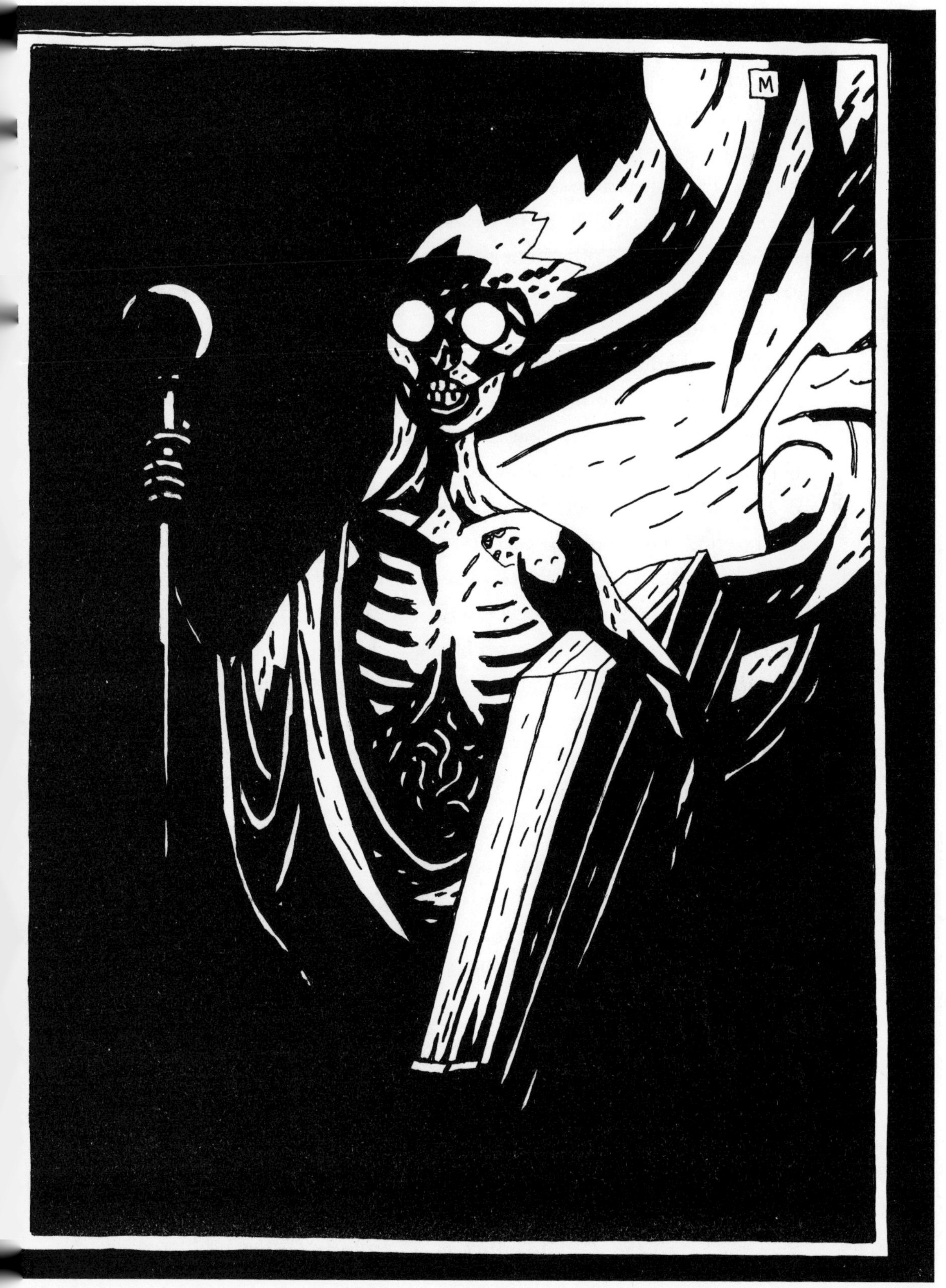

and reaching inside his coat for the pistol he had carried back from the war.

"Why, it's my masterpiece," the artist replied. His expression was blissful.

Doctor Rose wished he had a weapon. His cigarette case and the little wooden matchbox would do him no good. He glanced around, his eyes finally adjusting in the moonlight and lamplight, and now the walls and corners of the room resolved themselves further, and he saw that the piles he had seen were not anything so mundane as kindling.

They were bones. In the corners, and in the eaves of that high ceiling, human bones had been arranged into arcane and intricate designs. Skulls stared, hollow-eyed, from niches within the nests of bones. There must have been hundreds of human skeletons in the room, all contributing to the hideous architecture of this chapel of death.

"I hear his voice, you see," the artist told them, pleasant as any good host. "My master speaks to me from the mouths of the dead, through their skulls, from the echo of their bones."

He raised the lamp higher, smiling amiably. "Now, what about that brandy?"

A sound like the moaning of the winter wind began to thrum in the room, and then it shrank down into a single, richly resonant voice.

"Don't trouble yourself, Bentley," said that silken voice. "I think we can safely skip the brandy."

3

Aischros flexed his fingers and set himself into a fighting stance. This was no bar brawl, but he knew only one way to fight, and that was with everything he had. Heart and soul and fists. Sometimes, that wasn't enough. Quietly he drew his dagger from the sheath at his hip. In the pale yellow flicker of the artist's oil lamp, he saw a thin figure emerging from the shadows.

For most of his life he had been aware of things lurking just outside the edges of his vision. In the ghost of that hilltop village of Cicagne, he'd gotten his first real glimpse of the evil that infected the underbelly of the world. His friendship with Lord Baltimore, and his meeting with that strange monk on Trevelyan Island, had given him another. It seemed to him that, ever since, he had been waiting for the moment when the wretched fiend would show itself.

The moment had arrived.

Childress had a pistol. Doctor Rose was unarmed. In truth, Aischros was not sure how much it mattered. The dark slither of the thing that whispered from the corners of the room—whose voice seemed to come from the mouths of all of the moonlit skulls built into the alcoves and eaves—was the sound of death approaching. They could not hope to defeat the vampire. But they would fight.

Aischros held the dagger loosely. He'd been forced to use it in the past, and had found himself equipped with innate and grisly skill. A kind of preternatural calm filled him. An insidious sort of pressure had been gathering within the walls of the inn for hours. It felt oppressive and wrong, but more than that, it felt *unnatural.*

For a moment, under the weight of that foul presence, the doctor faltered. He swayed and fell to one knee, only keeping himself from sprawling on the floor with an outstretched hand. Grimly, eyes narrowed and jaw set, the slender little red-haired man forced himself back to his feet.

The artist, Bentley, lips curled in a madman's grin, raised the lamp higher. His masterpiece, with its paint wetly gleaming, seemed to flow and shift, almost as though the Red King could step out of the painting, his crimson shadow flowing across the world. But Aischros could not focus on the art, or on his two companions. All three of them stared rigidly at the silhouette that moved toward them.

For a moment, the gauzy yellow light and the shifting gray shadows conspired to create the image of a hideous devil. The reed-thin vampire had a single black eye, rimmed with red, and a scar that glistened like mother-of-pearl running down the right side of its face, across the hollow orbit of the other. Its commanding presence was unlike anything Aischros had ever encountered. Its gray flesh was cloaked in elegant fabrics of black and crimson. A death's-head grin slashed its mouth, revealing the jagged maw of a predator.  Baltimore had imagined a goblin, a demon, the Jack-in-the-Box of a grim fairy tale come to life, and that was precisely what Aischros saw.

But only for a moment.

He did not blink, but it seemed to him that the artist's studio did; that the shadows themselves blinked, the midnight gloom rearranging itself before their eyes. A sickening ripple passed through the shroud of malice that cloaked them all.

The vampire stood revealed. In the illumination cast by Bentley's oil

lamp, he looked like little more than a sickly old man, touched by the plague. His black eyes seemed too large for his face. The creature Baltimore had first encountered on a battlefield so many years before seemed decrepit now, with long bony fingers and a stoop to his back. Upon his scalp were wisps of white hair. The only part of his visage the shadows had not hidden was the pearl gleam of the scar that ran from forehead to chin, through the gouged hollow of his eye, and across his lips.

Yet despite the horrific countenance of that brittle, rustling thing, the vampire's most terrible aspect was his voice, so elegant that when it came from those dry lips, each syllable was an obscenity.

Childress cocked his pistol and pointed it at the devil's head. He appeared pitiful, but the aura of wickedness that radiated from him belied that impression.

"Not another step," Childress said. The way he stood, it was as though his body had just remembered what it had been like to be a soldier.

The vampire laughed softly and shook his head. "Now it has come to this?" he said with that silken voice. "Little men and their bullets?"

Aischros tightened his grip on the dagger. It felt comfortable and familiar in his hand. He took a step nearer to the wretched thing, picturing in his mind the swift, sure motions he would make, gripping the vampire's thin skull in one massive hand, even as he hacked the blade of the dagger through its neck. Unnatural or not—evil or not—it couldn't live without a head.

He hoped.

"Where is Baltimore?" the vampire asked, a kind of melancholic disappointment in his voice and his eyes. He tilted his head to one side, studying them, almost birdlike. "I can smell him on you. Bentley overheard some of your talk downstairs, and I heard through him. You are his friends. The stink of idiotic courage comes off you in waves."

Aischros bared his teeth in an odd sort of smile, the way he did whenever he was confronted by impending violence. In the moments before a bar fight, he could never stop that grin from coming. It was not purposeful, but it gave his enemies the impression that he would enjoy the pain and the blood. That might have been true—he had never given it much thought—but the baring of his teeth was instinct alone. Much like the vampire.

"Where is he?" the vampire said.

The artist, Bentley, gestured with his oil lamp. "I don't think they know."

Aischros felt certain that the vampire would slay them now, the way he had all of those Baltimore loved. Instead, a look of utter grief crossed the vampire's face.

"But they must," the monster said. "Bring him forth, you fools. The time has come, at last, for the hunter to capture his prey. I grow tired."

Sorrow haunted the devil's single eye as he raised a tremulous hand to trace the scar upon his face. "I took so much pleasure in the vengeance I wrought upon him. We were content, you see. We had slipped into a blissful simplicity, soaring upon the night wind and feasting upon whatever carrion we found, only rarely taking the flesh and blood of the living. The

damned soldier woke me with the slice of his bayonet...woke us all...and the disease in our hearts woke with us.

"Oh, how I hated him for that. I shook with pleasure when I tasted the blood of his mother, and father, and sister. I left his wife alive so that I could save her for another day, and draw out his torment. When at last I returned for her, I left her broken on the floor for him to find. And when I called Lady Baltimore from her grave, and then bade his family to rise up from the crypt, I knew that would destroy him."

The vampire shook his head.

Doctor Rose whispered something that might have been a prayer or a curse. The pistol in Childress's hand did not waver.

Aischros shifted two steps to his left, toward the artist. Bentley would help his master, of course. But Aischros would kill him before he could interfere.

"My joy," the vampire said, lowering his gaze, as though he had forgotten they were there, "was short-lived. I thought I had destroyed Baltimore, that these things would break his spirit and tear the heart from him as surely as if I had done it with my own hands. Instead, I had made him into something else . . . something terrible.

"Some other fire fuels that furnace now."

Doctor Rose stepped to the right, putting more room between himself and Childress. Beyond him, against the wall, stood a column of human bones.

"If exhaustion weighs so heavily on you," Childress said, "we'll relieve you of the burden."

The vampire's single eye widened and he hissed, fangs bared. He had not moved, but a dark power emanated from him. Aischros nearly took a step back, so terrible was the menace that seeped from the vampire then. He held his ground, but only by force of will.

"Not you." The vampire sighed. "Him. I have run for so long—for years now. I put oceans between us and called up storms to wreck the ships upon which he sailed in pursuit of me. But, always, Baltimore kept pace. I am tired now, and will run no more. He will come. Of course he will. He always does.

"Let it end. Let it end," the vampire said, but with these last words he glanced at the painting of the Red King. "Now, my dark majesty, before I meet my end, grant me a boon—a final blow, the last laugh upon my enemy. I have not the strength to do it, but if these three are all that he still cares about in this world, let him find them dead when he deigns to arrive."

A beatific smile touched his ruined face and the vampire fixed them with that single red-black eye. "His *friends.*"

The last word, spoken with utter contempt, seemed to unfurl across the room like evening mist.

Aischros saw motion out of the corners of his eyes. Flexing his grip on the dagger's handle, he glanced to the left, at the macabre arched columns Bentley had built against the wall. Birdlike shadows, black as oil, began to slip from amongst the bones and out through the dark, empty eyes of gleaming human skulls. The bird-shadows caressed those bones, slithering amongst them, covering them.

The liquid dark formed wretched shadow flesh over the skeletons, and with a wet, cracking sound, they began to tear themselves away from bone arches, from the ossuary the artist had made of this place. Bone and shadow and malice joined together, and red eyes opened in the dark.

4

The wraiths ripped away from the walls and began to flow toward them. The air in that room was thick with evil so oppressive it had driven Doctor Rose to one knee, but he would not succumb again. Fear burned like poison through his veins, but he refused to be crippled by it. His nostrils flared, his heart thundering in his chest. His weaponless hands clenched and unclenched as he glanced frantically around in search of some way to defend himself.

Childress fired his pistol. The sound echoed in the cavernous chapel of death that Bentley had made of his studio. The bullet struck one of the wraiths dead center with an audible crack of bone. The thing staggered, but kept coming. The decrepit, scarred vampire retreated into the shadows behind the artist, who still held his oil lamp high, smiling as though the horror was unfolding purely for his amusement. Aischros lunged at one of the wraiths and several of them drove him down to the floor, where his head banged off the wood.

That was all Doctor Rose saw before they swept over him. He had watched the shadows coalesce over the bones that had been built into columns and arches and bring those bones to hideous life.

Yet these things of death and darkness had substance, and terrible strength. A hand clutched his throat, searing his flesh with frigid cold unlike anything he'd ever felt.

Doctor Rose thrashed against them. Claws raked his back as they tried to drag him down. He struggled to keep his feet under him, staggering backward into a small table he had not noticed before. Bottles fell and shattered on the floor and he slipped in something slick and viscous. The strong smell of paint wafted up to him, accompanied by a chemical odor. Bentley's colors—his palette.

The light from the artist's lamp seemed to brighten. Doctor Rose looked up as the wraith in front of him thrust its face nearer. For the first time he saw the dreadful, hellish features of the thing, the burning-coal eyes and the awful bestial snout. In that moment, he felt sure he understood what these things were. Bentley had built a chapel and filled it with death and worship. The monk had shared his vision with Aischros, and in it there had been black-winged wraiths coming up from graves, the spirits of vampires whose bodies were too ruined to inhabit, and thus were abandoned. The wraiths could only be those same vampire spirits, the intangible evil essence of monsters, drawn here by the artist's devotion.

The wraith hissed—baring rows of gleaming needle teeth—and with a crack and pop of bone, wings pushed out from its back, shadowy drapes that

spread wide and began to beat against the thick air of the room. It grabbed him and tried to pull him upward, toward the ceiling, even as another tried to swipe talons at his abdomen.

Doctor Rose kicked away the blow meant for his gut. He stared into the nightmare face of the winged wraith and felt as though he were a child again, and all the things he feared were just outside his window, scratching against the glass, had finally come for him. It opened its jaws wide and tried to drive its teeth toward his throat.

The doctor screamed, terror burning away any thought of shame.

He thrust out his hands. With the left, he clutched its throat. But his missing fingers made the grip of his right hand weak, and he could not get a firm grasp. A thousand images cascaded through his mind now, of his childhood, of his years as a surgeon, and his life after losing those two fingers. Somewhere along the way, he had lost his faith. A crucifix had hung above his bed as a boy, and as a young surgeon he had worn one on a chain around his neck. He only wished it hung there now.

Rigid, unbreathing, unable to fight the strength of the wraith as it forced its yellow teeth toward his throat, Doctor Rose surrendered to despair. All his life he had combated his size with intelligence and arrogance and discipline, but he was a slim, boyish man, and this unnatural thing had all the strength of the Devil. Doctor Rose would die now.

His left hand gave way, elbow buckling. The winged wraith darted that damp, bestial maw toward his throat.

Powerful claws clutched Doctor Rose from behind, gashing his flesh even as they dragged him down. The winged wraith's fangs clacked shut only inches from his flesh, and he was torn from its grasp. In a tangle of limbs as the greedy vampire things reached for him, colliding with one another, he sprawled on the floor in a puddle of paint and turpentine. Glass slivered through his trousers and into the flesh of his right hip and leg. He cried out, and the pain seemed to shock his mind to life again. He could bleed. He could hurt. That meant he was alive.

"And by God," he whispered, "I'll stay that way."

A vampire wraith came at him, sliding in smeared paint. Doctor Rose kicked its face as he reached into the inside pocket of his jacket and drew out the wooden matchbox. It rattled as he flicked it open. The winged wraith approached, and two others as well. He heard more gunshots, and Aischros shouting in a kind of animal fury, but he could pay them no mind.

He plucked out a wooden match, pressed the box shut between thumb and forefinger, and with the remaining fingers of his mangled hand, he struck the match. It hissed as it flared to life. The shadow-sculpted demon faces of the wraiths drew back slightly in surprise.

Doctor Rose threw the match into the spilled paint and turpentine. A blaze of heat and flame bloomed upward, consuming the winged wraith and igniting one of the others. The third backed away, and all of the shifting, moving shadows retreated from the area around Doctor Rose and the burning paint. The winged wraith staggered off ablaze and knocked over a pedestal upon which sat an elegantly gruesome sculpture. It slammed into the wall, igniting the wood and a pair of framed portraits that hung there, the fire licking across the canvases and the wall with ravenous hunger.

But the winged wraith was not dying. It slammed against the wall again and again, and it took Doctor Rose a moment to realize that the shadow creature was attempting to put out the flames that flickered upon the shifting darkness of its flesh. Whatever the true substance of the shadows that comprised the creature, it would burn, but it would not be consumed by fire. It would not be killed.

The fire began to race along the ceiling and wall. Near his feet was a long shard of broken marble, the statue that had been knocked over. It had the smooth body of a woman and the head of some wretched, infernal thing. The legs had broken off, making it both the perfect club and a stabbing weapon as well. It would have to do. He had nothing else.

Doctor Rose stood as close to the fire as possible, given that his clothes were smeared with paint and turpentine. The vampire wraiths were reluctant to come for him with the fire burning. But the fire would not burn forever.

5

When Childress's first bullet passed through a wraith without doing any visible damage, his breath had caught in his throat. The gun barrel had risen in his hand and he'd almost lowered it. What good would the other twelve rounds in the pistol do? He had nothing else with which to defend himself—only a useless gun and his fists. His fate seemed determined.

The thought liberated him.

Thomas Childress, Junior, had never surrendered in his life. Twice during the war he had looked into the barrel of a gun pointed at his face and not broken. On leave in Spain he had plunged into a burning villa time and again, trying to save the life of a girl who had loved him. He had earned the scars on his face and neck in the fire that night, but when he carried Graciana outside at last, she was already dead.

On all of those occasions fear had enveloped him, of course; that was only natural. But in the face of fear—in those moments when death loomed near, only one stroke of the reaper's scythe away—action was the only recourse. He would not accept death calmly. He would strike.

The wraiths slipped across the room toward him, all the more horrible for the putrid yellow light that flickered from the oil lamp and played across their tar-black forms. Childress backed up a single step, searching the shifting shadows of the room for some other weapon. There was a simple wooden stool a dozen feet away, beneath a cornice of human bones, but getting to it would not be easy.

The gun felt light in his grip, as though it yearned for a target.

Damn you all to Hell, he thought. Shadow and bone, perhaps, but he had twelve rounds left. He would make use of them.

As the vampires continued to close a circle around him, slowly, perhaps even warily, he sought their master, the scarred creature that had summoned them. He caught sight of it, retreating into the darkness of a corner of the room, beyond that gruesome painting of the Red King with its devil's crown, its crimson-black shadow raising the dead. The pale, withered vampire seemed nothing like the painting, but Childress felt the evil that pulsated from the thing, and had Baltimore not pursued it, these many years?

With a flutter like a flag whipping in the wind, a wraith slid toward him across the room. Childress sneered wordlessly and raised the pistol. Time seemed to slow around him. Evil was no stranger. The things he had seen by the lake in that Chilean mountain village had engraved horror upon his soul. His terror had lain in wait all of this time, and now it awoke screaming inside of him.

But he would not break.

He pulled the trigger. The pistol bucked in his hand. The bullet struck the wraith in the center of its abhorrent, monstrous face. There came a splintering of bone, and it staggered backward, midnight talons whipping up to clutch its face as though keeping its head from falling apart. A shriek of pain rose up in an ululation.

Icy pleasure raced through Childress, and he smiled thinly. He had caused the wraith a great deal of pain. Unnatural the things might be—magic beasts constructed of pure iniquity—but they had bones within those dark sheath bodies, and bones could be broken. They could be harmed.

He shouted to Aischros and Doctor Rose, but did not seek them out. The wraiths had flowed away from him when the one he'd shot began to scream. Now they tried to slide in from the sides and from behind him. Some veered away, and he heard Aischros shout as the creatures dragged him down to the floor again. The mariner had some kind of blade that flashed in the lamplight, and it seemed he had also discovered that the wraiths could be hurt, that their bones could be broken.

But there were far too many of them. And though they might be hurt, there seemed no way to stop them.

Childress ran to help Aischros. The moment he moved, the wraiths came for him. He raised the pistol and fired twice, taking one wraith in the head and shattering its skull. The other he shot in the leg, hoping broken bones

would slow it down. It spun around once, then came on, dragging its leg behind it. The bones were only structure.

There would be no stopping them.

One of the shadow vampires reached for him and its talons raked furrows in his back. Childress cried out in pain, spinning and firing a bullet through its head. It flew backward with such force that the liquid shadow splattered across the floorboards and the bones fell out of it, clattering to the wood. The oil-black shadow slithered over to cover the bones again. Soon, it would rise once more.

None of us shall live to see the dawn, he thought.

Amidst the wraiths, Childress saw the artist, Bentley, with his bright eyes and mad smile. Bentley raised his oil lamp high, then turned it down and blew out the wick, snuffing the light. Even as the artist disappeared into the darkness of that corner, an unholy shriek tore through the room, echoing off bones and shadows, and then a new light blossomed in an instant.

He glanced over to see a winged wraith on fire, and Doctor Rose backing away.

Well done, Childress thought. *Good show, Doctor.* They would die, but they would not succumb to the poisonous taint of evil. Even as the silent vow entered his mind, he heard Aischros shout again and turned to see the mariner rising from the floor with several of the wraiths clinging to him like lampreys, their mouths fastened on his flesh, blood flecks spattering the  ground as he tore one of them off him. Then Aischros lumbered across the room and slammed one of the wraiths into a ridge of bones that had been constructed against the wall. He beat it with his fists, stabbed it in the eyes with his dagger.

Hands gripped Childress's legs. He pointed the pistol down and squeezed off two rounds, destroying its skull. Then he stomped on its arm, breaking bone. How many bullets were left he did not know, but he didn't have time to wonder.

Talons slashed his left shoulder. Barely looking, he fired again.

The blaze Doctor Rose had set raged against the far wall, licking up toward the high ceiling of the studio. When it reached the skylight and the glass broke and oxygen flooded the room, it would burn all the more swiftly. The heat blistered the air, and Childress felt the hot air sear his lungs. He clenched his mouth shut and breathed through his nose.

The wraiths had not terrified him enough to break him, nor had the presence of the ancient evil Baltimore pursued. But he felt the scar tissue tightening on his neck where he had been so badly burned long ago, and part of him shut down. He would fight the Devil himself, but feared the flames of Hell or Heaven equally.

A stream of curses rose in the midst of the room, and it took him a moment to realize they came from Aischros. The mariner called upon God to intervene, or be damned Himself. Childress thought that He had turned a blind eye to this place, to this night.

"Damn you," he whispered, hating the heat of the flames on him and the scent of burning wood. Smoke began to haze the air near the ceiling.

He saw that the wraiths seemed reluctant to go near Doctor Rose as long as the surgeon remained near the blazing fire. A terrible determination filled him. Something moved above him. He saw it in his peripheral vision and glanced up in time to see the wraith tear away from its perch on a column of bones and skulls and swoop down toward him.

Childress shot it three times in the chest. From weight alone, he knew the pistol was either empty or nearly empty, and it wasn't going to make them hesitate to tear him apart much longer. He ran for the stool, crossing the eight or nine feet in three long strides. As he moved, he fired the pistol until it clicked empty, and then he hurled it at the face of a wraith. The darkness flowed out of the way and the gun clattered to the floorboards.

He picked up the stool.

Fear and righteousness churned in him, combined with his despair and resignation. He screamed at them, and swung the stool. Wood and bone both shattered, and then he held only a single thick shaft of wood that had been one leg of the stool.

A soft, chuffing laughter filled the burning room. That single painting still stood spotlighted in the moonlight on its easel at the center of the studio. The vampire lurked in the shadows somewhere. Black smoke from burning paint roiled along the ceiling.

Hope departed, but Childress had had little of it to begin with.

He waded into the wraiths, swinging the stool leg. Bones broke within those shadow bodies, but there were far too many. They dragged him down.

6

Aischros bled. Their taint filled him. The wraiths had torn his flesh with their teeth and he knew he would be infected now. The plague burned in his veins. Fresh blood soaked into his trousers and his shirt, and the sharp copper smell of it must have driven them wild, for the wraiths rushed around him in a frenzy.

Aischros plunged the dagger into the neck of one of the wraiths, lodged it into bone, and twisted. He drove his elbow into the chest of the one behind him with such force that ribs shattered. They slashed him, tore at him, tried again and again to keep him down. Aischros crushed and splintered them, turning them into misshapen bags of broken bones.

The soft laughter of the dead black-eyed vampire echoed in the room, heard above the roar of the fire. Tendrils of liquid shadow caressed the bones on the wall nearby and hanging in a cornice above him, and more of the wraiths pulled themselves away from the wall with a wet pop.

Too many. There were simply too many.

Even as he thought it, three of them took hold of him at once. He began to retaliate, trying to shake them off, but one of the things opened its massive jaws, black nostrils flaring, and sank needle fangs into the meat of his thigh.

Aischros let out a bellow of pain and dropped to his knees. He tried to fight, but they swarmed him. His right wrist shattered and the dagger hit the floor and was kicked, spinning off toward the fire.

He caught a glimpse of something rising up behind Doctor Rose, silhouetted in the fire, and then the slender little red-haired man let out a cry as it grabbed him round the throat and tossed him into the shadows where the vampire and the artist must still have lingered, away from the fight and away from the fire.

Aischros began to scream his fury to God. If He still endured, somewhere, why did He not intervene? He damned the Lord to an eternity in His own Hell for allowing such evil to plague humanity.

His right wrist broken, his blood flowing freely, one of the leeches attached to his leg, Aischros still attempted to fight them. With his left hand, he plunged his fingers into the shadow stuff of a wraith, hoping to strike bone. So many of them were on him now that he could barely see the light of the fire.

Long talons punched into the flesh of his chest. He felt one of them slide between two of his ribs, spreading the bones apart, and he knew the next blow would open his chest, break his ribs, and then the vampire would tear his heart out.

For just a moment, he thought he heard the distant sound of a flute, playing a happy little melody.

Childress screamed.

Aischros shoved one of the wraiths aside just enough to see the broad-shouldered blond soldier tear loose of his attackers for a heartbeat; long enough to cock his arm back and hurl a length of wood—the leg of some shattered piece of furniture—upward. It turned end over end and then struck the glass of the skylight, shattering it. Shards of glass rained down around the hideous painting of the Red King, but it was untouched.

The fire roared like a dragon and raced for the oxygen brought by the broken window. Half the ceiling was engulfed, and now the blaze spread far more quickly.

Startled, the wraiths pulled back toward the far wall. Aischros was free. He knew it would not last, and so he started to rise, thinking to go to Childress and get out of there. Survival was the only triumph they could even dream of against such malice.

Broken wrist held against his body, he got one foot beneath him and tried to stand. Disorientation swayed him and he sank to his knees. Childress shouted his name. Already, though, the wraiths had begun to slink back toward them.

The door had caught fire.

The frame cracked as it burst open, tearing from its hinges and falling, ablaze, to the floor. Yet, somehow, Aischros felt a chill in the room, as though the fire had suddenly been robbed of its heat.

Lord Baltimore stood upon the threshold, cloaked in his military great-coat, weapons hanging all about him. Firelight flickered and gleamed upon his shaven head, and wide dark eyes.

He drew his saber, and charged into the burning studio, coat flapping behind him like the black wings of a wraith. For a single instant, the entire room seemed to hold its breath. The wraiths hesitated, just as they had when the skylight had stoked the flames burning the wall. But Baltimore did not hesitate.

His saber flashed silver in the firelight as it descended in an arc that slashed a diagonal path through the shadow and bone of the nearest wraith. Its oil-black flesh puffed away like drifting smoke and its bones clattered to the ground, yellowed with age.

Aischros stared with his mouth agape, the throbbing of his wounds somehow far away. He could only watch as Baltimore thrust his blade into another slippery wraith, with the same result. The room filled with a black smoke that quickly dissipated, some of it sizzling as it blew into the fire.

Bones rattled as they struck the floor all around him. Yet Baltimore moved with such grace and agility that it seemed unnatural. His wooden leg thumped the floorboards as he leaped toward a wraith that abruptly sprouted wings and tried to fly toward the broken skylight.

Baltimore slashed it from the air.

Aischros recalled his conversation with the monk in the cemetery on Trevelyan Island, and the vision the monk claimed to have had, and to have shared with Baltimore. Perhaps his old companion had been chosen for some dark and terrible destiny after all, a knight in an eternal struggle against evil. He had been transformed, and somehow his weapons had been altered as well. Baltimore had been forged into a weapon against the darkness, and his saber had an uncanny effect on the wraiths, destroying them and countering whatever dark sorcery their master had infused them with.

If the vampire was darkness, Baltimore must then have been infused with light. Yet in his heart Aischros almost did not believe it. Baltimore's vengeful savagery made him even more terrible to behold than the devils he slaughtered.

Throughout the bloody melee, Aischros and Childress had remained close to the door. The artist's portrait of the Red King separated them from the other side of the room, where a dozen paintings and sculptures stood near the shuttered windows. Even with the fire that blazed along the inner wall, the darkness there was thicker than ever, the shadows swimming together. The vampire and the artist hid there, invisible in the blackness.

From that eclipsed corner came a terrible scream. Aischros recognized the voice.

"Doctor Rose!" he shouted.

Baltimore swept into the darkness. A gust of wind seemed to accompany him. The fire paced him along the wall and ceiling, blackening plaster and beams and casting its light, at last, into those shadows.

Three vampire wraiths crouched like vultures over the thrashing, screaming form of Doctor Rose. The surgeon swung a long, sharp shard of statuary at one of them, and it was batted from his hand. One of the wraiths hissed and lowered its sickening maw toward him, darting like a bird feeding its children. Doctor Rose barely raised his hand in time to protect his face. Instead of his throat or eyes or cheek, the vampire's needle teeth snapped down on his left hand. As it drew back, blood fountained into the air from the raw stumps of two fingers. His left hand had been mutilated to match the right.

Then Baltimore was there, wooden leg punctuating his every motion upon the floorboards. His saber whispered as it swept through the air, and the wraiths attacking Doctor Rose were smoke. Their bones struck the floor around the doctor, and some even hit the man himself, as Baltimore grabbed him by the wrist and pulled him back toward the fire.

"Henry!" Childress cried triumphantly, the greeting of an old friend.

Baltimore seemed not to hear him. The wraiths peeled away from Aischros and Childress and focused solely on their master's nemesis. They swarmed around Baltimore, but the grim soldier was steadfast, deadly, and silent. He seemed to urge them on with a gesture and a nod, his saber slashing the air. His guns remained holstered, for they would have done him no good, but he brandished a small hatchet that had been clipped to his belt, and with it split the skull of a winged wraith that had gathered up the folds of his coat in its talons.

Smoke and bones.

Doctor Rose moved along the burning wall, and Aischros shared the concern he saw etched on the surgeon's face. The wall was black, parts of it burned away completely. The ceiling creaked and popped and the fire ran along the beams, spreading above their heads. How long before the whole roof caved in? How long before the fire had spread through so much of the top floor of the building that they would have no way to descend?

With the saber in his right hand and the hatchet lost to him, Baltimore unsheathed a long, thin Italian dagger. He pivoted and leaped, slashed and thrust, and with a nauseating churn of his stomach, Aischros watched that strange, hinged wooden leg moving and leaping—almost dancing—and could only think of the marionettes that had once haunted him, and tangled him in their strings. Fresh terror spilled from his heart like blood, and for the first time he truly understood how much that peculiar wooden leg had always troubled him.

He held his broken wrist against his chest, dagger in his left hand, and dragged his bloodied leg toward Baltimore, thinking to help him. Childress staggered toward him, his left cheek gouged by talons, his clothes tattered and bloody, and reached out a hand.

"Wait, Demetrius," the man said.

Aischros stared at him. They had to retrieve Doctor Rose and get out of there. The fire would bring the whole place down upon them. But Aischros saw a strange resignation in Childress's eyes, and an understanding as well.

"He might've been late, but Henry did not call us here to fight alongside him."

"Really? What in hell are we doing here, then?" Aischros demanded.

"We're witnesses."

Aischros trembled, vision hazy from blood loss, and perhaps the infection of the plague already making its way through his body, corrupting his flesh. He blinked and looked around. The abominable cruelty of the place remained in its bone towers and cornices, in the piles of skulls, and in the vile images of the paintings the fire had not yet claimed. Yet the evil that had so oppressed him seemed to have ebbed, flowing entirely toward Baltimore now. Doctor Rose stood near the gaping rectangle of the door, their fire-ringed exit, watching Baltimore. Aischros and Childress were a dozen feet from the wretched crimson and black painting of the Red King, which still stood, miraculously, on its easel, framed in the moonlight that filtered in through the broken skylight. Beyond the painting, in the last corner of

the chapel of death that Bentley had built, he could at last see the withered, bent silhouette of the scarred vampire, watching it all unfold.

Childress was right. They were, all of them, witnesses.

As Baltimore dispatched the last of the wraiths, they could only watch. The wraith screamed and Baltimore thrust his saber through its open maw. Black smoke eddied on the breeze drafting through the place, and the last of the bones fell.

The thing's skull dangled from the tip of Baltimore's saber. He flung it into the fire, and spared only a single glance at the three men he had summoned to meet him in this place before striding toward the easel at the center of the room. His wooden leg scraped along the floorboards now, heavy with the metal of hundreds of nails—some of them rusted and others gleaming in the illumination provided by fire and moon.

He paused before the portrait of the Red King, and then peered into the shadows beyond it, and the vampire shambled forth to meet him.

FINALE:

LIBERA ME

—

*"He looked at the little maiden, and she looked at him;
and he felt that he was melting away, but he
still managed to keep himself erect, shouldering
his gun bravely."*
—The Steadfast Tin Soldier
by Hans Christian Andersen

IN THAT MOMENT, surrounded by fire and darkness, Baltimore is the steadfast tin soldier once again. At the end of that old tale, the soldier has been thrown into the fire, and now it has come to pass in reality. Once more he faces his own devil—the goblin, the Jack, now out of his box.

Scarred, one eye socket hollowed out, skin rough and brittle as papyrus, the thing comes toward him from the shadows. All of these years, he has pursued the creature that fed upon the carrion of his fellow soldiers; the winged demon that dragged itself across the battlefield and crept onto his bloodied, broken body. Baltimore has crossed oceans and continents in search of the fiend that breathed its hellish breath into his wounded flesh, rotting his leg as sure as gangrene, ruining him. He has scoured the world in search of the gray, flat-eyed evil that stood by his bedside that day and promised vengeance, who murdered his wife and made monsters of his family.

Every nail in his wooden leg represents a lesser creature, a bit of vampiric vermin, just another leech he has dispensed with as he hunted for the Red King, the lord of them all, the one who had begun the plague and named Baltimore as his nemesis.

Now, at last, he stands face-to-face with the devil again.

He will not accept what his eyes tell him.

The vampire is a shabby thing, more scarecrow than Satan. The thing of his nightmares, the Jack-in-the-Box goblin whose laughter has haunted even his waking hours and made him forget, at times, what was reality and what mere remembrance of childhood fancy...this pitiful wretch cannot be that thing. This stooped, desiccated husk is more beggar than king of vampires.

Doctor Rose, Childress, and Aischros are all wounded. The fire rages behind them, consuming the entire wall in which stands the only exit from these rooms. Still, no one moves.

"What are you?" Baltimore asks, unaware of any intention to speak.

It begins to laugh, softly, the sound barely a rasp. In the damp, black eyes set inside that withered skull, and the insidious tone of that voice, Baltimore finds the truth. Somehow, this is he. Yet now the fiend is merely a shadow of a shadow, an inglorious shell of its former grandeur, diminished over the ages by Baltimore's constant pursuit and drained by the inability to rest, to feed, to grow strong again.

"What are you?" Lord Baltimore asks again. "Why do dead men rise up to torment the living?"

With a rasping cough, the vampire shakes its head. "It was you called us. All of you, with your war. The roar of your cannons shook us from our quiet graves. And all of your spilled blood. Even then, we were as sleepwalkers, lost in our ancient minds."

The vampire touches a brittle finger to the scar on its face. "But this woke my mind, and that awareness spread like infection amongst us, just as our contagion spread through you. We were your plague, and you were ours. You killers. You berserkers. You warriors. You will never be rid of us now. So long as man endures, we will be his red shadow."

Baltimore feels a terrible weight upon him, as though the nails that cause him to drag his wooden leg have been driven through the rest of him as well. It is as if his entire body is burdened with a chain mail of iron spikes, driven into his flesh.

"No." His hand tightens on the grip of his saber. "It began with the two of us, that night in the Ardennes. It ends with us as well. Both awakened, both transformed, both destroyed. At last, we both may rest."

With dreadful dignity, the vampire straightens its back and raises its chin. Its single eye gazes unwaveringly at him. And it begins to laugh, weakly at first, but then more powerfully, head shaking. Hatred, disgust, and pity roil in Baltimore. The fire is reflected in the dull black eye of the vampire, as though in its gaze he can see Hell itself.

"Now we rest," Baltimore says, through gritted teeth.

He runs the vampire through. It collapses around his saber like some gossamer fabric, deflating, and then its gray flesh crumbles further and spills like sand to the wooden floor.

The fire rages. The heated breeze whips the ash of the vampire's destruction into a whirling frenzy along the floorboards. Something cracks in the ceiling. Burning embers fall like rain.

"Henry," a voice calls, loud and frantic, but Baltimore does not look up until a powerful hand grips his arm. He raises the saber and nearly stabs Childress before he realizes who it is.

Doctor Rose stands on one side of Childress, and Demetrius on the other, all of them bleeding, all of them ready to collapse. The urgency in their eyes does not move him. Childress's exhortations seem to come from far away.

"Thomas," Baltimore says. "I feel nothing."

With the death of his tormentor, all purpose is drained from him. In its place, there is only emptiness. Destroying this fiend has been his mission, and now it is fulfilled. He has survived for this, and expected to die when it ended. Yet he lives. Why does he still live?

"We've got to go, Henry!" Childress shouts over the roar of the flames.

The room is an inferno. Smoke and the chemical fumes from burning paint sting their eyes and heat sears their skin. Baltimore nods and turns to go, but out of the corner of his eye he sees the huge canvas sitting on its easel in the center of the room. The firelight plays across the hideous portrait of the Red King.

With a cry of rage and frustration, Baltimore slashes the canvas, the saber cutting the image in twain.

In the very moment that the blade splits the canvas, a terrible weight fills the room. The air grows heavy and so cold that its frigid density snuffs the flames. Charred ceiling beams crack and buckle, but do not collapse. Not an ember still burns. The blackened, fire-ravaged wall looks as though the blaze was extinguished months ago, rather than seconds.

Baltimore feels it there in the room with them, a presence so massive that it seems the whole building might explode from its intrusion. The artist had built a temple to his god, but the ancient malevolence had never taken notice until the moment that saber defiled its image.

Realization staggers him as, at last, he understands. In all the years he has stood against the darkness, for all of the filthy vermin he has exterminated, he has been fighting the symptoms instead of the plague itself. The true enemy has barely been aware of him.

Until now.

Now the Red King has noticed him.

The image on the slashed canvas seems to shift, the paint flowing as it stares at him. Its crown burns with red flame and the stink of death fills the room, assaulting him with the memory of that predawn hour on the slaughter fields of the Ardennes when he awoke buried beneath the corpses of his men.

It lasts only a moment.

Then the painting is just a painting. The crushing pressure, the dreadful

278   *Mike Mignola & Christopher Golden*

weight, withdraws. The cold recedes as well, though the charred wood is rimed with crystals of ice.

The columns and eaves of bone and skull collapse with a clatter.

And Baltimore stands with the three men he calls friend, and stares a moment longer at the ruined painting. They gather round him now, these wounded, bleeding men, and together they turn him and lead him toward the charred ruin of the door. The artist lies bleeding in a far corner. He has slit his own throat with a shard of glass from the skylight. For years, he has labored to build this chapel, ignored by his dark god, and his death will go equally unnoticed. Unmourned.

CODA

———

"By this time the soldier was reduced to a mere lump, and when the maid took away the ashes next morning she found him, in the shape of a small tin heart. All that was left of the dancer was her spangle, and that was burnt as black as a coal."

—The Steadfast Tin Soldier
by Hans Christian Andersen

DOCTOR ROSE LEADS THE WAY down the stairs. He has already wrapped a torn bit of his shirt around his hand to stanch the bleeding in the stumps of the two fingers the wraith has bitten off. He tries not to think of the symmetry of his injuries. The cloth is sodden with blood, but the pulsing in his arm has diminished and he thinks perhaps the clotting has begun. The doctor is keenly aware of his last cigarette, carefully conserved and sitting now in a pocket. They have been victorious—or, at least, have survived—and it seems the perfect time to smoke it. But he finds that he no longer has the desire. Such things have lost their allure.

Behind him, Childress accompanies a weakened Baltimore. The hunter's eyes are narrowed and alight with strange emotion. Doctor Rose cannot decide if he reads fury or desperation in that gaze, and at last decides he sees both. Baltimore's wooden leg drags and thumps on the steps like Marley's chain of sins. Aischros brings up the rear, his broken wrist swelling and bruised black.

Several of the doors on the second floor have been left open by guests who fled when the smoke from the fire began to spread. In the midst of the conflagration of flame and shadow, he heard nothing, but he imagines there must have been screaming. Perhaps the innkeeper had raised the alarm.

Doctor Rose opens the door to an unoccupied room and strips the sheet off the bed, hoping it is clean. He is careful not to use his left hand, fearful that he might start the bleeding afresh.

"What are you doing?" Childress asks when he emerges.

"Bandages. We'll all need them," the doctor replies. "Not that it will matter, in the end. Even once I can get my hands on a needle and thread, I can stop the bleeding, but not the infection."

The words rouse Baltimore a bit. He stands straighter, but his gaze remains distant. "The source of your wounds, those shades that infected you, have been destroyed. You will not be tainted by the plague."

Doctor Rose cannot disguise his relief, nor mask the sense of awe that fills him at this revelation. The vampire wraiths had survived the destruction of their physical bodies, but Baltimore has eradicated them, and in so doing has cleansed the doctor and his companions of the filthy taint of the plague. It seems almost miraculous. Perhaps they will all survive, after all.

When they reach the bar, its gray gloom illuminated only by the moonshine coming through the windows, he leads them all to the nearest table.

"Demetrius, fetch some alcohol from behind the bar, would you?" Doctor Rose asks.

Aischros nods, a wan smile on his face. "To drink, or to clean our wounds?"

"A bit of both, I should think," the doctor replies.

Childress begins to tear the sheet into strips. Doctor Rose is grateful. With his newly mutilated hand, he would not have been able to do the job. He watches Aischros move behind the bar, already thinking about what he might use to set the mariner's broken wrist.

When the man returns with a bottle of rough whiskey, Doctor Rose sets about seeing to their wounds, ignoring the throbbing of his missing fingers—for now. Baltimore only sits and stares, the faraway look never leaving his eyes.

Not until Childress speaks.

"Henry. It's over, old friend. Your nightmare is ended."

At last, Baltimore's gaze wavers and he turns to regard Childress.

"Ended?" he says, glancing at each of them in turn. "You don't understand. I have been no less among the dead than the devil I have just destroyed. The

fiend murdered all that I might ever have been or done. From that time until now I have been dead inside. I had thought—I had hoped—that with his defeat, I would finally know the peace of the grave. That is why I called you all here. I hoped that when I fell, you would bring my body to Trevelyan Island and burn me there, and then spread my ashes across the harbor, putting me to rest in the sea where I had scattered the ashes of my mother and father, and my sweet sister. At last I would be reunited with my darling wife, my Elowen."

The faraway look returns to his eyes.

"But it has not ended. The vampire was correct. It will never end. The cold inside me remains."

Doctor Rose shudders. A dull ache spreads through him, bone-deep. He attributes it to blood loss and exhaustion.

With his good hand, Aischros pours a glass of whiskey and slides it across the table to Baltimore.

"This will warm you," the mariner says, moonlight gleaming on the tiny white scars all over his ugly face.

Baltimore takes them all in with a look. "Warm me?" he asks. "Warm this?"

They can only look on in silent horror as Baltimore opens his shirt and presses his right hand to the center of his chest. Flesh and bone give way as he draws out his heart and sets it on the table. Without pain. Without blood.

"I had thought my quest would end here," he rasps. "But I see now that it is my enduring curse. I understand, now, what fate has forged of me."

The heart of Lord Henry Baltimore is a misshapen lump of cold tin. A bit of gold glimmers from one side—the missing wedding ring of his wife, the Lady Elowen, located at last.

"So long as the Red King reigns, there must always be Lord Baltimore."

THE END

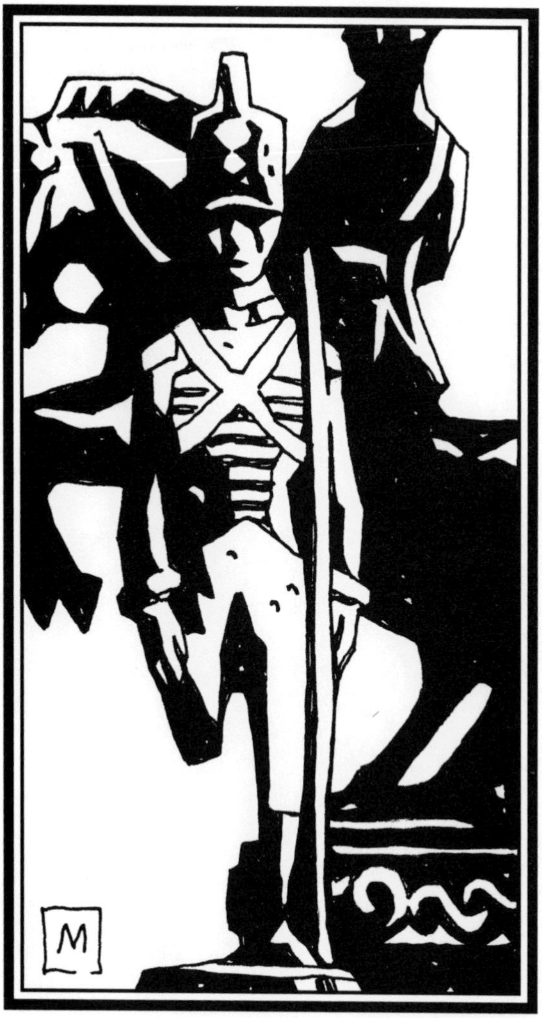
M

ABOUT THE AUTHOR/ILLUSTRATOR

Mike Mignola was born September 16, 1960, in Berkeley, California, and grew up in nearby Oakland, the eldest son of a tough and leathery cabinetmaker. His fascination with ghosts and monsters began at an early age (he doesn't remember why) and reading *Dracula* at age twelve introduced him to Victorian literature and folklore, from which he has never recovered.

After graduating from the California College of Arts and Crafts in 1982 (hoping to find a way to draw monsters for a living), he moved to New York City to begin a career in the comic book field. Starting as a bad inker for Marvel Comics, he swiftly evolved into a not so bad artist on comics like *Rocket Raccoon, Alpha Flight,* and *The Hulk*. By the late 1980s, however, he began to develop his own unique graphic style and moved on to higher profile commercial projects like *Cosmic Odyssey* (1988) and *Gotham By Gaslight* (1989) for DC Comics, and the not so commercial *Fafhrd and the Grey Mouser* (1990) for Marvel. In 1992 he drew the comic book adaptation of the film *Bram Stoker's Dracula* for Topps Comics, which led to his working (briefly) with Francis Ford Coppola on the film.

In 1993 Mike joined several other comic book creators (John Byrne, Frank Miller, Geof Darrow, etc.) to form the Legend imprint at Dark Horse Comics, and there he created *Hellboy,* a tough and leathery occult detective who may or may not be the beast of the apocalypse. The first *Hellboy* story line (*Seed of Destruction,* 1994) was co-written by John Byrne, but Mike has continued writing the book himself and, as of this writing, there are six *Hellboy* graphic novels (with more on the way), several spin-off titles (*Hellboy: Weird Tales, Hellboy Junior, BPRD*), two anthologies of prose stories, several novels, two animated films, and a live action film starring Ron Perlman. *Hellboy* has earned numerous comic industry awards and is published in many countries.

Mike has also worked as a production designer for the Disney film *Atlantis: The Lost Empire* (2001) and was the visual consultant to director Guillermo del Toro on *Blade II* (2002), *Hellboy* (2004), and currently on *Hellboy 2: The Golden Army* (in preproduction). In 2001 Mike also created the award-winning comic book *The Amazing Screw On Head* (recently adapted into animation).

Mike lives somewhere in Southern California with his wife, daughter, and cat.

ABOUT THE AUTHOR

Christopher Golden is the award-winning, bestselling author of such novels as *The Myth Hunters, Wildwood Road, The Boys Are Back in Town, The Ferryman, Strangewood, Of Saints and Shadows,* and *The Borderkind.* He has also written books for teens and young adults, including the thriller series *Body of Evidence,* honored by the New York Public Library and chosen as one of YALSA's Best Books for Young Readers.

With Thomas E. Sniegoski, he is the co-author of the dark fantasy series *The Menagerie* as well as the young readers' fantasy series *OutCast* and the comic book miniseries *Talent,* both of which were recently acquired by Universal Pictures. Golden and Sniegoski also wrote the upcoming comic-book miniseries *The Sisterhood,* currently in development as a feature film, and *BPRD: Holly Earth,* a spinoff from the fan favorite comic-book series *Hellboy.* Golden authored several original *Hellboy* novels, including *The Lost Army* and *The Bones of Giants,* and edited two *Hellboy* short-story anthologies.

He has written a great many novels, nonfiction books, and comic books—and two video games—based in the world of Buffy the Vampire Slayer. Working with actress/writer/director Amber Benson, he co-created and co-wrote *Ghosts of Albion,* an original animated supernatural drama for BBC online, from which they created the book series of the same name (www.ghostsofalbion.net).

Golden was born and raised in Massachusetts, where he

still lives with his family. He graduated from Tufts University. He has recently completed *The Lost Ones,* part three of a dark fantasy trilogy for Bantam Books entitled *The Veil.* At present he is collaborating with Tim Lebbon on *Mind the Gap,* the first novel in their series *The Hidden Cities.* There are more than eight million copies of his books in print. Please visit him at www.christophergolden.com.

FIC   Mignola, Mike
Mignola   Baltimore

             $25.00   9/07